Chapter 1

A DESPERATE VOICE ECHOES THROUGHOUT the warehouse, stopping me in my tracks. "Clarence!"

I cringe.

"Clarence! Help me, Clarence!" the voice continues, warbling tones filling the cavernous area, echoing off metal racks filled with pallets of machine parts.

A round of groans comes up from the other dads, who have just huddled around freshly arrived boxes of pizza.

Turning to look back, I spot Oliver Parkin up on the Christmas float being constructed in the center of the open warehouse. Hands folded as if in prayer, leaning over the railing of the barely completed replica bridge, he cries out to the ceiling with a terrible impression of Jimmy Stewart from the Christmas classic *It's a Wonderful Life*. "Get me back!"

"Oh, don't worry, I'll get you back!" Out of the corner of my eye, I see someone hold up a slice of pizza and wave it menacingly.

"I don't care what happens to me!" Oliver yells, louder, face piously turned up to the fluorescent lights.

He's really hamming it up, and I can't help but grin at him.

"You will!" another dad's voice yells back.

"Especially when we start back up with the 'Oliver reindeer' jokes again!" comes another.

Laughter breaks out, and Oliver's melodramatic mask begins to crack

3

into a smile. "Get me back to my wife and kids!" he pleads.

"They don't want you either!" I shout at him, joining in the fun.

That finally does it. Oliver loses it and starts laughing along with the others. Nothing like a good divorce joke between divorced dads.

He hooks his hands on the railing and swings under, dropping off the side of the float and landing on the sealed concrete floor. "It's finally starting to look like a real bridge, Jeff!" He beams as he catches up with me.

"I'm telling you, it's gonna work," I say. We fall into step and head for pizza.

"Yeah. I knew it would. But, jeez... A friggin' bridge. I'm glad the new parade rules limit the size, or you'd have wanted us to build the river below it, too!"

Bob Candler, reaching around behind the backs of Mark Thorndyke and Jimmy Hazlehurst, hands a half-empty pizza box to us. "With boats, likely," he says. "Jeff never thinks small when it comes to these floats. Remember that first one?"

Groans go up from everyone again, and I roll my eyes. Here it comes. Ten years, and six first place float entries later, and they can't let it go.

"What was that monstrosity supposed to have been again?" John King goads.

I ignore him and fish out a piece of pizza. Oliver, scrunching up his nose at the sausage pizza, shakes his head and leaves me holding the box as he goes looking for a different kind.

"Wasn't it Tom's Diner?" Mark asks.

"I thought it was a Gunther Toody's," Jimmy says through a mouthful.

"Y'all know it was *supposed* to be the Polar Express," I say, falling into the same routine we've been through for years now. It's friendly camaraderie, and I enjoy the ribbing more than I'm irritated by it.

I think.

"I thought it was supposed to be that really long camping trailer from *I Love Lucy*!"

We all stop eating to stare at Thomas Hackett. He is the youngest member of the Decanter Elementary School Dad's Club. By far. He could be my kid, if I hadn't waited until my thirties to have a kid.

A MID-LIFE CRISIS THRILLER

LOST ANGEL

SAM KNIGHT

CASTLE BRIDGE MEDIA
DENVER, COLORADO, USA

CASTLE BRIDGE MEDIA
Denver, Colorado
Cover Photo by Jake Blucker/Unsplash

This book is a work of fiction. Names, characters, business, events and incidents are the products of the authors' imaginations. Any resemblance to actual persons, living or dead, or actual events is purely coincidental.

"You know, after it fell off the cliff," Thomas continues.

Jimmy busts out laughing.

"For starters, that wasn't *I Love Lucy*." I try to deflect. "On top of that, I'm pretty sure the trailer doesn't fall off of the cliff in that movie."

"Your nose is still wet. How do you even know about *I Love Lucy*?" Oliver, who is the oldest of the dads after me, cocks his head accusingly at Thomas.

"From *WandaVision*," Thomas replies gleefully. "That was such a great trip down memory lane for all of those old shows."

"Down memory lane? Just exactly when—"

Thomas is saved by the shrill, piercing voice of an eight-year-old boy screaming, "Pizza!"

"Uh oh." Jimmy says. "Coffee break is over."

"Someone grab a box for Bill!" Chip Burbank hollers. I appreciate that he thinks of it. Bill Petterson, whose kids grew up a long time ago, owns the warehouse and has been kind enough to let the Decanter Elementary School Dad's Club use it to build parade floats for more years than I know of.

"Got one," Oliver calls out, holding a pizza box high.

We all grab for a last slice of our own and hurry out of the way as two dozen of our progeny stampede through the open garage door, giggles and shrieks preceding them like horror movie music warning something terrible this way comes. Their faces, ashen gray with sunken black eyes and dark lips, match their threatening approach.

They are upon us in seconds, screaming wildly.

Or, rather, they rush past us as we scatter and watch them tear into the pile of pizza boxes like crazed zombies ripping random parts out of a cornered victim.

If pizza boxes could scream...

"What *is* all of this?" Bob waves his arms wide, a pizza slice dangling from each hand. "Are we doing a Skeletons on Parade Christmas float this year? I didn't realize it was Halloween again already!"

Bob's son, a second grader named Danny, laughs, holding his stomach tightly and bending at the waist, delivering deep, heartfelt, yet totally fake guffaws that end abruptly as he stops to take another bite of pizza.

"We're *dead* angels!" one of the girls says gleefully, eyes sparkling with mischief. I don't recognize her through the heavy face paint at first, but, as she cackles, she gives herself away to be her mother's daughter. Brandi Hazlehurst, who is nothing at all like her reserved husband Jimmy, could have told us that she had cloned herself to make her daughter and none of us would have doubted it for a second.

Watching all of the excited kids, my heart begins to ache. I miss my own daughter, Coney, who hasn't come tonight. Or any night this year, for that matter.

The whole reason I joined the Decanter Elementary School Dad's Club, and took up the heavy mantle of building and entering the Decanter Elementary School Christmas float into the Decanter, "Christmas Capital of Texas," Annual Christmas Parade, had been to spend more time with my daughter.

And, for ten years, it worked. Actually, more like eight and a half years. Last year Coney missed most of the nights we worked on the float. But I couldn't really blame her. She'd finally made it to high school. They had their own float to build, and she had friends to do it with.

And they didn't need any dads to help them.

Except for money for materials, and to supply tools, and to give advice on how to make it all work. And maybe fix it when it doesn't. I suppose they especially don't need Dad's help when Dad is the competition. And when he's won the best float award six out of the last seven years, he probably shouldn't be invited to come stakeout his competition. Why would any highschooler want my advice?

This year is even more different than last. This year, I don't even know if Coney is working on the high school float. As soon as she got her driver's license, as soon as she didn't need me for rides anymore, I lost my major line of communication with her. Now, I barely know what she is up to at all.

I continue to watch the kids swirling around the table and clinging to their fathers, and I do my best to enjoy the moment. Each of these men around me, each of these dads, will feel what I am feeling one of these days. And, if they don't, it will, God forbid, likely be because they experience something even worse.

games until someone loses a wiener.

"Really?" she says.

I shrug. "It's the only one I have besides the one I'm using. You can have this one, if you want it, but it's already covered in stuff."

"I'll use this one." She puts on the big apron and looks around suspiciously, as though someone might jump out and take a picture to post on social media.

"Do you want to do the frosting?" I hold up the electric hand-held mixer. "Or watch the last ones in the oven?"

"Hmmm… Do something or do nothing… I'll take the something." Coney reaches for the beater, and I hand it to her.

I check the oven. The whirring sound of the mixer fills the kitchen and drowns out the Christmas music. Trying not to look like I am paying too much attention to Coney, I fuss with the cooling gingerbread men and organize them for decorating. If she decides to talk about whatever has her upset, I will hopefully be able to keep my "dad feelings" out of it and talk with her rationally. If she doesn't bring it up again, I won't either.

It's just nice to have her here.

Chapter 7

"GO! GO! GO!" I YELL along with Coney, Dana, and Trent, all of us joining a hundred others in rhythmic chant. The kindergarteners' heat of the Santa's Delivery Helpers race is well underway, and the tiny kids truly look like elves under the weight of the giant red bags full of foam block 'presents' they are hauling across the field.

More awkward than heavy, the bags cause the kids to sway side to side as they run and sometimes fall over or into each other. Fleming, lagging a little behind, but still in the first half of the kids to reach the other side, dumps his sack out into a pile, the foam block presents bouncing everywhere. He hands the oversized bag off to another kid on his team who takes off running back to the diminishing pile of blocks at the far side. Fleming, now working with the other four kids on his team on this side of the field, starts grabbing at yellow foam blocks while avoiding the kids grabbing for the other colors.

"Go! Go! Go!" The chant continues as kids fumble over each other and race to sort the blocks into boxes of the same color. People laugh as one of the kids, on a different team, trips and throws a double armful of blocks up into the air, mixing them in with the teams on either side of his.

Fleming throws his own armload at his team's yellow box from two feet away and misses nearly all of them, sending the foam blocks bouncing around in all directions. "Over there!" Coney yells to him, pointing out some he misses picking up. "Over there, Fleming!" He doesn't hear her. There is too much noise, too many people, too much laughing and cheering.

I push that thought away. I don't need to think like that. None of us need to think like that. The last few years have been rough on everyone. We all need to enjoy this, to enjoy each other.

I need to enjoy this.

As the kids begin to break away from the table with double-handfuls and triple-mouthfuls of pizza, nearly a dozen of their mothers appear in the doorway, chatting and walking slow. For a half a moment, my heart does a stutter. I momentarily forget exactly where, or more accurately *when* I am, and I expect to see Dana walk in the door with the other mothers. It is so easy to imagine her moving among them, graceful hands gesturing as she speaks with that big smile of hers that never seems to go away.

But she isn't here.

She hasn't been here since the divorce, over five years ago.

"Hey!" Oliver hits me on the shoulder. "You okay? You look like you've seen a ghost."

Oliver does a good job of keeping tabs on me, just as I try to keep an eye on him. He's in pretty much the same situation as I am. Divorced two years ago, he's here to spend time with his kid, too. Of course, his son and daughter actually are here.

"Skeletons," I answer, looking around at all of the 'dead angels.' "This wasn't exactly what I had envisioned."

I look back to the women, allowing myself one last indulgent moment of pretending Dana was walking in with them. I notice several of the women keep looking back, over their shoulders. Some of the words they exchange are hushed whispers. While gossip isn't unusual, the worried looks on a couple of their faces is.

"Don't worry, Jeff. We were just having a little fun." Stacy Thorncyke, having heard my comment, says, arriving at the table. "The kids looked great before we started playing around with the makeup."

Ahead of most of the other women, and arriving along with Stacy is Summer Christmas, whose bright and cheery smile somehow always lives up to the unfair expectations created by her name. Summer holds out her cellphone for me to see. "Here. This'll make y'all feel better. I got pictures before things got silly. Jeff, I think your idea is going to work out just fine."

Some people are just a little too perfect to be real. Summer Christmas is one of them. Over-the-top name aside, she always looks like she just walked out of a fashion catalog. Her hair is always perfect, her makeup subdued but accentuating, her clothes always fashionable, and she always seems to be in the right place at the right time to say the right thing.

Honestly, she scares me a little bit. Oliver, on the other hand, is completely and obviously infatuated with her, and he moves closer to see her phone as well. Much closer, accidentally bumping me out of the way with the pizza box he's holding.

At least, I think it's accidental.

Summer is fairly new to Decanter, having taken over the job of librarian at the middle school only last year. I haven't ever asked why she joined the elementary school's PTO instead of her own middle school's, though the thought crosses my mind pretty much every time I see her here. Really, it just falls right in with all of the other things about her that are just a little too good to be true.

I tear my eyes away from her dazzle to look at her phone. She is right. The group photo of the kids looks great. This is going to work. I am—I mean *we are*—going to win best float again this year.

Out of the corner of my eye, I see Stacy give Summer a look and a nod of her head and, at first, I think she's teasing Summer about Oliver, but then Stacy points back to the door with her nose, and I follow their gazes out into the night.

Just outside the reach of the light I see a figure moving at the far end of the parking lot. They are far enough away I never would have noticed them, and neither, I believe, should have Stacy—unless she was specifically watching for someone.

Chapter 2

"YOU'RE RIGHT," I SAY TO SUMMER, stepping back away from her outheld phone and smiling at her. "The kids look great. Thank you." I move farther away, giving Oliver the space he seems to need in order to stand even closer to Summer to see the photo on her phone.

Dropping my voice, I lean in and talk to Stacy. "I saw that look you gave Summer. Is there a problem?"

She shakes her head but keeps her voice low as she answers. "There was some guy watching us out there. Probably not a big deal." She picks up a slice of pizza and takes a bite. "I mean, you can't expect people walking by not to come see why a full choir of little kids is singing outside after dark, right?"

"I guess But...?" I ask, hoping to prompt her for more information. I realize women need to keep an eye on the world around themselves more than men do, or even more than most men realize, but they don't usually broadcast being spooked. I'd always figured it's kind of like showing weakness or something.

"But," Stacy answers, "he came right on up to us to watch. Like uncomfortably close. Stood right there with the rest of us. I mean, he was fine, but..." She shrugs and takes another bite of her pizza.

The blank look on my face leads her to say more.

"He was young. Twenties, maybe? He didn't seem to be... What are we supposed to say now? Cognitively challenged? He seemed normal. And normal young guys don't generally have any interest in little kids doing stuff like that. When a young guy sticks around, just watching, there's probably something else on their mind. And he wasn't eyeballing any of the mothers." She gives me a pointed look that tells me that if I'm not smart enough to start figuring things out on my own from there, she's not going to tell me.

But I already understand. Having a daughter changed my outlook on the world years ago. Anymore, I don't trust most guys as far as I can throw a Mack Truck. At least not when it comes to women.

I grab a pizza box that still has two slices in it and head outside. Before I even make it out the door, Oliver catches up with me.

"You look like a man with a plan. Where you headed?" he asks as we reach the parking lot.

"The kids had a fan. I figured I'd take him some pizza."

"Homeless guy?" Oliver turns his head back and forth, scanning between the cars parked around us.

"I don't know. Maybe. I was hoping to find out. Doesn't really sound like it though." The rise in the homeless population has been in the news a lot lately, though there haven't been any real issues here in Decanter. It's the other kinds of recent news stories, the bad kinds about sex trafficking, that have me nervous.

"A weirdo, huh?"

"Maybe. I hope not. I thought I saw someone heading this way." I point with my chin and aim for the end of the street.

"Just now?"

"No. When we were still inside, before I came out."

Glancing around the temporary choir stand, set up for the kids to practice on and learn their positions on the float, I don't see anything out of the ordinary, and the small clump of trees at the edge of the property seems empty, though it's a little hard to tell in the dark. The chill air is a bit warm for this time of year, but it's cold enough I'm still surprised the kids' rehearsal lasted this late.

"Hey!" I call out, holding up the pizza box even though I don't see anyone. "We've got extra, if you're hungry."

Looking around, Oliver and I walk on down to the end of the street before stopping. No one answers my call, and there's no signs of life anywhere, not even a car parked anywhere up or down the street.

"I don't see anyone," Oliver says.

"Yeah, me neither. I'm sure they're long gone."

"Starting to get chilly," Oliver says. "Maybe it was just someone out for a walk, and he decided to head on home."

"Yeah, maybe. Or maybe he'd rather look at a bunch of women and kids than a couple of old dudes with a box of half-eaten pizza."

"Speak for yourself, you old fart. I'm not even middle-aged yet." Oliver gives me a mock sour look.

"Really? How old you gonna live to be? A hundred and fifty?"

"Geez! You and your math skills. That would make seventy-five middle aged. But maybe. A hundred and fifty sounds a lot better than the sixty-five you seem to be shootin' for."

"If that were true, I really would be way past middle-aged already. Eighty-five would be good, I think," I say, digging one of the slices of pizza out of the box. I offer Oliver the other, but he shakes his head. "That still puts me climbing the hill."

"Really? You have to push Over-the-Hill all the way past forty? Damn! You're even older than I thought, Grandpa!"

"Don't be wishing that on me yet! You've got a daughter, too, you know. Karma can go both ways."

Oliver and I walk back into the warmth and chaos of the warehouse, still bickering with friendly jibes. The kids, mostly done with the pizza, are playing tag around the Christmas float, and the parents are chatting animatedly, with broad smiles and laughs. It makes me smile to see it all. It does me good to be around so many friends.

Oliver heads straight back to where Stacy and Summer are stacking up empty pizza boxes and laughing, the possible weirdo outside probably all but forgotten.

Which is good. Chances are he was just a random passerby anyway.

Chapter 3

MY KEYS CLANK DULLY AS they land on the empty dining room table. I hate the lonely sound they make, the way it feels like they're being tossed into a vast space so large there isn't anything for it to echo off of. But I do it every time anyway. And, every time, the empty house feels cavernous.

I can't explain why I never turn on the light until after I've tossed the keys. Hearing them land in the dark is worse, but maybe that's what I want.

Some nights I manage to come home and not just stand in the doorway and stare. Tonight is not one of those nights. I can feel the spring-loaded tension of the fire door, from the garage into the house, pressing against my shoulder as I stand there, telling me I should move on. I give in and press the button to close the overhead garage door and tell myself I am waiting, making sure the big door finishes closing behind me, but really, I am still looking into the shadows of the past.

Christmas lights on the porch shine through the sheer front window curtains; fuzzy red, green, and gold orbs of light, matching the Christmas tree in the living room, and, just for a moment, I can almost feel like none of it ever happened.

Almost.

But there are no bright, shiny presents under this tree, no smell that anyone has been baking anything in the kitchen, and not a single mess or thing out of place to be picked up. No dirty dishes in the sink. No shoes by the door. The house doesn't look lived in. It doesn't look like a home.

It doesn't feel like a home anymore, either.

The cranking sound of the motorized garage door stops with a *thud*, and the big door seals off the garage from the outside world, making me feel shut off, too. The engine of my truck ticks loudly, seemingly mournfully, as it cools in the dark silence of the garage behind me. Sometimes I feel like my truck is sad to be home, sad to be the lone vehicle in a two-car garage.

I try not to think about how it's kind of like how I still sleep on the same side of the bed, on *my* side of the bed. But I can't help it. That thought entered my mind a couple of years back, and having it is an automatic part of coming home now.

I sigh deeply, turn on the light, and tell myself that tomorrow I will park in the middle of garage instead of close to the left side, where I have to squeeze by to get in and out of the truck, to make room for a car that's never going to park there again. And to prove it, I'll sleep in the middle of the bed tonight.

I ignore the fact I know those are both lies and try to believe myself.

Dropping my handful of mail next to the keys on the empty table that's too big for one person, I head for the kitchen, turning on the lights as I go. I dig into the freezer and pull out a Salisbury steak meal. I went for years without eating these because Dana hated them. Since the divorce, I've eaten enough I can't say that I like them anymore. Coney, who loved them at first, refuses to touch them now. If she were here, she'd be upset there is nothing fresh and green in the fridge to eat.

But she isn't here either.

I tear the plastic film off the dessert and put the frozen dinner into the microwave. Stabbing the minute button with my finger, I count to seven in my head. The light inside comes on and the microwave hums to life, finally making the house feel like there is something happening in it. But it is still a lonesome sound, and it feels artificial, like using a plastic plant to liven up a cube-farm office space with no windows. It just doesn't quite fix the unnatural ambiance.

I go back to the table and sort through the mail, quickly picking out brightly colored Christmas cards. The envelopes are still cold to the touch after being in the mailbox. The weather has been strange this year. Extra

13

warm days for December, warmer than jacket weather even, but still with cold nights pushing down into near freezing temperatures.

The bright red and green Christmas envelopes taunt me. I feel chastised just looking at them. I haven't sent out Christmas cards since the divorce. To be honest, I wasn't the one who'd sent them out before either, but I'd helped. I'd stuffed envelopes. I'd signed cards. I'd posed for pictures.

Now I don't know what to send. Or really, who to send them to. I don't have any other family left, and all of our friends and acquaintances are mutual. Though none of them took sides—they didn't have to, because Dana and I split amicably—it feels wrong sending out blank Christmas cards with only my signature. But what else do I have to add? There are no recent family photos, no great career changes to crow about at the print shop—just the opposite really.

Dana already keeps everyone updated on Coney and Fleming, Dana's new stepson. My Christmas letter would not only be short, it would be redundant and still only half of what Dana's was. Or less. I'm no longer current on Coney's comings and goings. Hell, at this point, I may end up getting *my* information from Dana's Christmas letters.

That is not a good thought. I push it aside. I know better than to let myself hold onto things like that. I can't stop a thought from crossing my mind, but I can stop myself from believing it or dwelling on it.

I get most of the way through tossing the junk mail into a recycle pile before the microwave beeps and shuts off. The new silence is nearly overwhelming. It makes me feel like my own home is suddenly someplace I'm not supposed to be.

I shake off the feeling, like I have hundreds of times before, and head back into the kitchen. Dutifully, I crunch up the ice still glazing the top of the apple dessert and the mashed potatoes, stir them up, and return the plastic tray to the microwave oven, adding another couple of minutes to the cook timer. The smell of the warming cinnamon apples is a little Christmassy and slightly takes the edge off my mood.

I sit down to go through the rest of the letters. One catches my eye as I start to throw it into the junk pile. It's addressed to Coney, and it looks like something official from Texas A&M. Which surprises me. She hasn't said anything about colleges yet. At least not to me.

My gut tightens. She's only a sophomore in high school. It's still too early to be worried about college. Isn't it? Is she already applying to colleges?

The microwave shuts off again. Have I really been staring at the letter for a full three minutes? I take a deep breath and set it next to the Christmas cards that spite me. The letter is a mixed blessing; a terrible reminder of how fast Coney is growing up, growing away from me, yet it is also a good reason to stop by and see her in the morning, to talk to her and see how she's doing.

And I'm grateful for that.

Chapter 4

THE COLD, WET SENSATION STARTS at the top of my belly and creeps downward slowly, making my abdominal muscles quiver. It's a sickening kind of tickle, and I can feel the viscous fluid sticking the fabric of my shirt to my skin.

Holding the waste ink reservoir out, away from me, I see black ink spreading across the front of my shirt. It's already seeping into my pants, and I can feel a clammy wetness creeping down the inside of my thigh as well.

A steady stream of black drips falls from the corner of the plastic tank, splashing on the rubber mat I'm standing on, spraying droplets onto my shoes.

"Shit, shit, shit, shit." I cuss all the way to the recycling, holding the plastic tank against my stomach to catch the leak, trying not to slosh as I weave through the equipment. The shirt and pants are already ruined, there is no point in spilling more ink everywhere else. There must be ink on the bottom of my right shoe, too. I can feel myself slipping with each step.

"Hello?" A woman's voice startles me. I hadn't heard the front door chime, and the shop doesn't open for another two hours. The sun isn't even up yet.

"Just a moment!" I call, fighting the urge to look at the clock and continuing to quickstep my way to the back of the shop, trying not to slip every time I put my right foot down.

Reaching the recycling holding tank, I pour the waste ink in. The pile of shop towels is right where it's supposed to be—just out of my reach on the next bench. The leaking tank drips more than I like as I take the extra step to grab towels and my foot squelches under me. I wrap two around the tank and then grab two more, pressing them against my shirt. I drop the tank into a trash can. I'll have to come back later and figure out why it is leaking. If it was leaking while it was in the printer, I'll have an even bigger mess to clean up.

I snatch two more towels, reducing the pile by half, and drop them on the floor. Wiping the bottom of my foot on the towels, I turn to see the trail of right-foot prints I'd left. I take a deep breath and blow it out, squeezing my eyes tight and wishing it all away.

Opening my eyes, I'm not surprised to find it's all still there. I grab more towels to blot at the ink on my pants, and I head for the front of the shop, sliding the towels under my right foot along with me as I go, trying to mop up some of the ink before it dries.

"Sorry," I say, moving into the reception area, searching to see who'd entered my shop so early.

Margret Atwater, shaped like a church bell in her overcoat and clutching her handbag in front of her as though it is a permanent fixture sewn into her gloved hands, stands in front of the picture windows, admiring the shop's Christmas display from the backside.

"Really very clever, Jeff," she says without looking at me. "You really created a wonderful diorama, with a lot of depth. It looks so good from out— " She finally turns to see the mess that is me, and her mouth keeps moving up and down though no sound comes out.

"Oh, my," she finally manages. One hand reluctantly breaks away from the small purse and waves in my general direction before snapping back into place as though tethered by an invisible rubber band. "Don't you normally wear a bib?"

I sigh and hold my hands wide, pulling the rags away to show her my clothes. "I thought I was only going to be a minute, so I didn't put my apron on," I lie.

Really, I forgot. My mind has been on taking that letter to Coney this morning. I came in early because I wanted to get over there before Coney left

17

for school, but that also means there is a good chance I'm going to run into Dana, or worse, her husband Trent.

Though I am sure Margret would like the opportunity to express her many opinions on the subject, I do not want to talk to her about that.

Shaking my head, I force a smile. "I won't make this mistake again."

"No. I imagine not! Those seemed such nice clothes, too. Did you have a meeting to go to?" Her eyes, as gray as her hair, are steeled and disapproving, as though she thought I couldn't go now. Unpresentable as I am.

Margret is a very judgy person. I've privately wondered if she judged her husband to death, or at least seriously contributed to his heart attack by driving him crazy with her nattering opinions of other people. It took a couple of years after my divorce before she made eye contact with me again. Partially because, like so many of her generation, she frowns upon divorce so hard, and partly because I stopped attending church after the divorce. Sitting behind Dana and Coney and staring at them felt only slightly better than sitting in front of them and feeling like they were staring at me. And when Coney wanted to move back and forth between us and didn't understand why we didn't all sit together… Well. It was just easier not to be there.

Which I'm pretty sure Margret doesn't agree with or approve of. I think the only reason she talks to me now is that she is the church's head coordinator and I'm the only local print shop.

But I try not to judge her back. She's a lonely old woman doing the best she can, and when I'm not cranky, or covered in ink, I generally know that, and I relate a little too well.

The way her hands wring the top of her purse remind me of that again now.

"Just some errands to run later," I tell her. "Not a big deal. What can I help you with?"

"Yes," she nods firmly, moving back into a conversation she is comfortable with, where she can be fully in charge. Her eyes leave me and go back to the Christmas display. I assume because she finds it painful to look at me. "I have to confess I have been so wrapped up in preparing the layout for the Christmas service program handout that I completely forgot to send you the one for this week's service until last night.

"As I was passing by, I saw that your lights were on, and I wanted to make sure you received the email and would still be able to print them up on time."

"Of course, I did, Mrs. Atwater." I smile warmly as I can. "That is exactly why I was here so early this morning," I lie again.

"Oh. Is that…" her eyes come back to me, looking me up and down, "…what *that* is?"

"No. Of course not." I easily let yet another lie fall off my tongue. Something about her brings that out in me. Or rather, seems to force it from me. "This was from some last-minute calendars I was printing up for advertisements. It's not a big deal. I can't hardly give calendars away anymore anyway. Everyone uses their phones nowadays."

Margret nods curtly, as if granting me her approval of that explanation, and turns to leave just as the door opens again. Cold air swirls through, and Margret steps back from it, but carefully not in my direction.

"Oh! Good morning, Mrs. Atwater!" Paige Walker says, entering quickly and pulling the door closed behind her, almost shutting her luggage-sized purse in it. "How are you on this lovely, but chilly morning?" Her voice is too bright and too cheery, and it matches her smile, clothes, and makeup, but not always her eyes. I'm sure the mask she wears is a permanent affliction caused by her real estate agent job. She is always trying to keep herself upbeat, both to keep her clients happy and for self-promotion. She once told me, *You never know which interaction may lead to a possible future client— or worse, cost you one.*

Her eyes give it away for me though.

People are suck, I'd heard someone else say a long time ago. I have found that to also be true. At least sometimes. Case in point, the woman in front of me trying to murder her handbag as she scowls at Paige.

Paige has to work with people, strangers, for a lot longer, and a lot closer than I have ever had to. I know she routinely meets people who absolutely *are* suck, and then she has to pretend they don't and keep working with them. She also had a rough time as a kid. Teenage pregnancy is never easy, and, twenty-some years later, people like Margret Atwater still look down upon her even more than they look down upon me.

"*MIZZ* Walker," Margret says, disdain dripping from her more thickly than the ink covering me.

Paige, not missing a beat nor giving an inch to the insult, turns to smile at me. "Good morning, Jeff!"

"Good morning, Paige."

She looks me up and down and apparently decides not to comment.

Margret does it for her. "I hope you weren't coming for one of his calendars. They aren't ready."

"Oh?" Paige, becoming perfectly concerned, raises her eyebrows at me. "I thought you did those last week."

"Most of them," I agree and nervously wipe at the ink one more time. Nothing like getting caught in a lie in front of the town's self-appointed moral compass.

Margret *harrumphs* and pushes past Paige and out into the still-dark morning without looking at either of us.

Unfazed, Paige turns back to me again. "I saw your lights were on and wanted to ask about the mailers…?"

Paige, like Margret Atwater, is one of my few regular customers. She is always ordering mailers and flyers to keep herself at the front of the minds of the locals, should they ever choose to sell their houses. I am always sure to get her orders done as soon as I can, just like I do Margret's. Maybe even a little sooner than Margret's.

Actually, if I am being honest, always sooner than Margret's.

"They all went out to the post office yesterday," I assure her. "People will definitely get your holiday cards before Christmas."

The relief in her eyes is real.

Chapter 5

THE MORNING SKY IS BRIGHT enough I can see Coney's car is still parked on the street in front of Dana and Trent's house when I turn the corner. A mixture of excitement and dread churns inside me. I really want to see Coney. I really don't know if I am up to seeing Dana. And I really, *really* don't want to see Trent. Especially not with all of this ink on me.

It's stupid, I know, but some thoughts, some feelings, come back over and over again, no matter how many times you push them away and try to ignore them. And it's like he won, and I lost. And every time something like this happens, I feel like he gets to look down at me from the winner's podium and sneer about yet another reason why I deserved to lose Dana.

None of which is true at all. He's the nicest damned guy.

Which makes it all the worse.

I park my truck behind Coney's car, the brand-new one Dana and Trent bought for her sixteenth birthday, and I try not to give headspace to thoughts about what I can and can't afford to do for her. I should be grateful for everything they can provide for her. And I am. It's just another one of those stray thoughts I have to ignore.

I get out of my truck, the drying ink pulling at the skin of my belly as the fabric of my shirt shifts. After I'd fixed the ink problem, cleaned up the mess, and made sure Margret's programs were printed up and ready, there wasn't enough time left to go home and change. The last of the clean towels, which

I'd used to sit on in the truck, still look clean. The ink doesn't seem to have spread to the truck, which is good. It'll ruin just about anything, including me. I'm sure I'm going to have temporary tattoos on my stomach and thigh that make me look like a walking Rorschach test for the next month. Fortunately, no one ever sees me naked.

I shake my head at my own joke; even I don't find it funny.

The morning air is brisk and stings my sinuses. The chill transfers almost immediately through the still-damp ink on my clothes, making cold spots on my stomach and thigh. And crotch. I probably should have my coat on, but I don't want to ruin that too.

Someone a half-block away starts their car. I look up just in time to see a perfect white smoke ring blow out of the tailpipe and float neatly up the street, undisturbed in the still morning air. I smile and try to enjoy it. It's the little things like this you have to pay attention to, you have to hold on to, to keep enjoying life. The car takes off in a hurry, tires crunching and throwing the gravel that has accumulated in the gutter, and I feel bad they didn't get to enjoy the smoke ring. As it turns the corner, I think I recognize it as Paige Walker's, though it's probably too early for her to be driving lookie-loos around.

Maybe she's got a new listing. Maybe that's why she was out so early this morning; excited about a new prospect. The housing market has been strange lately.

I look back to the row of houses where the car had been parked, searching for a For Sale sign, momentarily having a crazy thought of buying a house here, next to where Coney lives. I'm still entertaining the fantasy, which I know would more likely turn into a nightmare for all of us, when something akin to a gunshot booms out from the house beside me.

It's Coney, slamming the front door hard enough to rattle windows. She stomps down the front walk, head down, her black, hard-soled boots clomping against the cement like she's trying to break it. I can't help but notice her outfit. Ripped jeans, cutoff t-shirt showing her belly button and maybe the bottom of her ribs, flannel shirt tied around her neck like a shawl, and all of it covered by an unzipped hoodie with the hood up, hiding her face. Her sleeves are pulled up, revealing long, thin jewelry chains connecting bracelets on her wrists to rings on her hands.

"Hey, Sugar Cone," I call out. "You okay?"

Coney stutter-steps when she sees me, then she changes direction toward me. She lifts her face up, raising her chin almost defiantly, and I see what looks to be another chain hanging down from one earring and draping under her cheekbone then coming back up and connecting to a ring in her nose. I suspect it's the reason she stormed out of the house and started stomping down the sidewalk. Dana would never have given permission for Coney to do that.

Would she?

I don't know anymore. I'm too far out of the loop.

But if it's done, it's done, and all I can do is cause a problem. Or more of a problem. I do my best not to stare at it as she approaches.

"Just running late." She sounds exasperated. "What the hell happened to you?" she says, looking me up and down.

"Hey. Language."

"That's what the words comin' out of my mouth are. And you didn't answer my question. Industrial accident? Is there a hazardous waste spill at the shop that the EPA's gotta come clean up? They gonna burn those clothes?"

"Hey now. I didn't comment on your wardrobe."

Coney makes an ugly face at me. I deserve it. I knew I shouldn't have said that as soon as it came out of my mouth. It's the same kind of thing her mother does. Making a comment on her clothes while saying she wasn't. I'm just glad I didn't blurt out anything about the chain following the contour of her left cheek.

"This came for you," I say, holding out the Texas A&M letter and hoping to change the subject before it's too late. I notice her hair, under the hoodie, is different, too. Wild on the right side and neatly braded from the temple back on the left, probably to show off the earring the nose-chain is attached to.

"What is it?" Coney asks.

"I was hoping you would tell me."

I try to ignore her baggy jeans but finally look at them just so I don't just keep staring at the piercing in her nose. Ripped into little more than strips of frayed cloth across the front of her legs, the pants show a lot more skin

23

than I like to see my daughter showing. Which is silly, because it's still more clothing than a swimsuit, but it seems different when I think my daughter is trying to look…sexy.

I hate that thought and force it out of my mind and focus on not knowing how she can stand wearing the pants, if you can call them that, with how cold it is out here.

She takes the envelope from me and turns it over, quickly looking at both sides. She shrugs. "I dunno. I gotta go. Bye."

"Wait!" I hear desperation in my own voice and regret it.

"What?" She has learned her mother's agitated voice, and I almost cringe away from it.

"I love you." I step in to give her a big hug.

With a grimace, she steps backward, away from me. "I love you, too, but you're *not* touching me." She points to the ink stains. "I gotta go." Coney spins on her heel and heads into the light breeze that has come up. Her loose pants billow out, catching the air, reminding me of the parachutes dragracers use to slow down their cars at the end of a race. More than from the actual cold breeze hitting my face, I shiver at the thought of how cold that must be for her.

I watch Coney all the way to her car. The sun is finally coming up, the golden light beams streaming between the houses, and I suspect it is going to be another warmer-than average day.

"Jeff?"

I turn at the sound of my name. Dana is in the garage, Fleming on her hip. With one hand she opens the passenger door of her car and tosses her purse and briefcase in. She shifts Fleming's weight for a better grip and then starts toward me. I notice she parks on the left side of the garage, where she's the one who has to squeeze to get out.

Fleming buries his face into her shoulder. Whether from the cold wind or at the sight of me, I don't know. Probably both. Even after two years, the little guy and I haven't quite figured out how we fit into each other's lives, and, I have to admit, things in his house always seem to get awkward and uncomfortable whenever I'm around.

Which doesn't really happen too often.

"Hi, Dana," I say awkwardly. Her name feels weird in my mouth. It's not what I used to call her. Or at least not the way I used to say it. I've never gotten the hang of being divorced. The new boundaries between us never manage to block any of my feelings for her, so I always try to stay formal and courteous. In the end, I always feel like a jerk. Like I'm pretending. Which, I guess I am.

I hear Coney start her car, and I turn and watch. That conversation hadn't gone anything at all like I had imagined or hoped it would, but at least it hadn't been disastrous.

"Is everything all right?" Dana asks as she reaches me. She looks good. Healthy. Prim and proper, dressed for business at her law office. Just like I remember. Just like I miss. Her ever-present smile isn't there, though. Somewhere along the line, I became the one person she doesn't smile for.

"I could ask the same," I say, nodding toward Coney, knowing it is the wrong thing to say before I finish saying it.

The not-smile hardens. The whole argument goes through my mind in an instant: She'll say something like, "It's not easy raising a teenager," and I'll comment I would help more if she'd let me, and then, somehow, I'll be an asshole for both being around and for not being around.

I swallow it all down and do my best to avoid it. "Yeah. Everything is fine. I was just dropping off a letter off for Coney." I shove my hands into my pockets as Coney drives away. "She got something from Texas A&M."

I feel like Dana's face is too hard. She is taking too long to say anything, and I am afraid I didn't manage to stop that argument after all, so I push the topic before it can get changed. "Is she applying to colleges already?"

"No. She took the PSAT. Colleges always start sending out letters after that." Dana shifts Fleming's weight again. At nearly six years old, he is getting too big to hold for long.

"What happened to you?" Dana asks.

I look down at myself and realize the mess is likely why Fleming is peeking at me so curiously. "Little accident at work."

"Not sure 'little' is the right word." Her eyes rove up from my pants to my shirt and then lock onto mine with her piercing, lawyer-stare mode, and I find myself bracing for what's coming. "Look, I know Coney hasn't been to your house for a couple of months—"

"Yeah," I agree, raising my voice more than I want to. The automated defenses are still on a hair trigger. That's never good.

"—but you were the one who told her it was her choice. You were the one—"

"I know! I know," I interrupt, trying to stop Dana before she escalates because I accidentally escalated. "You're right. And I didn't say anything about that. And I wasn't going to either. Honest. I just brought her the letter because I thought it might be important. And because I wanted to see her."

I lower my voice a little, pretending to myself that if I say it quieter Fleming won't pay attention to it. "Was that a piercing?"

The look on Dana's face tells me it is, and now I'm sure I know why Coney was slamming doors and stomping out of the house.

"Hey, Jeff! What a nice surprise!" Trent, coming out of the garage, walks toward us looking perfect in his business suit, and suddenly this morning is everything I had always never wanted it to be.

Trent reminds me of the happy-ever-after in a Hallmark movie. Big City lawyer comes to small town, meets greatest woman in the world who changes everything about him, they fall in love and live happily ever after in said small town. As he reaches Dana and Fleming, and Dana's smile returns to her face, the illusion of perfection is complete. The troubled teen from the first marriage has left, and now it's just the perfect fucking family left standing in front of their perfect fucking house.

I brace myself, breathing the cold morning air in deeply, letting it burn my sinuses and cool my hot head.

Like many of the feelings I don't seem to have much control over anymore, these ones are not fair, because it really isn't like that.

Trent lost his wife, Fleming's mother, in a car accident a year or so before he married Dana. There were a lot of rough times there. Nothing remotely perfect about it.

I guess just I feel this way because he's perfect in every way I'm not: young, fit, good-looking, good career, well-off. Married to my wife. Has my daughter living under his roof. Buys her nice cars for her sixteenth birthday.

More bad thoughts. I push them away and force myself to be civil.

Fleming reaches for Trent with both arms, learning out and away from Dana, trying to get his father to take him. Trent, who is nearly a decade younger than me, takes him effortlessly with one arm and simultaneously reaches the other hand out to greet me.

"Hi, Trent." I meet his gaze, and I shake his hand. I can't stop myself from disliking the man who is taking care of the people I love, but I can stop myself from showing it. He doesn't deserve it, and neither do they.

Trent takes his hand back, his genuine grin still wide. I don't understand how he always seems happy to see me. It just seems wrong.

"Someone throw an octopus at you?" he asks.

Fleming laughs. Safe in his father's arms, he finally turns and fully looks at me, as if he thinks he can spot an octopus still crawling around.

"A little less exciting than that," I say. "Just a mess at the shop is all."

Looking at Dana, Trent says, "So, what did he say?"

"I haven't asked yet," Dana says, eyes still on me, smile fading. I know that look, too. She uses it to nail me into place, to make me listen. And then she refuses to let me go until she gets what she wants.

"Ask what?" I ask, despite knowing I don't want to know.

"Fleming would really like to be on the Christmas float in the parade," Dana says. Her voice is softer than I expect. She really is just asking, not telling me what it is I am going to do for her.

"He's learned all the songs the music teacher said you would be doing," Trent adds. "I know we didn't sign up when the permission slips went out, but he changed his mind and really wants to. Don't you, buddy?"

Fleming meets my eyes and nods solemnly.

"What do you say," Trent whispers to him.

"Yes, please." Fleming's eyes are as big, brown, and hopeful as I ever remember Coney's being when she was that age.

How could I say no to those?

Chapter 6

THE GINGERBREAD BAKING IN THE oven smells great. The Christmas music is festive. The lights are lit on the tree, the gas fireplace is on, spreading a warm glow through my living room. And yet, my house feels like a house instead of a home like it had been when Coney and Dana were here with me.

I count the stacks of gingerbread men one more time. When the last batch comes out of the oven, I will have enough for each volunteer parent, both moms and dads, and their kids to have two apiece. In the past I've found that works out well to balance the kids who take four against the parents who don't want any.

Just as I pick up the beater to start whipping the buttercream frosting, I hear keys rattle in the front door lock. My heart does a stutter. My first instinct is that someone is breaking in, but who would break into a house with lights on and music playing? And why would they use keys?

Poking my head out of the kitchen, I see Coney letting herself in. It's a new experience for me. This is only the second time she's driven herself over here, and the last time I came home after she was already here.

"Hey, Sugar Cone!" I step back into the kitchen, set the mixer down, and wipe my hands clean on my apron. I take the messy garment off and drape it over the back of a chair.

"Hi, Daddy."

Her words stop me, still just out of sight, at the doorway. She only calls me 'Daddy' when something is wrong. Considering it's a Friday night, I assume it's boy problems. At least, I hope it's only boy problems. I mean, easy-to-deal-with boy problems.

Or, if I'm lucky, it's just the nose-chain thing. I can deal with that.

I take a deep breath and do my best to put on a smile that hides any worry that might show through to my face. Braced, I come out and catch her in a big hug.

Her leather jacket is cold against my skin, but I hold her close and press my cheek to the top of her head. We stand there for a long moment before I realize she's crying.

"Hey." I step back, hands on her shoulders, and look at her. "What's going on?"

She doesn't meet my eyes. Instead, she shakes her head and steps close again, resuming the hug. I hold her tight, refusing to let any thoughts go through my mind, until she finally pulls away. It's hard not to assume the worst about everything, all at once, as I watch her.

"It smells really good in here," she says, going for a tissue from the box on the end table.

"Gingerbread men for the float team."

"Tomorrow is all-hands on deck?" She finally looks at me. Her face is puffy and red, but her eyes are bright and full of life. I take that as a good sign. As she wipes her nose, I notice all of the chain jewelry is missing, including whatever had attached the chain to her nose, but I know better than to say anything about it. Maybe, hopefully, this is what she is upset over. Maybe Dana finally won the argument.

"Yeah. Last full day to get it all done," I say.

Wadding the tissue and shoving her hands into her jacket pockets, she shifts her weight to stand in an accusing stance, one hip stuck out. "So, you're making them work through the Reindeer Games then?"

"What?"

"You forgot they moved the Reindeer Games up a week, didn't you?"

"Crap."

Coney clicks her tongue and shakes her head at me. "Looks like you might not win first place this year."

"Looks like…" My voice is falsetto and completely unconcerned.

29

"Are you teasing me?" Coney's eyes go wide, and she leans forward.

I laugh. "Yeah. Even if I had forgotten, none of the kids would have. I'd have been reminded *real* quick."

"So, when are you guys going to get the float finished?"

I wink at her.

"Really? It's already done? That's like a record!"

"Well…" I shrug. "It was an easy float this year."

"That's *not* what I heard." She takes off her jacket and hangs it up in the closet, tissues still in her hand.

I try not to let tears form in my own eyes as that simple act suddenly makes my house feel like a home again.

"Have you been spying?" I ask. "How do you know what our float is?"

"I live with a five-year-old who won't shut up about being a *dead* angel. Which, of course, meant Mom had to look into what the hell you were up to."

"Language."

Coney rolls her eyes at me. "Okay, Captain America."

"That 'dead angel' thing never went away, huh?" I ask.

"Nope. It sounds like some of the kids are planning to sneak face paint to put on themselves after they get on the float."

I raise my eyebrows at her, considering the idea. "I guess… If they really want to. I mean. It could work. But probably no one would notice."

"*Of course* someone would. Your floats always get the most scrutiny. Everyone wants to find *something* wrong with it so they can belittle it somehow."

"Ah, the price of being famous!"

Coney laughs at me, and it feels good. "You want help with the gingerbread men?" she asks.

"Of course! But don't eat more than three, or I won't have enough."

She follows me into the kitchen. I open a drawer and pull out her apron, which says *I'm cuter than the chef, kiss me!* and I toss it to her.

"I can't believe you still have this," she says. "I don't think it'll fit." She holds it up and it reminds me of the half-shirt I'd seen her in two days ago.

"Yeah. Sorry." I pull out another apron, a less cute, but much larger one with a drawing of a barbeque grill with hotdogs on it. It says, *It's all fun and*

My face hurts from grinning. With Coney cheering for her little brother, I have to, too. I can't not. And the next thing I know, I feel like I am part of the family again. Despite Trent being here, too.

He isn't a bad guy. I know he isn't. But sometimes it is hard to not feel bad things about him. Or, more accurately, *at him*, I guess. Now, cheering alongside with him, for his son—for all intents and purposes Coney's brother and Dana's son—I finally feel…if not kinship, then at least a complete lack of hostility.

It is a first for me. And I like it. I like feeling like we all get along. Like we can be a family, even if it is a little confusing.

A whistle blows and the cheering gets louder. A team on the far end has moved all of their blocks across the field and sorted them into colors. One kid, on the team furthest behind in the race, all alone and still dragging his big red bag full of foam bricks, falls down in the middle of the field and flops out, spreadeagle. At first, I think he is going to throw a fit, but I see his tiny belly heaving as he breathes, and I realize he was just really giving his all.

"Hold on! Hold on!" A voice comes over the PA system. It's tinny and the echo makes it hard to understand. "It's not over until it's over, folks! We still gotta check the boxes and make sure the elves delivered the good kids the right presents and not someone else's coal!" I spot the referees, three of them, all dressed like Christmas elves, jogging toward the winning team. One of them, of course, is Summer Christmas.

"Ah-ah-ah! Put that back!" the announcer says, and I spot which elf has the microphone because he is pointing at a kid using his foot to move a block closer to his team's finished piles. "Everyone has to stop!"

Fleming, dressed only in jeans and a Christmas Grogu t-shirt because it is so warm today, leans out around his teammates, trying to see the judges. Instead of walking out to where a referee might call foul on him for still doing stuff, he lifts one leg and leans so far over he loses his balance, windmills his arms, and finally falls down.

Trent and I both laugh. Dana gives Trent a mock dirty look at the same time Coney gives me the same one. There is a symmetry here that feels right, and my heart feels light for the first time in as long as I can remember.

"He did so good for his first time, didn't he?" A voice carries from behind

33

us and, at first, I don't realize it is directed to our group, but Dana and Trent both turn, so I do too.

Paige Walker is there with her bright, always plastered-on smile. Today it seems real, though. It seems to have reached her eyes, which are as bright as her LED lit Christmas sweater. She has a handful of pamphlets I quickly recognize as something I printed up for her a month ago, and, for a moment, I wonder if she is going to try to hand me one.

She doesn't. Instead, she keeps talking to Trent about Fleming. "He looked so *strong* carrying that bag across the field, didn't he? Oh, he's getting so big!"

"Growing like a weed!" Dana says. Paige looks at her, and I see the smile in Paige's eyes flicker.

It looks like there's a story there, but I don't know it. Or not much of it, anyway. I know Paige was best friends with Nancy, Trent's deceased wife, but even if that is why, it's really only a guess. Dana hardly talks to me about Trent, let alone Trent's family or friends, and even then, only when she feels I have a right or a need to know because it might affect Coney. Beyond that, I really don't have any input or inside information in Dana's life anymore.

Which is as it should be, I tell myself, feeling all of those good, family feelings from earlier slipping away.

"Oh! Jeff!" Paige turns her attention on me. I'd kind of lost myself in the moment, and I actually jump a little. "People are already telling me they got my Christmas mailer! Thank you so much!" She reaches out and pats me on my chest in an entirely too familiar gesture. I do my best to ignore it. I'm pretty sure, like the permanent smile, it is an acquired affectation designed to endear her to her clients.

She starts to turn away but quickly comes back to me with wide eyes and a too-practiced, not really surprised, "O" on her lips. Her hand comes right back to my chest and stays there while she speaks, pressing her words into me. "The lights in my little house aren't working! I can't figure out why. Do you have time to look at it for me?"

Her 'little house' is a parade float built on top of a travel trailer. It is a scaled down, ranch-style house, complete with white picket fence and a swinging For Sale sign in the front yard. She bought it online somewhere a couple of years back and has had constant problems with it since. Mostly because she doesn't take care of it.

I made the mistake of volunteering to look at it once. It's haunted me ever since.

Her hand lingers, waiting for my answer, and I wonder if it is some kind of high-pressure sales technique she learned somewhere.

"Sure," I answer, hating myself for agreeing but knowing I'd feel guilty later if I didn't. "I can do that."

Receiving the answer she wants, I can see her attention leave me faster than she can pull her hand away. She quickly turns to Trent. "Have you seen Tommy?" Paige asks him.

"Who?" Trent's brows furrow.

"My son, silly!" She reaches out and pats Trent's arm, pushing a little, like she is trying to wake him up. Like a best friend punching another friend in the arm for being stupid. The hand she lays on him, keeps on him to keep his attention, is just as familiar, just as friendly as when she'd touched me, but, unlike when it was on me, it draws a scowl from Dana.

It's just a tiny one, one I'm pretty sure neither Trent nor Paige will recognize even if they see it. But I've had years of practice reading Dana's face, and I can tell Dana doesn't like Paige's handsiness.

"He's home for the holidays," Paige continues excitedly. "He's around here somewhere. I know he wants to see you again. It's been so long!" She looks around us, into the crowd, then shrugs dramatically. "He probably ran into some of his friends. Oh, well. Gotta go! People to see!" She holds up the pamphlets then looks back to Trent again. "If you see him, make sure to say hello. He's too shy to come up and say it first."

Before she can leave, Fleming comes running up, panting hard, and throws himself at Trent while still three feet away. Trent catches him out of the air and effortlessly lifts him up to hold him as high as everyone else.

"Did you see me?" Fleming asks excitedly, looking to all of our faces for a response. "We almost winned!"

"You did great!" Coney says.

"You were *soooo* good!" Paige steps forward and tweaks his cheek.

"Auntie Paige!" Fleming falls forward out of Trent's arms into Paige's.

35

She deftly catches him without dropping any pamphlets and easily puts him on her hip as though he belongs there.

More scowling from Dana.

I step back. This no longer feels like family to me. In fact, I feel like a complete outsider watching things I don't understand. Before I can fade into the crowd, Coney catches my arm. I can see from the look on her face she is feeling the same way, and it saddens me. I don't ever want her to feel out of place in her family.

"Where are you going?" she asks. "You're not trying to skip out on the three-legged race, are you?"

"Don't you have a partner?" I ask.

"Yeah, the same partner I always have. You!"

I put my arm around her and pull her close, pretending to match leg sizes. She is still a good foot shorter than me, and her hip lines up with the bottom of my back pocket. "I suppose it would only be fair to handicap ourselves and give everyone else a chance to win."

I have been her partner every year except last year when she had first decided to start dating. I can't even remember the boy's name anymore. Steve, I think. I never really met him. There was too much going on at the time, and it didn't last long enough. I was still reeling from Dana and Trent's marriage, and to be fair, Coney was too.

But if she was going to pretend that didn't happen, so was I.

Chapter 8

GASPING FOR AIR AND NEAR passing out, I pull Coney into my arms and hold her close, protecting her with my body as I give up and fall to the ground, pulling her down across the finish line with me. The dry grass of the soccer field crunches beneath us, and our tied-together legs fly up into the air. We roll all the way onto our backs, joining the hundred or so people around us who have also just finished the three-legged race.

Coney is laughing so hard she can't hardly breathe. I just can't hardly breathe.

"I guess you're gonna need a new partner if you ever want to win," I finally manage to say. "We didn't even make the top ten this year."

"Top ten?" Coney guffaws and then covers her mouth, looking embarrassed. "We didn't even make the top hundred!"

"Hey! At least we finished!" I point to a young couple still in the middle of the field. Having fallen opposite ways, they had somehow twisted themselves around and now faced opposite directions while still tied together at the knee and ankle. Their attempt to finish the race, with arms hooked at the elbows and the girl trying to run backwards, is still raising laughter from the crowd as they fall yet again.

"You can do it!" an elf referee encourages them over the PA system.

Coney fumbles at the elastic wrap joining our knees and says something I can't make out.

"What was that?" I ask, still laughing, though I don't know if it is at us or the couple in the field. The woman bends over at the waist, in what looks like some kind of ballerina move, and lays herself in the man's arms with her unbound leg sticking straight out. He tries to carry her in his arms but has problems lifting his leg that she's tied to. She tries to help by hopping, and they go down again.

"Oh, noooooo!" the overhead voice groans. "Get up! Get up!"

"I said, you've let yourself get out of shape." Coney pulls the wrap off our knees and starts unwinding the one at our ankles. "You should start working out again."

With a deep sigh I stop laughing. "You're right," I admit. "I haven't been to the gym in a couple of years."

She pulls the wrap off our ankles and looks at me, shaking her head. "It shows." She pats me on the belly and jumps up before I can react. She's laughing and gone, off to put the wraps back in the box we got them from, before I can even get my tired, old, fat butt off the grass.

I'm glad to see her laughing. Remembering how upset she'd been last night, I hope it was just a passing teenage thing, a random flyby of emotions. I can still see the little girl she used to be as I watch her run past Trent and Dana, who beat us by a mile. She stops to high-five Fleming, who apparently ran the race with his short little leg tied to 'Auntie Paige,' as they are still hopping around with Fleming pretty much completely standing on Paige's foot.

"You got it!" the referee calls again. "You got it!" The woman has, mostly, climbed onto the man's back, with one leg thrown around his waist and her arms around his neck. He carries her piggy-back across the finish line to a round of cheers.

"Looks like you're out of practice, old man!" Oliver, arm in arm with Summer Christmas, comes up on me with a big grin on his face. I know the grin isn't because he's happy to see me. It's because he's just run the race with Summer, whose one lock of hair out of place on her forehead still looks like it was planned and intentional, and maybe even a required part of the referee elf uniform she is wearing.

Oliver has been flirting with her since they first met, and, up until now, I wasn't sure she was going to have any interest in him.

"Hi, Jeff!" she says, casually pushing her hair back into place under her green cap as she unhooks her arm from Oliver's. "I have to go," she says to Oliver, putting a hand on his arm. "That was really fun. Thank you."

"No, *thank you*," Oliver says.

Summer smiles at both of us and jogs off for the far side of the field, the jingle bells on her shoes and the end of her cap ringing with each step.

"She's running the ornament hunt," Oliver explains.

"Brave of her." I nod.

Like an easter egg hunt, but with Christmas ornaments hung from the trees and bushes along the path and throughout the manicured forest on the far side of the park, the ornament hunt brings out the worst in people. Now limited to kids between three and ten years, it used to be for everyone, but, as some of the ornaments once had money and gift certificates hidden in them, a particularly nasty fistfight, which led to a shooting later that night, prompted a reimagining of the event a few years back. Now the fights are between little kids who find the same pretty ornament at the same time, and then between their upset mothers, which, arguably, is harder to understand and deal with, in my opinion.

Sooo....?" I look to Oliver and raise an eyebrow.

He shrugs and shakes his head. "I dunno. She's just so nice and polite that I can't tell if she's just being nice and polite."

"That sounds about right."

"You've got grass all over your butt."

"Thanks." I brush it off. "Where you headed?"

"Welp." Oliver makes a show of making a resigned face and hooking his thumbs into his front pockets. "Since Lara decided to take Steven and Katie to her mother's this year instead of coming to this, I was just going to follow her around." He nods toward Summer's receding figure. "But...like I said, I can't tell if she's just being nice and polite, so I don't want to overstep and shoot myself in the foot."

"Are Steven and Katie going to be back for the parade tomorrow?" I'm not worried about them missing out on being on the float so much as I am concerned for my friend that he's not getting to spend any of this time with his kids.

His answer is a shrug and another face. He's never really been sure if Lara does things like this to spite him, or if she just doesn't realize, or maybe doesn't care.

I kind of understand what he goes through, but then, he had a terrible divorce and Dana and I split as friends, so I can only guess at some of his feelings. Like what it feels like to not have his kids around, but not what it feels like if that is because their mother is being hateful.

"My wife's stepson is doing the ornament hunt," I tell him, "so that gives me an excuse to be there, which gives you an excuse to be there, too." I pat him on the shoulder and give a gentle shove to start him walking along with me.

"*Ex*-wife," he says.

"What?"

"Your *ex*-wife. Dana is not your wife anymore, brother. It's been five years. You need to stop making those kinds of Freudian slip-ups. You're not doing yourself, or anyone else, any favors like that."

We take a few steps in silence. His words running through my mind. "Do I do that often?" I ask.

"Often enough to be too often. I can't say anyone else would have noticed, but I have. You really need to move on, Jeff."

I nod, considering Oliver's words. How often have I thought of Trent as married, not to Dana, but to *my wife?*

Often enough to know I've done it. Which is too often.

Chapter 9

SUMMER IS ALL SMILES WITH the kids as she explains the rules of the ornament hunt. There are dozens of children, each holding a large Christmas stocking to put found ornaments into, and they are all so eager to start down the path into the trees that Summer and the six volunteer teenagers have to keep holding their arms out wide and herding the kids back into place.

Summer's gentle manner and skill with the kids evinces her experience as a school librarian. "Shall we count down from the Twelve Days of Christmas?" she asks them. The response is a confusion of unenthusiastic answers from the kids and chuckles from the surrounding crowd of parents.

"No. You're right. That's too long. How about we just count down from *Five Golden Rings?*" She sings the last few words, and her voice carries beautifully, as though she were a professional singer.

Some of the older kids groan while some of the younger ones cheer.

I spot Coney, Dana, Trent, and Paige on the far side of the crowd from Oliver and me. They are all standing behind Fleming, with Coney bent down and whispering in his ear. I imagine she is giving him tips on where to look for the best ornaments. When she was little, she devised a whole set of elaborate rules about where to look and where to not bother looking because other kids would have already been there.

My eyes flick from Dana to Paige, and I wonder again at what I'd seen

41

pass between the two of them earlier. Whatever it is, Paige is still right there with them, and it likely isn't any more awkward than me still calling Dana 'my wife.'

I really hope I haven't done that in front of anyone besides Oliver, though I probably have.

"You're right," Summer says to the kids with a mock exasperation, her eyes wide and fingers outstretched. "That's still too long, isn't it? Tell you what, let's all just count down from five!"

A cheer goes up from all the kids and, as Summer starts counting backwards, they all join in. When they reach one, Summer yells, "Go!" and pandemonium incarnate is released into the one-acre forest. The kids, heedless of the paved path before them, spread out in all directions, tearing through the bushes and screaming their precious little heads off.

The teenagers quickly follow after them, carefully picking up the half dozen three-year-olds who went down in the initial rush.

"Be careful!" Summer calls out. "No pushing! Remember to be nice and help each other! Christmas is about charity and giving, not…" Her words are lost to me as she follows them into the trees.

"Those were the days, huh?" Oliver asks me.

"Yeah," I answer. My eyes are still on my not-so-little Coney, who only has eyes for her new brother as he chases off into the Christmas Forest in search of his treasures. "Any idea what the prizes are this year?" Last year it had been coupons for ice cream cones and cookies. Something valuable to the kids, but not to asshole adults.

"More of the same, I think. I didn't really hear anything different."

A scream, unlike the other screams of joy and fun we've been hearing all day, catches our attention. This one is terrible.

I find myself reflexively responding to the sound of the distressed child and suddenly I'm running into the tiny forest, dodging little kids, trees, and bushes. Oliver and a handful of other parents are right beside me, and we all home in, changing our direction as a second scream, this one for help, leads us farther into the foliage.

The scream for help seems to have come from one of the teenagers, who still has her hands over her mouth and nose, eyes looking over the tops of her fingers, when we arrive. The three little kids with her are all wild-eyed, looking back to the arriving mob of parents and pointing to show us where to look, into the bush, at the man, in a pool of blood.

His unshaven face, laying on a bed of shining leaves still wet with blood, is gray as ash, and his dark eyes are staring into eternity, unblinking. There is no doubt in my mind he is dead.

Chapter 10

"GET THEM OUT OF HERE!" Oliver takes charge, directing parents to grab the kids and move them away just as Summer arrives with more parents. "You, you, you, and you." He points to me last. "Make a big circle around this, keep everyone away. A *big* circle. We don't need any more kids seeing this."

Summer's eyes go wide when she sees the body, but she doesn't hesitate to start blowing her whistle. "Everyone back to the starting line!" she calls, moving back and forth through the trees and herding children and adults alike out of the area.

As soon as he's done giving orders, Oliver pulls out his cell phone and is calling for help. The other parents Oliver has assigned to guard duty take up closer points around the body, so I head on around to the other side to close up the circle, unable to keep my eyes off the man.

He's young. Too young to be dead. The scraggly beard, nose piercing, and ear gauges almost look fake on his chubby baby face. The stark black tattoos across the knuckles of his hand mar the illusion he is about to suck his thumb. I recognize one of the tattoos is a logo from a video game. The other three are similar and probably also from games, and they are all shakily drawn, like he'd done it himself, at home, which reinforces my feeling he is too young to be laying here.

I take my place in the circle and find myself looking across the body at the other parents. They turn away a couple kids and other adults who approach to see what's going on, but, being on the far side from the start of the ornament hunt, no one comes up on my side.

I find myself staring at the body.

I've seen bodies before, in caskets at funerals, and once at a car accident while driving by, but this is different. This man was murdered.

And he's right here in front of me. Too close, too *real,* to ignore.

Blood has turned the soil dark near his neck, which is where the majority of the bloody leaves are, and I wonder if his throat was cut. The blood on the leaves looks fresh, wet, and I wonder how long ago he was killed, if this happened today, while everyone was here at the Reindeer Games, if maybe the kids would have even seen it happen if Summer had started the hunt sooner.

More kids and parents are waved off by the others surrounding the body despite Summer's whistles and calls for everyone to come out of the trees.

I don't recognize the dead kid, but I can't help but think maybe he came here with family. Maybe he snuck back here to get high, so he could put up with being around his parents and whiny kid sister, and then got killed for his drugs. Or the money he was going to use to buy them.

"Over here!" Oliver calls out and waves his arm in the air. I spot an officer approaching us through the trees. He sees the body and says something into his shoulder mic.

"Has anyone touched anything?" he asks, looking at all of us.

"No one has gotten any closer than they are right now," Oliver answers. "Unless one of the kids did when they first found him," he adds.

"Which kids?"

"They're over there." Oliver points to the parents who took the kids away. They are all still huddled in a group separate from everyone else, just at the edge of the treeline. The teenager looks like she's crying.

"Stay here," the officer tells us all. "Don't get any closer. Don't touch anything. I'll be right back." He heads over to where the kids are, and I can barely hear his voice as he tells them something along the same lines.

Another officer arrives before the first can return, and he takes the scene in with calculating eyes. "Y'all just got here? No one actually saw nothin'?" he asks.

We all nod.

"Okay. I want y'all to come over to me and be careful where you step. Stay away from the scene." He points to me because I'll have to walk around it again. "I need y'all to pull out your I.D.'s so I can find you later if we have questions, and then y'all can clear out."

I walk back around the body the way I'd come, and then stand in line behind Oliver to show the officer my driver's license.

"You did a good job taking charge," I tell him.

"Military training kicked in," he whispers back.

"I didn't know you were in the military."

"I wasn't."

I look sideways at him, and he grins at me. Before I can ask about it, the officer is snapping images of us and then our IDs with his phone.

"Thank you," he says. "We'll be in touch if we have any questions for you. Please vacate the area."

"I didn't recognize him, did you?" Oliver asks me as we walk away.

I shake my head. "No, but that doesn't mean anything. He looked old enough he would have probably been in high school when Coney started middle school, so I wouldn't have met him."

"That's what I figured, too. I don't remember ever seeing him around town. And I'm pretty sure I would have remembered that jean jacket about tea bagging your enemies."

Chapter 11

I LET LOOSE A SIGH that sounds deep and bone-rattling, even to me. Paige's 'little house' has a lot more problems than just the lights not working.

"Do you think you can fix it?" she asks.

I try not to laugh, or cry, as I look at the miniature broken For Sale sign leaning up against the miniature, broken, white picket fence. 'White' isn't really accurate anymore. The float has been left outside, in the elements since the parade last year. The paint is faded and starting to peel. The plastic windows are fogged with sun exposure. Even the artificial turf comprising the front lawn looks like it's turning brown from neglect. And both tires on the trailer are flat, maybe rotten.

"Well," I say, trying for a chipper tone, "it's definitely a fixer-upper!"

I get a friendly punch in the shoulder and a forced laugh from her. "Thanks, Jeff. I really owe you for this!"

Before I can reply, she drops her voice low. "Wasn't that just awful yesterday? Those poor kids that found that man! They will probably have nightmares forever!"

Before I can decide whether or not I want to tell her I've already had nightmares about the baby-faced kid, dreaming he was crying and sucking his thumb while bleeding all over the leaves, Paige keeps talking.

"Is it true that he was hanging around watching the kids practice Wednesday night?"

"I didn't see him there," I tell her, "but most of the moms at the rehearsal did, and they're all sure it was the same guy." After the police found out they guy had been acting weird around the warehouse, they'd contacted me again about it, but, other than explaining that Oliver and I went out to look for the guy that night, I had no information to offer.

"Isn't that creepy!"

"Yeah, it is." It makes me feel sick. I still feel like he was just another kid, and something terrible happened to him in that park, but at the same time, after hearing he was the one who'd been weird around the moms and the kids at the warehouse, I'm kind of relieved the guy is dead. Which is a horrible thing to admit even to myself. The whole thing makes me wonder how close we came to having something bad happen Wednesday night, but then, I guess something bad did happen, but it was on Saturday, and it was to that guy.

Paige's phone sounds off with a cringe-worthy, obnoxious giggling voice ringtone that I am sure she thinks is cute and friendly, but it damn near physically hurts me to listen to it.

"Oh! It's Tommy! I gotta take this," she says and vanishes back toward her house, already talking.

Taking a deep breath to clear my mind, I look around her backyard. It's in pretty much the same shape as the little house. It doesn't look like anyone has done any upkeep, other than maybe mowing, in years. Beyond the overgrown weeds and the brambles that were once a neatly trimmed hedge lining her fence, I spot the field of dormant grapevines that made this a prime house to own when Paige originally purchased it. She occasionally did some house flipping on the side. This one was a foreclosure, if I remember correctly.

Decanter, almost as famous for being wine country as for being the Christmas capital of Texas, still uses a photo of people, in this very back yard, toasting each other with red wine, with the green grapevines stretching out behind them toward the lake, for the summer tourist promotional fliers I print up for the city each year. Come spring, that vineyard will be green again, but this yard…

I don't really know Paige well enough to know her reasons for letting everything go to pot like this. Sometimes people just give up on some things in their lives. I'm surprised the HOA hasn't said something about the state of her yard. It has to be dropping the property value of the neighbors. Which is something Paige should totally understand.

I shake my head and look back to the decrepit scale replica house. There's symbolism going on here, I can feel it, but I don't know what it means. Sometimes I feel the universe teases me with things like this, puts them right in my face, with flags all over them, and dares me to recognize them for what they are.

But I don't see it. Instead, I recall I once heard that when you're juggling life's problems and have to drop one, make sure it's made out of plastic and not crystal, and I have to admit, a backyard is a plastic problem, not a crystal one.

Two of the four hinges that hold the roof on the little house, which opens up like a storage box, are rusted through, and the top doesn't sit square anymore. I carefully lift the top and look in. The wiring for the lights is all gone, chewed up, eaten by mice. I wrinkle my nose at the musty smell and the nest in one of the corners. I'm not looking forward to crawling around inside of there and cleaning it out. It's too big to just reach into and work on, and too small to comfortably get inside to work.

I close the roof and do my best to latch it. The top alone needs some serious work, or it will tear itself apart just bouncing down the road. At least it will give me something to do, I guess, something to take my mind of that poor kid in the park.

Taking a step back from the smell, I pull out my phone and start making a list of what the little float needs, besides a good pressure wash: wires, tires, paint, plastic windows, battery…

With the parade only a day away, I wonder if it can even be done, let alone if I can do it by myself. I decide the first thing I need to do is fix the tires so I can tow it back to the warehouse where the other float building supplies are.

"Jeff!" I turn at Paige's voice. She's standing at her back door. "Can you help me with my laptop?"

I shove my phone into my pocket and head toward her. "I can try. I'm not really an expert with computers. What's wrong?"

"I can't connect to the internet," she says and beckons me to come on in.

The inside of Paige's house is completely different than her backyard. It reminds me of a show home. Everything is strategically placed for maximum 'this is what you could do with it' effect, but nothing looks like it has ever actually been touched or used. Ever.

Paige leads me to the kitchen table, where her laptop sits open to a blank browser tab. "Ever since Tommy put in the new Wi-Fi, it just won't connect."

I poke around with the internet settings for a moment and don't like the error messages I am seeing. "Do you use cellular or internet on your phone when you're at home?" I ask.

She shrugs and hands me her phone. The lock screen is a cute picture of a little kid, barely a toddler, in a Tigger Halloween costume, roaring at whoever was taking the picture.

"Is that your son?"

"Ha! No, silly! That's Fleming!" Her voice lowers. "That was right after Nancy died. Um, Fleming's mother." She nods to make sure I understand, then her perky voice comes right back. "I took Fleming trick-or-treating that year. Oh, we had so much fun!"

"I didn't recognize him." I'm not sure what else to say. "He's grown a lot since then." There's a lot here I'm really not privy to, and, not sure if it was one of those boundaries I shouldn't cross with Dana, I'm not sure I *want* to know anything, so I don't press Paige for more.

Almost as if reading my mind, Paige puts her hand on my shoulder and says, "I don't know why Dana ever let you go."

Startled at her forthrightness, I glance up at her, but don't know how to respond.

Different than the fake familiarity of her hand on my chest yesterday, her touch feels like a genuinely friendly gesture.

I swallow. Hard.

"Oh, stop it!" Paige's voice changes, her eyes, her face goes back to the practiced persona I am used to. She slaps my shoulder lightly, the forced friendliness again present. "I'm not hitting on you. I'm just saying you're a good man. A good person. I know she couldn't have had a good reason for leaving you."

"Thank you," I say, not sure what to say. It isn't common knowledge that Dana left me. We both tried very hard to tell everyone it was a mutual decision, so I assume Paige is fishing for gossip. Instead of offering any, I look back to the laptop.

"You should have fought harder for her. I can see it in the way you look at her. You still love her."

I open my mouth, but, again, I don't know what to say. Hopefully I never called her 'my wife' in front of Paige. Lamely, I say, "There wasn't anything to fight for."

"There's always something to fight for." Her tone is different again. I look up to see a determination in her eyes that was never there before, not even when the smile didn't reach her eyes.

She quickly looks away, to her phone still in my hand, still on the lock screen with the photo of Fleming. "Oh, it's just all ones," she says with a handwave. Her voice is bubbly salesperson again. "Same as my laptop." She takes the phone and enters the passcode. "I had to upgrade to a new Wi-Fi, to make the new security system work, and I haven't been able to make any of the other things work since. Tommy said he had it all working, but it doesn't." She hands the phone back to me.

"Did I mention I'm selling home security systems now? I can get you a special discount if you're interested. I don't know why I didn't think of it years ago. It just fits in so well with selling a house. People love new security systems in their new houses!"

"Uh… Lemme think on that," I say. I go to the settings screen on her phone and search for local internet connections.

"That one," she says, pointing to the list.

"Panopticon?" I ask, looking at the names. It is nestled between GetOffMyInternet and blackFBIvan.

"Yeah," Paige says. "Tommy says it's the name of the 'All Seeing Eye,'" and he thought it was funny because it was for a security system. I don't think so, because to me, the All Seeing Eye is that weird Freemason pyramid eye thing. The illuminati or whatever. Generational thing, I guess. I'm just not hip anymore!" She sticks her hip out sharply and giggles.

It might have been cute, if she hadn't already unnerved me earlier. And if it hadn't seemed so rehearsed.

"Password?" I ask, pointing to the screen.

"All ones! I can't remember anything else, so I use that for all of my passwords."

"That's not really secure, you know."

Paige shrugs. "What have I got to hide?"

Chapter 12

THE SOUND OF EXCITED KIDS echoes, doubles, and then triples inside the warehouse, competing with the loud warning beeping, pulsing in our ears as we all watch Bill Petterson back his semi-tractor in to hook up to the float. The semi has gone through a major make-up job to match the theme of the float. Piles of fake snow wobble on top of the cab, fenders, and hood, and a white, stick-on plastic film has been stretched tight across the bright red paint job to mute the colors down to gray.

A scattering of small, white LED fairy lights and paper snowflakes, cut out by the kids, hang from a nearly invisible mesh of wires tethered to stay out in front of the rig, making it look like the truck is driving through the night in a light snow. Or rather so that it will look that way when it is moving forward instead of in reverse.

"Hey! Stay back!" A voice cuts sharply through the din.

Jimmy Hazlehurst herds a couple of the kids back out of the way. The kids, forty-two of them if they are all here, all look alike now. Dressed in white choir robes with glittering, sliver halos floating above their heads on wire tiaras, their faces are all painted a light shade of gray. The kids with dark hair have had it covered with spray-on color to turn it all the way black, and the kids with lighter hair have had theirs sprayed into gray. Fortunately, none of them have used any dark paint to make themselves look dead.

Yet.

After the incident at the park, I'm hoping that idea is no longer on any of their minds, but I'm sure it's just wishful thinking on my part. I try not to think about how much their chubby white faces look like the pasty, pale face of the dead kid in the park.

Mrs. D'Arby, the music teacher whose first name I still don't know after ten years of being around the elementary school, stands out from the crowd in her own white robe and gray face. She is twice as tall, and maybe three times as wide as any of the kids. And ten times as loud.

"Settle down!" she calls out. The parents all turn instantly at her voice. The kids, and some of the other teachers who have come along, are more used to her commanding presence at school and react much slower. "Y'all know where we're meeting, right? At the corner in front of Betsy's Bakery. That's where we will all meet again *after* the parade, too, right? And then, if everyone has behaved, we'll *all* get cake pops."

The cheer from the kids momentarily drowns out the big rig's warning beeps.

"BUT," Mrs. D'Arby continues, "no food *before* we do the parade, right?" Her warning tone is enough to make me clench my jaw, purse my lips, and look away.

No one has said anything directly to me, but the mess the kids made of their gowns with my gingerbread men, during the full-dress rehearsal, did not go over well. Fortunately, I didn't use any food coloring in the frosting. Also fortunately, John King owns The King's Robes Dry Cleaners, and he got the choir gowns all cleaned, pressed, and taken care of in less than twenty-four hours.

I'm pretty sure I owe him for that.

The other person who stands out is Oliver. He's a tall splash of gray moving back and forth in front of the bright, colored lights of the Christmas tree set up in the corner of the warehouse. Thanks to his stunt the other night, shouting movie lines from the railing of the bridge, he was unanimously voted in by the other dads to play Jimmy Stewart's part. Which, despite Oliver's groaning protestations, is probably what he wanted all along anyway. As demonstrated by the wide grin on his face now, as he flirts with Summer Christmas.

She's dressed in a Mrs. Claus outfit with a hem just high enough to prove she's not the older version but still low enough to be acceptable anywhere. Pretty much perfect, like she always is. I swear, it's uncanny.

I have to admit, Oliver looks good in his suit and tie. Better than I could have hoped. Mary Candler, owner of the sometimes a little too racy Mrs. Claws' Corsets and Curios, outdid herself with Oliver's black, gray, and white tweed jacket, shirt, pants, and tie. After watching the quick photoshoot she did of Oliver earlier—which he really hammed up—I am sure she's going to be advertising a new Black and White line of clothes on her website. And I think it might do well, with the right people.

The giant metal *clunk* of the semi-tractor hooking up to the float's trailer all but shakes the walls, and the kids all cheer again. I nervously watch the as bridge on the float jerks around, but it holds solidly.

I knew it would. We did a good job constructing it, but some worries you just can't let go of until you know for sure.

As I relax a little on the inside, my eyes finally land where I've been trying not to let them linger: on Dana. And Trent and Fleming, of course, but Dana is the one I can't stop looking at, can't stop picking out of the crowd. Seeing her here, with all the kids, and a Christmas float… All that's missing is Coney, and it would be just like before. Like we were a family again.

"Nervous?" a voice at my shoulder asks. It's Summer Christmas. I didn't see her approaching.

"Should I be?" I feel like I'm trying to act casual, trying not to get caught looking at my *ex*-wife and thinking thoughts I wish I could prevent from ever going through my head.

Summer shrugs. "Probably not. I think you're a shoo-in to win again this year."

"*We*," I correct her. "We *all* did this. And I'm not so sure. I hear we've got some pretty stiff competition. I hear the Fire Department finally got permission to use real flames with their Heat Miser float this year, and it sounds like the Elks Club built that giant reindeer they've been talking about for the last five years. You know, the one that poops out giant Hershey's Kisses? That's sure to be pretty popular."

Summer wrinkles her nose in disgust, a gesture every bit as perfect and cute as I'd expect it to be on her. "Only with some people," she says. "Some of us don't think of poop as very Christmassy, chocolate or not."

She is the epitome of Mrs. Claus, and I can't imagine anyone who could have lived up to being named Christmas as well as she does.

"Not a big fan of Mr. Hankey, then I take it?" I ask.

"Who?"

I turn to look directly at her and raise my eyebrows. "Are you kidding? You don't know who Mr. Hankey the Christmas Poo is?"

Her wrinkled nose turns into a grimace. "Eww. No. Really?"

I laugh and nod.

"That's just…wrong!"

"It's from South Park."

"Like that explains everything and makes it okay? Yuck!"

She walks away shaking her head, and I can't keep the grin off of my face. I know she is some sort of miss perfect, I've come to expect it of her, as does everyone else, but even so, she still surprises me.

"Okay!" Bill Petterson calls out. "I'm all hooked up! Where's my escort?"

I step forward and merge into a group with five other dads who volunteered beforehand. "Here, Bill!" I call.

He waves to us, and I wave to the guys around me to take up position. As we move, I hear Brandi Hazlehurst and Stacy Thorndyke calling out individual kids' names, herding them out to be loaded into cars, trucks, and minivans. Of course, I spot Dana again. She's like a magnet for my eyes. I can't help but pick her out every time.

Fleming is jumping up and down with excitement. I can tell he wants to ride with some of the other kids even before I see the concerned look on Dana's face.

Trent puts a hand on Dana's shoulder, much like I would have, and nods for Fleming to go on ahead with Stacy's group. Just like I would have done with Coney.

It's like watching a Twilight Zone episode of my life, where I've been replaced.

Oliver screams, "I want to live again!" and laughter breaks out. The excitement in the air is palpable, and despite my mixed emotions, I'm smiling.

This is why I do this. These people all love making the floats, but they love being on the float and in the parade even more. And the camaraderie that goes along with it.

And I love being a part of it all.

As our group of float escorts moves forward, I follow Chip Burbank, who moves to the right front corner of the truck. I stop a few feet in front of the left front fender and look back. Mark Thorndyke has taken a position behind me at the center of the rig, and Jimmy Hazlehurst has stationed himself at the right rear of the float. I give them each a questioning thumbs up and they look through the float to spot their counterparts on the other side of the truck. I can't see them, but I am sure John King and Randy Marks are there. I wait for a return thumbs-up from Mark and Jimmy anyway.

Once we hit the actual parade route, we will be surrounded by teachers and parents and students who want to walk along with the float. My guys and I will make sure no one gets too close and gets hurt, and we all take the job seriously. I trust them to be thorough. We all have kids here.

When Mark and Jimmy both give me the all-good thumb, I look across the path of the rig to Chip and give him the questioning thumbs-up, which means I raise my eyebrows and look like I'm waiting for an answer. He turns to look behind him, and I visualize the same process happening all over again on the other side. Chip looks back to me, with an enthusiastic thumb shaking at the top of his fist, and grins.

"We're good to go, Bill!" I call up to the cab. I see Bill's hand move and I quickly cover my ears. Still inside the warehouse, he blasts the horn three times, rattling the windows, the doors, and my bladder.

At least I remembered to cover my ears this year.

Chapter 13

THOUGH I CAN'T SEE HIM, I know Thomas Hackett is in place and ready when the float's lights come on. I hear a murmur of *oohs* and *ahhs* from the people manning the other floats around us, and it makes me smile.

The lights, strategically hidden around the float, create deep, emphasizing shadows and bring it all together, and suddenly, with the night sky dark behind it, I am staring at the bridge where Jimmy Stewart delivered his classic lines near the end of *It's a Wonderful Life*. And it is all in perfect, glorious, original black and white.

Oliver, in his black and white suit, and wearing gray face paint, appears at the railing of the bridge, and the resemblance is uncanny. Spontaneous applause breaks out, and I couldn't be prouder.

"Clarence!" Oliver cries out, and I get chills. He's obviously been working on his Jimmy Stewart impression, and he's nailed it.

The only thing different about our scene is at the very end of the bridge, where a gray Christmas tree stands decorated in silver and gray ornaments, silver tinsel, and a silver star. Beside it, held in a stand half-hidden in fake snow and bolted firmly to the floor of the float, is a large silver church bell.

"Wow, Jeff!" A hand falls heavily on my shoulder. "Just wow." I look to find Mayor Sean Dunn next to me. Although his patronage is seasonal, coming and going with political campaigns, he's always been one of my biggest customers, and, like with Paige and Margret Atwater, I plaster a smile onto my face whenever I see him.

The car he is going to be riding in, waving to all of his constituents, is two floats ahead of us, and he's been out pressing palms while we wait for the parade to start.

"I think you just might win again this year," he says.

"You haven't seen it all, yet." I grin, for real, knowing what's still coming.

"Really? Oh, of course! Where are the children?"

As if on cue, the angels, led by Mrs. D'Arby, appear from the crowd of people. She leads them to the steps on the back end of the float and supervises and directs them as they march up. They whisper and giggle, and their halos bounce atop their heads as they line up, taking their assigned spots all around the float. In the special lighting, their makeup is as perfect as Oliver's. They are all black and white angels.

And, as far as I can tell, not a one of them is a 'dead angel.'

"Oh, my gosh! Look at them!" Paige, walking up to the mayor and I from where her little house float is waiting next in line behind the bridge, claps her hands. "They look so darling!"

The first row of kids lines up along the length of the bridge while the smaller second, and even smaller third rows fill in the choir stands built up behind the first rows.

Thomas Hackett, who was nice enough to volunteer because he is young and flexible, and maybe a bit naïve, is hidden somewhere inside that choir stand. I can't see any lights or movement through the vent grates we installed, but I know he's in there or the lights on the float couldn't have been turned on. And I know the stomping feet of the kids situating themselves above and all around him must be loud as all get out.

I'm happy to see the thin safety cables we installed between the rows doesn't wiggle in the slightest as the kids pull on it and lean against it. The last thing any of us want is someone to get hurt.

"Oh! There's Fleming!" Paige bounces excitedly and waves at the boy. "Fleming! Fleming!"

I quickly spot Fleming near the center of the first row. Part of me is becoming attuned to him, I think, like he is my own kid. My brain easily picks him out of the crowd. He's grinning ear to ear, and I know that look; little kids get it when they finally get to play with the big kids and it's the most exciting thing in their lives.

Paige continues to wave until Fleming finally sees her and waves back. Paige snaps photos of him with her phone, then he spots me and changes the aim of his wave toward me. His excitement is like a sudden energy boost for me, and it makes me feel good. I wave back and, just for a moment, wonder if this is what it would have been like if Dana and I had had another child. A son.

Suddenly regret washes over me, and I'm sure my smile falters. It shouldn't have been difficult for Dana and Trent to ask me if Fleming could join in with the float late. Anyone else would have just asked. And they aren't just anyone.

Unlike most of my bad thoughts, I don't push this one away. I need to hold on to this one, to remind myself I have to work harder to be a part of their family, even if it is only an extended, peripheral kind of role. That grinning kid up there does not deserve to watch his father and new mother and sister have problems with his... I don't know what I am to him. The not-fun uncle, I guess.

Whatever it is, I resolve to make it better.

"They look fantastic!" Mayor Dunn says about the angels, interrupting my thoughts. I make sure I'm smiling again when I look at him.

"Don't they?" Summer Christmas is standing next to him, her eyes twinkling. She has to raise her voice to be heard over the excited crowd. "We had so much fun doing the makeup and costumes!"

Mayor Dunn takes a dramatic step back and looks Summer up and down with raised eyebrows. "You look fantastic, too!"

"Thank you." Summer curtseys in her Mrs. Claus Christmas dress and blushes appropriately, and somehow turns a moment I feel is a bit creepy into a sweet compliment.

Paige moves closer to the float, putting her back to them, perhaps a little too quickly. I wonder if it is a bit of jealousy, and if maybe that is what goes on with her and Dana as well. I never stopped to consider Paige may be a bit more insecure than she lets on. She is so outgoing when it comes to looking for clients and selling houses.

Mayor Dunn, perhaps realizing his eyes have lingered too long in places they ought not to have been in the first place—or perhaps because of the look Paige gives the two of them over her shoulder—quickly turns back to the float. "What are those pillars behind some of the kids? Some kind of support? So they don't fall?" he asks

"No." I grin. "That's the *big* surprise."

Summer bounces on her toes. "That's my favorite part! You'll see!" she tells the mayor with an eager smile. "Jeff had an absolute stroke of genius with those!"

I have to laugh. Now I'm just as excited as Summer is.

"No, I won't!" Dunn protests. "I'll be too far ahead of you."

The kids finish filling in, and now the float has three layered rows of angels on each side of the bridge, twenty-one kids looking out each way into the crowd.

"Maybe you will," Summer says, pointing. And like magic, Summer Christmas seems to make things happen again. Uncanny. I swear.

Mrs. D'Arby comes up the steps and joins the angels on the float, beaming and looking radiant despite being as monochrome as the rest of the float. In her commanding presence, the kids all settle down, though nervous giggles and shivers still roam about the float, flitting through the kids like wind on tall grass.

A police siren whoops, followed by the grinding *blaaat* of a firetruck's warning, signaling the parade is starting.

"Thank you for fixing my little house, Jeff!" Paige quick-waves to me and starts heading back toward her car, which is hitched up with the small float.

"You're welcome." My eyes flit to the little house. If I had to guess, I'd say some of the paint is probably still wet, but I have to admit, it looks good again. It had gone quicker than I thought it would, and I'd even had time to re-string it with miniature Christmas lights and put a tiny wreath on the front door.

"Time to go," Mayor Dunn says.

"Hold on, Sean." I catch him by the sleeve. "We still have a couple of minutes until we get to move out. This is worth it, trust me."

I can barely hear Mrs. D'Arby, saying something to the kids, but I can tell when she starts counting. Then the choir begins to sing.

There is nothing quite like the sound of children singing "Silent Night." It pretty much represents everything I think Christmas is, at least on the more religious side of the holiday. And I feel the sanctity swell up, filling the night, and my own heart, as the kids, as one, sing out *ho-oly niiight.*

"Truly angelic," Mayor Dunn says. He tries to pull away, and I realize I am still holding his sleeve. I don't let go. I keep him there a moment longer, until the silver bell at the back of float rings.

And then angel wings suddenly appear behind Fleming.

Chapter 14

FLEMING GRINS, BOUNCING WITH PURE joy when he realizes he is the first angel to get wings.

The applause around our float turns heads up and down the street around us, drawing looks even from people around the corner, where the first float is starting up the parade route.

Mayor Dunn, no longer trying to pull away, just stares at our float.

The bell rings again, and another set of wings magically appears behind one of the children. Reveling in the moment, the choir's voice grows stronger, and their song carries out into the night like a magic moment in a movie.

I can't take my eyes of Fleming's excited face, and I feel like I have never been prouder of anything I have ever accomplished than I am at this very moment, for making these kids this happy. For making *him* this happy.

I hear a *"Woot!"* I instantly recognize, and my eyes fall on Coney in the group of teenagers walking by, heading for the parade route. Her face is so alive with enthusiasm, I nearly forget where I am. I had no idea how badly I needed to see my daughter happy. Dana and Trent aren't far behind her in the crowd. They are all smiles, waving wildly at Fleming and taking pictures as they pass by.

Someone whistles sharply, and I spot Paige standing in front of her car and waving wildly. Next to her is a young man I assume is her son. Dressed in a suit, he's a sharp-looking kid with a broad grin. Putting his fingers in his mouth, he whistles again.

"I told you, Jeff! They look great!" Summer is bouncing and clapping like a little kid. Her smile and enthusiasm are infectious and, in that magical way she has, they seem to spread throughout the crowd up and down the street.

"Hell yes, they do!" Mayor Dunn claps, too. He turns and slaps me on the shoulder. "Outdone yourself!" He leans in close. "This is great. This will make people forget about what happened in the park." He grins at me and heads for his car.

I hope he might be right. It had made me forget.

An elf on stilts, heading toward the front of the parade, strolls by with an oddly graceful incoordination, almost stepping over, almost tripping over the mayor. They both whirl around trying to avoid disaster, looking like a planned comedy routine the clowns might have put on.

"Watch it there, Luca!" Mayor Dunn cries out.

"Sorry, Mayor!"

I never would have recognized Luca if Dunn hadn't said his name. The kid makes a good recovery and continues loping down the street in log strides. Coney and Luca had been best friends in second grade. Dana was sure it was puppy love, but Coney always denied it. They were just besties.

I hadn't seen him in a couple of years. I wonder if Coney ever talks to him anymore, or if high school had ended the friendship.

"Jeff?" Summer asks over the cheers of the people and the singing choir.

"Yeah?"

"Bill Petterson is trying to get your attention."

Turning, I see Bill waving at me from the cab of his truck. "I need my spotters!" he calls.

I give him a thumbs up. "Thanks, Summer," I say and hurry to start rounding up the guys. We take our places and go through the whole routine of checking on each other again before I tell Bill we're good to go when it's our turn.

Bill looks satisfied and waves at me. I almost throw my hands over my ears before I realize he's not going to blast his horn. He notices, and his grin grows big enough to show all of his teeth.

The angels on the float finish their song and the world suddenly seems quiet.

A muffled clacking noise comes from within the float. The angel wings are slowly disappearing from behind the kids. Thomas Hackett, hidden inside the bleachers, is cranking the spring-loaded mechanisms back down to reset the wings. As the float goes down the parade, he will be able to pull a rope to ring the bell and then trigger the wings one at a time again.

Summer catches up with me and then moves on to one of the twelve baskets, six on each side, attached to the float and rig. The baskets have been filled with goodies for handing out during the parade. Summer's basket is full of Christmas trees, which she made out of silver Hershey's Kisses for stars, glued on top of two stacked, green-foil wrapped mini-Reese's placed on top of golden-brown Rolos tree trunks.

She grabs a couple of handfuls and puts them into her red Santa's Helper bag. She slings it over her shoulder, warily watching Luca, the giant elf, tramp back by again. He loses his footing again, and nearly stumbles over me and then Summer, sending us all scrambling.

"Be careful, Luca!" I call out. "Stay away from the floats when they're moving!"

"Okay, Mr. McKenzie! I will!" He does a pirouette on one stilt to turn back and salute at me before moving on. It would have been a great comedic gesture, if I'd believed for one second it was entirely on purpose.

"Oh, that makes me nervous," Summer says. Just for a moment, the first moment I've ever seen, she looks a bit disheveled. She takes a deep breath, puts the bag back over her shoulder, and suddenly, somehow, she looks perfect again.

"Christmas tree, Jeff?" She offers a treat that somehow magically appears in her hand.

"Never while on duty." I hold a hand up to wave it off.

The semi rumbles to life beside me. "Here we go!" I call out to the rest of the guys escorting the float.

"Everyone hold on!" Mrs. D'Arby's voice carries across the float. All of the angels' white-gloved hands take hold of the safety lines. The float begins moving with the slightest of jerks. Hardly an angel sways on the float.

I give Bill the thumbs-up again. The man is good with his truck. He nods appreciatively, and we make our way into the parade. We reach the corner, and I hear Mrs. D'Arby count again, and the kids begin singing, "We Wish You a Merry Christmas."

The crowd lining the street around us cheers as we round the corner. The double-handful of parents and teachers walking along with us wave and smile and begin handing out treats to the children in the crowd. When the bell rings, and the first angel gets their wings, there is applause and *oohs* and *ahhs*.

I can't help but look back to sneak peeks at the kids as they sing. Beyond looking angelic, they look happy, excited, and proud. Especially Fleming. He never fails to look surprised and thrilled when the bell rings and wings appear behind him.

My earlier thought comes back. I need to be something better in his life. If he is going to be Coney's sister, he needs to be my son. If not in name, then at least in spirit. If not in the eyes of the rest of his family, at least in mine.

Summer is in her element. Beaming ear to ear, she glides past me, nearly a red streak back and forth from the people on the sidewalk to the float to refill her bag of treats.

"Slow down, or you'll run out before the end!" I call to her.

She slows and matches pace with me, breathing heavily, yet looking like it is intentional. "This is so much fun! I can see why you do it every year. Thank you so much for letting me tag along."

"Tag along? You've been a huge help! We've been glad to have you."

Smiling, she looks down the road ahead of us, eyes wide, and takes it all in. The reflection of all of the lights in her eyes and the look of wonder on her face makes me realize it's been a long time since I've done that, and I take the opportunity to do the same.

The whole city, and many more, has turned out for the parade, and the street is decked out to the hilt. Decanter isn't called the Christmas Capital of Texas for nothing. The light poles are all decorated to look like trees, and the real trees are all decorated to look like a wonderland come to life. The stores have been turned into an alpine mountain village, with windows filled full of mini wonderland dioramas.

I can hear the marching band at the front of the parade when the choir behind me pauses between songs. A sudden glow of orange light happens somewhere up ahead, and I hear cheers go up from the crowd. I'm sure it's the fire department's Heat Miser float, finally getting to use real fire.

Maybe we won't win best float this year after all.

"Clarence!" Oliver's voice carries out from the float behind me. "Help me, Clarence!" Cheers go up from the crowd around us as people understand the reference and recognize the character Oliver is playing.

My concerns fade. It doesn't matter if we win or not. We did good. People will remember this float for years.

My print shop, on the opposite side of the street from me so I won't be able to see it through the float, is still a half a block away. I imagine the people in front of it enjoying the Island of Misfit Toys scene I put up, filling the sidewalk with jagged, snowy mountains and then merging them down into the valley with the toys themselves placed inside the shop window.

I don't expect to win with that display, but that's not the point.

Summer looks at me and smiles, and I can't help but grin back at her. Because *that is* the point.

For once, the whole world is good. After several rough years, this is exactly what I needed. What we all needed.

Luca stumbles past on wobbly stilts again. This time there is a definite look of panic across his face, and I am sure he is out of control and going to come down hard.

"Take my spot!" I tell Summer, pointing to my position at the front of the semi.

She pulls her eyes from the unsteady elf on stilts and looks to me with a nod.

I'm already on the move trying to predict where Luca is going to fall. I don't know if I can actually catch him, but when his elf hat goes flying off his head, I know he's going down.

Luca teeters sideways, puts one leg out too far forward trying to get his balance, and falls straight backward.

Chapter 15

A LONG TIME AGO, I discovered there is a terrible superpower that comes with being a parent. It is the ability to see a catastrophe happening to your child one or two seconds before it happens. The problem is you are almost always three to four seconds away...

As the world slows, I can see all of the children sitting on the curb scrambling out of the way when they suddenly realize the giant silly elf on stilts isn't playing and actually is going to fall down on top of them. The curb sort of clears, with children crawling over one another, and a sick feeling enters my gut, and that terrible, unwanted superpower kicks in. I *know* the back of Luca's head is going to land right on the edge of the curb. I can see the future, and it is not something I can live with.

Already running toward him, knowing I don't have a snowball's chance of getting there in time, I dive for Luca, hand outstretched like he is a fly ball and I am Mike Trout.

We hit at the same time, and by some miracle my hand is under his skull—I know from the flash of pain that shoots up my arm as at least one metacarpal gets crushed against the curb and snaps like a twig.

Then my face is in Luca's face, my momentum continuing to carry me forward, and I flip over him, like a ragdoll, landing with my back hitting the curb this time, and there is another flash of pain, seizing my whole body. My chest constricts in a spasmodic reaction, and air begins to rush out of my lungs, forcing a never-ending moan of the dead past my lips.

Time goes from slowed to all but stopped while the air continues out of my body, uncontrollably, forever.

"Mr. McKenzie!" Luca is suddenly looking over me. "Are you all right?"

I can't answer. I can't breathe. Air is still being forced out of my lungs by a paroxysm of constricting chest and diaphragm muscles.

Then there are others around me, lifting me off the curb, holding me up, and, after an eternity and a half, I finally run out of air in my lungs. But my body keeps trying to get rid of more. My abdominal muscles are locked tight, trying to press against my spine. I feel like I'm collapsing in on myself and drop to my hands on my knees to keep from falling over. Then the spasm finally lets go and I suck air in like a drowning man.

"Oh my gosh, Jeff! Are you okay?" Summer is there with the other people from the crowd who lifted me up. I recognize a couple of the faces. Brandi, Greg, Mary; other parents who were passing out treats like Summer was. I try to answer Summer, but I still can't do anything more than gasp for air, so I nod, but the movement makes me lose my balance and I stumble.

Someone steadies me from behind while I try to straighten up. It's Mark Thorndyke. "You okay, Jeff? That was a hell of a tumble you just took."

"Jesus!" I hear someone in the crowd say. "Why'd you tackle that kid?"

"Fucking dumbass," Mark curses under his breath.

I try to laugh, but I don't have the air for it, so it comes out a grunt. Plus, it hurts like hell. I think I've broken a rib. "It seemed like the thing to do at the time," I manage to mumble.

"Not you," Mark says. "The dumbass back there."

I take a couple of unsteady steps forward, back into the street, carefully straightening up, stretching out my back as I go. Hands grip my arms. Mark and Summer are on either side of me, helping me along.

It hurts where Summer touches my arm, and I look down to see blood soaking through the sleeve over my forearm. It's dark and reminds me of the ink, and all I can think is I've ruined another shirt this week.

"Oh, you're bleeding!" she says.

"I'm okay," I lie, my voice croaking. "Be careful. Don't get any on your dress."

I take another step toward the float. It's still moving. The choir is still

69

singing, though the kids on this side are all looking at me with wide eyes. The world starts to come back into focus, but it is different now, sharper and uglier. Everything looks the same, but nothing feels the same.

I feel out of place. I don't belong here. The fun is gone, replaced by the pain in my hand, my arm, and my back. I'm a puppet pulled along by someone else's strings as I walk.

"Is Luca okay?" I ask, finally gathering my thoughts.

"He's fine," Mark says. "Already on his feet and gone. Kids are made out of rubber. You, not so much."

I turn back to see the gangly elf, hat back on his head, moving up the street again. But his steps are more measured and cautious.

"You're the one I'm worried about," Summer says to me.

I wave her off, just like the idiot man-child I am, and pretend I'm fine, even though my right hand is already swelling, and I can't bend my fingers. "I need to get back to my post. I have to watch the float."

"I think we need to get the paramedics to check you out, Jeff," Summer says. "I'm serious."

"Someone has to watch the float."

"I got it, Jeff," Mark says. "We'll get someone else to help. You go get checked out." He looks to Summer. "You got him?"

"Yeah." She nods. "I can get him to the paramedics. Their tent is set up just a block up the street."

My eyes leave the two of them and go back to the float just as the bell rings and a pair of wings unfurl in an empty space. For a moment, lost in my own strange puffy cloud of pain, the sight confuses me. There are way more kids than wings. There should never be wings without an angel in front of them. Then the singing kids shuffle around a bit, filling in the gap, and once again one of the black and white angels stands in front of the wings and smiles broadly.

This time I recognize Marci Hazlehurst even with her makeup on. She's just as excited about having the wings as Fleming had been.

I take two more limping steps, grimacing, knowing it doesn't look anything like the smile I intend it to be for the crowd watching the parade. The meaning of Summer's words start to sink into my addled brain, and I realize she's right. I should see the paramedics. I'm not thinking straight. I probably hit my head. Then, through the haze of the pain engulfing me, it finally registers.

Those were Fleming's wings.

Chapter 16

"DO YOU SEE FLEMING?" I ask Summer, looking back the way the parade was coming from. Worry tightens in my chest. Did he fall off?

I grunt and wobble unsteadily, trying to squat to look under the skirt of the float. There is nowhere on the float he could have moved to, and no reason for him to have moved.

Still holding my arm to steady me, Summer hesitates, searching the choir of singing angels on the float before answering. "No."

"He should be there." I stumble, walking sideways, trying to keep up with the float. The world swims around me. "Right there. In the middle of the first row."

Could he have gotten off? How would he have gotten off?

"I'm sure Fleming is fine. Jeff," Summer says. "Jeff." She squeezes my arm. "Jeff. I think you need to see a doctor. I think you're hurt."

I realize I'm leaning on her pretty hard. My hand is throbbing. My knee hurts. I'm taking shallow breaths because deep ones hurt. "Yeah. I do. You're right. Thank you. But—"

My head swims, and I feel like puking.

"Jeff?"

"I may have a concussion," I tell her.

Then more hands are on me again. The parade swirls around me. I stop walking and the bridge moves on past. I look to see who's got hold of me.

It's Trent. "Where did Fleming go?" he asks.

Numbly I look back to the float. Dana is there, sidestepping alongside it. Her face is twisted with worry. "Fleming?" I hear her calling over the choir, her head moving back and forth as she searches. "Fleming!"

"Jeff?" Trent asks again. "Where's Fleming?"

I shake my head. "He was right there." I wave my swollen hand at the float. "And then he wasn't."

"He has to be here somewhere," Summer says. "Ask the kids who were next to him."

"Ask Mark," I tell Trent, trying to point. "They guy walking next to the float. He'll know."

Trent lets go of me and hurries after Dana and the float. Trying to force my head to clear, I follow despite Summer's protestations.

"Jeff, you should really get checked out."

"I will. I promise. But I have to make sure Fleming is okay first."

As I get closer, I pick up part of Mark's answer to Trent. "...over helping Jeff. Check with Jimmy." Mark points to the rear of the float where Jimmy Hazlehurst is still walking in his position as one of the escorts for the float.

I change direction and head for Jimmy. "Did you see Fleming get off the float?" I ask him.

"Who?"

"One of the kids," I answer. "Did you see any kids get off the float?"

Jimmy shakes his head. "Not that I saw. Man! That was a hell of a digger you took back there." He points at my bloody arm. "You should get that looked at!"

Trent and Dana catch up with Summer and me, and I shake my head. "He didn't see anything."

The look on Dana's face rips my soul from my body and leaves me feeling panicked. If she's this worried, then something must have happened.

"Where's Fleming?" she yells to me.

I don't have an answer. I can only shake my head.

The choir ends their song, and the world gets eerily quiet despite the other sounds of the parade around us. I look up and see Mrs. D'Arby waiting for the wings to reset and for Oliver to do his thing before she starts the choir on the next song. She's got a slightly raised dais at the front of the bridge, facing the choir, where she can see all of the kids.

"Ask her!" I tell anyone who is listening to me. "Ask Mrs. D'Arby!"

Hearing her name, she looks at me.

"Where's Fleming?" Trent, Dana, and I all yell at once, our voices mixing over each other and garbling the words. Oliver picks that exact moment to plead to the sky to get back to his wife and kids, and Mrs. D'Arby raises a hand to her ear to show she didn't understand.

"Where's Fleming?" Dana screams the words, hysteria creeping into her voice.

Mrs. D'Arby furrows her brow and leans to the side to look down the row of angels. She obviously had no idea he wasn't where he was supposed to be. She looks back to us and, putting her hands palms up for emphasis, mouths the words *I don't know*.

"Jesus," Trent says. "He's got to be here somewhere." His face is flush. Even in my haze, I can see the terror deep in his eyes. The eyes of a man who's lost a wife and now thinks he may have lost his son.

Chapter 17

THE DARK WORLD AROUND ME is lit in flickering strobes, changing back and forth from red and blue impossibly fast as emergency vehicle lights flash all around us. Two police cars, two police motorcycles, and an ambulance, all going at once to show them off to the passing crowd, are enough to warrant a seizure warning sign be put out front of the First Aid Tent.

"Search the crowd!" I can barely make out Dana's angry words from this distance, but I can tell she is on the verge of a breakdown. Her eyes are wild and her gestures frantic. "How many kids can be wearing a white robe and white face paint?" Her whole body shakes as she pleads with the three police officers in front of her.

I can't hear what the officer says back to her, but I can guess the gist of the hollow reassurances by the placid look on the face of the speaking officer. The other two officers are only half-paying attention to her, their eyes flicking back and forth from Dana to the passing crowd.

Coney, standing next to Dana, is a mess of tears, running makeup, and snot. I can't stop staring at the way the lights reflect off the moisture on her face. Nothing hurts me worse than seeing my daughter upset or in pain. Except maybe when her mother is too. And when it's my fault because Fleming is missing.

I've never felt so goddamned terrible in my life.

We've already gone up and down the parade route twice searching for

Fleming, and there was no sign of him anywhere. No one we talked to saw anything. Marci Hazlehurst, who I'd seen step into Fleming's place on the float, and the other kids on either side of her, Bridget Wolfe and Ralphie Carter, just seemed confused by the questions. It was hard to not get upset with them, but they are barely older than Fleming, and they were distracted by being on the float.

I lost track of Trent and Summer a long time ago. I'm sure they are still looking for Fleming somewhere in the crowd of people flowing all around us as the parade breaks up. The rushing blur of faces, smiles, laughs, and excitement, don't fit my new reality. The noise of the parade, the motors, the bands, the people, have become a dull, steady roar in my ears. The flashing colors and blurs of motion are nothing more than white noise for my eyes. Visions of a nothing that refuses to stop, and I begin to feel motion sick, watching them stream past as I sit still.

I am in hell.

"Ung!" I grunt as a sharp, sudden pain shoots through my right hand.

"Yeah. That's broken," the paramedic says, testing the bone in my hand again, making me grit my teeth and bringing my full attention back to where I am, under the tent, with her. She's young. She looks as young as Coney, though I know she has to be older.

"Something in there is grinding together like rocks," I tell her. I shift my weight in the folding chair to my other butt cheek, because apparently, I've bruised my ass, too.

I turn my head away, so I don't have to look at what the paramedic is doing to my hand, which means I am forced to look away from Coney and Dana, too. Looking around the makeshift station set up behind the ambulance, there are a couple more folding chairs and a table set up inside the portable canopy tent. Another paramedic, along with another police officer, is standing just outside the tent, talking to a red-faced man in an expensive looking business suit and tie. The guy is so drunk he reminds me of a top that's just about done spinning, and his words are so slurred I can't understand what little I hear him say.

Irrationally, it makes me angry.

I don't want to be in here. I want to be looking for Fleming. The only reason I stay is that the cop talking to the drunk guy hasn't given me the okay. The officer all but dragged me in here get checked out after seeing me listing through the crowd, calling Fleming's name over and over. I guess I can admit that protecting and serving the public involves removing bleeding, shouting weirdos from crowded areas and finding out what the hell they are up to, but that doesn't mean I have to like it when it happens to me.

"You need to go get it x-rayed and properly splinted. They are probably going to have to cast it, too," the paramedic says. She wraps an elastic bandage around my hand, making me wince some more. "Try not to use it before you get it splinted, and don't put off having that done, or it won't heal right." To my great relief, she finally lets go of my hand. I really don't want her 'testing' it a third time.

"And make sure you get those ribs checked out while you're there," she tells me. "I don't see any immediate problems, but better safe than sorry, and, I have to be honest, it's a bit hard to see what is bruising and what is ink stain."

"What about concussion?" I ask, changing the subject. I had fully expected to never show anyone the ink stain covering a third of my body.

"Based on what you told me, I'd say yes, you probably have one. But really, that's for a doctor to say. Just because I don't see any indication that you actually hit your head doesn't rule it out. It's still possible. Are you feeling any better?"

"Yeah. I do. The headache and nausea are mostly gone. I just feel like a beat-up, old, fat dude now." I look down at my left forearm. It still stings a bit. The bloody shirt is ruined, but it only took two stitches to fix the problem. Just a small cut that bled like stink. It doesn't hurt nearly as much as my ribs, my hand, or my knee. Or my ass.

I'm just glad she hadn't insisted upon me dropping trou and showing her the rest of the ink stain so she could look at my knee.

"Does that mean I can go? I'd really like to keep looking for Fleming."

"Is he your boy?"

Such a simple question, so many mixed emotions. "No. Uh...my... stepson." The answer is all wrong when I give it, but it's close enough I let it go. It gets the idea across.

"I hope you find him soon." The concern in her big brown eyes reminds me of his, and the knot in my gut tightens even more.

There is a special kind of hell that comes with being a parent, with loving someone so much that you feel responsible for everything about them, even though you have no control over any of it. I hadn't realized I felt that for Fleming. And in all honesty, maybe I don't. But I feel that for Dana and Coney, and they feel that for Fleming, which means I do too.

And it hurts worse than everything else wrong with my body combined. Times ten. Especially since this was all my fault. I should have been watching him. They trusted me with him.

It hurts times a hundred million, and I feel the tears trying to well up again and the lump in my throat grows large enough to suffocate me. The urge to vomit comes back, but its stress, not nausea this time.

"You go slow and take it easy," the paramedic says. "Don't push yourself. If you do have a concussion, the last thing you want to do is make it worse."

I nod, taking a deep breath, and get up from the folding chair. My bruised butt muscle feels like it's going to cramp, and I fight to keep the grimace off my face, so she won't try to hold me here any longer. The pain helps push all the other emotions down.

The officer notices me standing and looks from me to the paramedic. She nods to him, and he looks me in the eyes and nods at me. Somehow that simple gesture carries a big warning at the same time it tells me I'm free to go.

I swallow and turn back to the paramedic. "Do I need to pay you now, or will you guys bill me?"

"Since we didn't have to transport you anywhere, this one is on the city."

"Thanks," I say awkwardly, and, for the first time, I notice the name on her uniform. Julie White. The name rings a bell, and I look back to her face, recognition setting in for the first time. "Julie. You grew up."

"Everyone does, Mr. McKenzie." She gives me a thin smile. Obviously, I touched on a sore spot.

"Sorry. I didn't mean it that way. I just... I didn't recognize you." She had been a fifth grader the first year I built a float for the elementary school.

"Well, ten years can change a lot of things."

I nod. "It certainly can." I had still been married and happy back then. Judging by the look in her eyes, I guess she feels those were happier times as well.

"Thank you." I hold up my bandaged hand, then point to the stiches on my forearm. "I really appreciate it."

"Just doing my job." Her face is still hard, and I wonder if something I said or did ten years ago had stayed with her, made her not like me for some reason.

I turn to look for Dana and Coney. There are more important things I needed to worry about right now. Like finding Fleming.

As I move to join my girls talking to the police, I remember that Julie White's parents were killed in a robbery of their vineyard's tasting room. Three years ago? Four?

I look back to her. She's still sitting at the table, looking out into the surging crowd, as apart from it as I am. I don't know where she's been for the last few years. I don't know what she's been through. Remembering the little kid she used to be, I wish I could give her a hug.

Not that she would want it, or that it would help her at all.

Maybe I really want to give her a hug for me, to make myself feel better. For not being there for her. For not being there for Fleming

Nothing seems to make any sense right now.

I turn away and head back into the crowd to keep looking for Fleming.

Chapter 18

MY KNEE HURTS MORE WITH each step. It feels tight, like someone put bubble wrap around the joint, but somehow placed it under the skin. It reminds me of the time I tore my meniscus sliding into home plate in high school, and I suspect that's what I've done again this time.

I press on through the remnants of the crowd that had been here. The street is oddly quiet now, with no music from the parade echoing off of the storefronts, and the few groups of people left are talking and laughing in hushed tones, almost as if they know it would be disrespectful to be loud.

A loose candy wrapper blows across the street in front of me, carried by the gentle night breeze. Although it's chilly, there couldn't have been a better night for the parade.

And it couldn't have gone worse.

On top of everything else, Oliver told me that, while I was getting patched up by Julie White, Paige found out Fleming was missing and went into hysterics, nearly running her car into the crowd before being sedated and taken to the hospital.

Now, limping through the thin crowd, my eyes flick to every face I pass by. I judge the size and age of every kid I see, trying to imagine if Fleming could be disguised to look like that, trying to see if they might still have white face paint around the edges of their mouths or eyes or ears.

Many of them see my limp and bloody shirt and judge me back, but I don't care. Pushing on, I refuse to allow myself to believe what, deep in my heart, I know: if someone took him, he is long gone by now. There is no way they would still be here, because why would they be?

I also feel stupid thinking he would have been kidnapped. Why would anyone kidnap him? What on earth possible reason could there be? Trent and Dana are doing well financially, but they are by no means rich, so holding Fleming for ransom is really out of the question. It just wouldn't make any sense.

But, if that's not what happened, then all of the alternative reasons my brain dredges out of the muck of horrible thoughts stagnating in the deepest sewers of my subconscious are even worse, and I refuse to imagine his little body dead in a ditch, his lifeless eyes staring into the heavens.

A real dead angel.

Looking just like the kid in the park, chubby cheeks and all, not even old enough for the scraggly beard and tattoos yet.

I refuse to let myself acknowledge that's what I'm really looking for every time my eyes go to the dark shadows of doorways, or lumps between parked cars in a parking lot, or the dimly glowing white of trash dropped behind trees set back from the sidewalk. But some part of me, the part that's watched too many crime dramas, is telling me the clock is ticking, that too much time has already passed, that if we don't find Fleming now, we never will.

There aren't any real alleyways in downtown Decanter anymore, but my eyes desperately search down what looks like one. A nice, paved walkway between the Decanter Real Estate Agency and The Coffee Cup. Both businesses are small and don't use up the rest of their long buildings, so there are other businesses, at the far end, that do.

On the left side of the alleyway is a small, dim, red lightbulb, the only indication there is a doorway there at all. It leads to a speakeasy type cigar bar called Smokey's.

Up and down the right side, nearly lost in the dark and the dim red light, is a row of outdoor tables and chairs used during the day by The Coffee Cup. The backside of the building behind The Coffee Cup is a warehouse for some kind of kitchen supply company, I think.

I don't know why, but I turn down the alley, somehow drawn by the red light. I walk through the pale pool of ruddy light in front of the plain industrial door set into the side of the brick building. It looks like it's used for deliveries, but The Decanter Real Estate Agency at the front of the building doesn't need anything delivered.

It hardly needs anything.

Owned by a couple of elderly women whose names I can't remember, the Decanter Real Estate Agency is likely one of the easiest business to run I've ever heard of. The women sit inside the storefront and chat, and knit, and play cards, and occasionally have socials with other folk a generation or two ahead of me. They wait for tourists to walk by, see the properties advertised for sale on printouts taped to the windows, and come in to ask about them. I suspect they only make a couple of sales a year, but that seems to be enough for them.

The only reason I know of them at all is, years ago, they had me print up a thousand tri-fold pamphlets for their business. They've never been back since. They probably still have a pile of the pamphlets to hand out if anyone asks for one.

I stop at the back of their building and stare at the weathered steel door under the red light. It belies what I know is behind it, and I can barely make out the sound of live music. As expensive and classy as I know the place is on the inside, all mahogany and brass and crystal—and cigar smoke—I've always found the idea of a "hidden" speakeasy to feel seedy. Which, I am sure, is why so many people like it.

I wonder if that is why I am drawn here now.

My mind, wrestling with nefarious ideas and thoughts, is pulling me toward a place I feel would naturally be home to cutpurses and sneakthieves. And kidnappers.

And murderers.

I hate myself for that last thought.

It's been on my mind a lot since the park, but despite how close I had come to the body, to the boy, it had still felt distant, unrelated to me. I hadn't carried the worry forward to someone I loved—until now.

The door opens, startling me. I'd been just standing there staring at it.

I step back from the escaping music that fills the alleyway ahead of a young couple laughing and leaning on each other. They ebb and flow their way out through the door with the rhythm, barely glancing at me. The door shuts with a solid, metal sound, and the alleyway is dark and silent again, save the giggles of the girl and whispers from the man.

Their silhouettes head back toward the light of Main Street, and I feel stupid again. Alone in the dark and stupid. I don't know why I am here or what I am doing. I don't know where to go next or what to do.

A crunch of gravel under someone's shoe, somewhere behind me, makes me turn to look the other way, behind me into the darkness beyond the gentrified alleyway.

Someone is moving around in the darkness behind the warehouse.

Walking quietly as I can, I move to the end of the alley and look around the corner, my heart pounding, though I know it's stupid of me to think there's anything—

A man, with long, scraggly looking hair sticking out from underneath a Longhorns knit cap, is looking me in eyes. His eyes go wide, and he jerks his arm out of the dumpster, pulling out a long white cloth.

A robe.

The metal dumpster lid slams shut as the man is already racing away from me, the white robe flapping wildly in his grip like a strangled ghost.

The knot in my stomach burns into rage, and I hear myself snarl as I take off after him, eyes focused on the weird way his spindly, bowed legs swing out sideways as he runs. Loose gravel crunches under my feet, repeating the sounds his feet make passing though the empty parking lot ahead of me.

Then my swollen knee gives out, and I fly face-first onto the pavement. Daggers of frustration twist into my soul as the scrawny man quickly moves away from me.

I try to get up, but I am betrayed. First by my hand that won't bear my weight, won't let me push myself up, then by my knee that won't carry me, and finally, by my ribs that won't even let me take in enough air to scream out my rage at the man as he vanishes into the night.

Chapter 19

"YES," I SAY TO DETECTIVE Littlejohn, answering his question. He had pronounced his name something like *loo-hawn* when he introduced himself and handed me his card. "I'm sure it was this dumpster."

"And he went that-a-way," he says. It isn't a question, so I don't answer. I just nod.

It's close to two in the morning and the town is eerily quiet. The parking lot behind the kitchen supply warehouse now has two police cars, two dark sedans, and some kind of big, gray police van filling it.

I'm so exhausted I can hardly stand without swaying, not to mention how badly everything hurts, all over my body. Taking a nosedive into the gravel had chewed up the palm of my good hand, and I was still picking at what I thought might be a rock or two buried in there.

Dana, with swollen eyes and trembling movements, looks as bad as I feel. Trent looks…old. No longer full of the youthful vitality I was jealous of, tonight has taken a toll of twenty years on him, and he walks slow and stooped. It's hard to tell if he's helping Dana or if she's holding him up.

Coney is passed out in the back seat of their car, which is parked on the street. All I can see of her are stockinged feet above the seat in the back window. She'd already been asleep when they pulled up, so I can only hope she's doing better than the rest of us.

Summer left hours ago, right after the parade broke up, to head back to Bill Petterson's warehouse, where the float would be, and where, after the cake pop party at Betsy's Bakery, carpool riders would be breaking up into individual cars as families went home. She had hoped to ask anyone there if they had seen anything, and she promised to call if she heard anything.

She hasn't called.

"Okay," Detective Littlejohn says, watching one of the officers start walking in the direction the guy with the robe had run, flashlight sweeping back and forth on the ground in front of him. "We've got all your statements. You should all go home and get some rest. You'll be contacted in the morning."

Dana mumbles something and Trent puts his arm around her. I don't even have the energy to feel jealous it's not me comforting her anymore.

No, that's not right. I'm not jealous anymore. It's like something inside of me, something stupid and petty, couldn't take the strain of something really terrible happening and has been washed away by the realization of things that actually matter.

"Please," Detective Littlejohn says after none of us move. "There is nothing else you can help with tonight. We will look into everything we can. I promise, if there is any news, or if there *is* anything you can do to help, I'll call. Go get some rest."

Dana starts to resist. She looks like she wants to say something but doesn't know what else to say, what words she could use that would stop the detective from turning her away.

Trent, no longer the perfect leading man, no longer someone with answers or solutions, shakes his head and pulls her toward the car. After two steps, it looks like they are holding each other up and both would fall if either failed.

Dumbly, I watch them go.

The only sounds in the night are the quiet voices of Detective Littlejohn and one of the officers talking about processing the dumpster. I would have horrible thoughts about what that meant, but I've already looked inside. There had only been trash. Styrofoam packing material, mostly.

"Jeff!" Trent calls to me. Even staring at them, I hadn't realized they had stopped to look at me. "Do you need a ride?"

"No, I'm fine." It's another lie, something I seem to be making a terrible habit of lately, but I can't imagine being in the car with them, getting dropped off, alone, at my empty house and watching them drive away.

Trent guides Dana to turn back the other way and they keep walking to the car. The sound of their shuffling feet on the asphalt is stark and heartbreaking.

"You should go, too, Mr. McKenzie." Detective Littlejohn is at my elbow. I hadn't seen him come closer either.

I stare at the man for a moment. His dark eyes reflect distant streetlights, which somehow makes them seem even darker.

"That wasn't a request," he says.

I nod and turn away, back to the alley with the red light, and start walking. My swollen knee hurts with every step, and my ribs with every breath, but I move up the paved alley feeling like my body is moving on its own accord, like I'm in a dream.

Fitting. Like a dream.

A fucking nightmare.

All the things I worried about before, even just this morning, are suddenly so petty, so stupid, I can't even remember what they were.

I walk half a block up Main Street on autopilot, heading, I think, to Bill's warehouse, where my truck is parked. I realize I have the keys to my print shop in my pocket, which is only a block away instead of a couple of miles. I turn around and head the other way.

Chapter 20

THE SUN ISN'T UP YET. Stepping out of the print shop and onto the sidewalk, I take in a slow, deep breath, trying not to hurt my sore ribs, and I let the chill air fill lungs and permeate my body, hoping it will somehow cool the pain of all of the things that are wrong with me right now. It doesn't help. It doesn't wake me, calm me, or do anything except make me feel more aware of the fact that nothing is right in the world.

The uncaring gray sky puts a morose winter chill into my soul that I hadn't felt yet this winter. The kind of emptiness that doesn't usually settle in until after the holidays, when the nights get long and the storms rage for days, and it feels like maybe the world will die.

Last night, trying to sleep on the couch in the print shop's waiting room, was miserable. I couldn't lay on my back or on my right side, because of my ribs, and I could neither bend my knee nor tolerate keeping it straightened out across the thin arm of the couch. On top of that, the couch was never made to be lain on to start with. I'm unhappy with myself for having such cheap furniture in the shop, but then, I can't remember the last time anyone actually sat and waited for anything there.

As I lock the print shop door, the rattle of the keys reminds me of how they sound when I drop them on the kitchen table, echoing into the darkness of my empty house. Putting them into my pocket, I turn and look out into the empty world around me, feeling that it is no different, no less empty than my house.

The Christmas decorations, with all of the lights turned off, are empty of life up and down the silent street. The echoes of the parade come only from my mind, from my imagination. There is nothing here to show that the parade, or Fleming, or any people at all were ever here, not really. It's just an odd type of desolation, a card-board cut-out set up to mask the nothingness; a forlorn hope that maybe, someday, somehow, there will be something worthwhile here.

But not now.

With a heavy sigh of weariness that goes deeper than the physical, I start the walk to Petterson's warehouse and my truck. The only sound this time of morning is the strange cadence made by the scuffling of my shoes on the sidewalk as I limp along in the dark between the glow of sickly-orange streetlights.

My eyes, searching the shadows, fall back into the habit I'd acquired last night, but I don't let myself think about what I am looking for as I take in and disregard unknown dark shapes between buildings and under park benches. I don't let myself think about how much time has passed. I just force my feet to keep moving.

Somewhere in the distance I hear the rumbling motor of a vehicle. Idly, I wonder if it is a delivery truck, and whose business would have to be open at this ungodly hour in order to receive goods. It could be someone delivering newspapers. Or maybe the local dairy delivering milk. A lot of the residents around here liked having their dairy delivered from local farms.

Eventually I run out of inane things to ponder, and, with unwanted images of newspaper headlines and photos on milk cartons, my mind comes back to what I'm trying not to think about.

I haven't heard anything at all about Fleming. I'm not sure if I will hear anything from the police. I'm not family. But Dana or Coney haven't contacted me, so they haven't heard anything either. And Summer never called or texted back last night, at least not me, so I am still assuming she didn't learn anything from asking the people returning to the warehouse after the parade.

And that's not good.

It's way too early to try to call and bother any of them to find out what I already know: that they don't know anything.

My mood couldn't be any darker as I limp on through the gloom, so lost in my misery, so numbly searching the shadows for the shape of a little boy's body—a shape my mind already thinks it knows after the poor kid in the park—that I arrive at Petterson's warehouse without realizing it.

My truck is the only vehicle left in the parking lot, adding to my feeling the world has been deserted. I remember all of the parties here over the years, after the parade has ended, and I wonder what it was like last night. Did the dads still break out the beers from their coolers for a toast to a job well done? Did the moms bring even more ice cream and cupcakes and cookies for the kids to celebrate their success with? Or was it silent and dead here, everyone not talking about the kid who was missing, trying not to scare their own children?

I realize I have no idea how the float placed in the parade, and as soon as the thought crosses my mind, I feel petty and selfish. My only concern right now is Fleming.

As memories of the cheer and joy of the participants in the float design over the years quickly flow away from me, leaving me alone and miserable in the dark again, I notice the walk-through door at the front of the warehouse slowly swinging open in the breeze. It opens all the way outward and hits the side of the building with a slight, dull *thunk* of metal on metal, before gently closing and then opening again, instead of latching closed.

While Bill Petterson has never been stingy about sharing his warehouse, some of the machine parts he stores cost as much as a house, and it would break him and ruin his business to have them stolen. He's always been meticulous about keeping it locked up, and if we weren't careful, we'd lock ourselves out.

Could someone still be here? Had they blocked the door open? Maybe a group of parents had organized some kind of home base for a search for Fleming. Maybe everyone was so distracted last night Petterson just didn't get it locked.

That thought leaves my mind when I reach the door. The door jamb has been splintered.

Chapter 21

CATCHING THE SWAYING WAREHOUSE DOOR with my good hand, I peek inside, unsure if whoever broke in would still be here. I suspect not, because there are no vehicles besides my truck here, but maybe some drunken idiot got a hair-brained idea there'd be money in here or something while they were walking by.

The lights are all off and, unlike so many idiots in movies I've seen, I don't think I would have any advantage in the dark, so I turn them on. The overhead fluorescents hum and flicker to life, revealing the black and white bridge float I had been so proud of such a few long hours ago. Seeing it now twists my gut hard enough to make me think about puking.

"Hello?" I call out. There's no reason to pretend someone wouldn't know I was here after I turned on the lights.

The only answer is the tinny echo of my voice, coming back at me from the metal walls at the distant end of the warehouse, nearly a football field away. I walk farther in and make a cursory inspection. I don't know that I would recognize if something was missing, but I don't see anything that looks any different than what I expect.

I move deeper into the building, working my way around the float. The angel wings are all extended outward and, though I saw them that way many times while we were building it and testing it, it now looks all wrong without the children standing in front of them. Marci Hazlehurst's words come to me like a bolt of lightning aimed at my heart.

We're dead *angels!*

I fight off tears welling up in my eyes, and I step closer to where Fleming had been, searching for any clue to what had happened, how he had gotten off of the float, where he had gone. But of course, there's nothing.

I pull out my phone and dial Bill Petterson. While it rings, I turn a circle, looking around to see if everything else looks right. I'm surprised to see Paige's car, hitched to her "little house" float, parked at the far end of the warehouse. Someone has expertly backed it in, fitting it neatly between two of the metal pallet-racks. My guess it that it was Petterson himself. Not only is he the best with a trailer that I know of, but I don't know anyone else who would have had the nerve to risk hitting his racks.

I keep walking toward it, listening to the phone ring in my ear.

"Yeah." Petterson's voice is gravelly when he finally answers the phone.

"Hey, Bill. Sorry to wake you so early. It's Jeff. I'm at the warehouse. I came by to get my truck. I wanted to let you know the front door has been busted open."

"What?" His voice sharpens as he wakes up.

"I'm standing inside now, and I don't see anything that looks messed with, but I figured you should know, and that you'd want to come take a look for yourself."

"Eee-yup," he says with a grunting sigh. "Thanks, Jeff. Be right there."

"I'll wait for you." I hang the phone up and finish walking to Paige's car, remembering what Oliver had said about Paige going into hysterics, nearly running into the crowd. I notice the little For Sale sign in the front yard of the float is broken again, hanging by one chain. I take a couple of steps closer before seeing the new latch I'd put on the house's roof. It's busted, too. The screws torn right out of the wood.

I try to imagine what Paige did with her car to jerk the trailer around enough to do that. No wonder someone thought Paige had to be sedated.

The sound of crunching of gravel under tires in the parking lot pulls my attention away. It seems too soon for Petterson to have made it, but maybe he was still in his pajamas or, more likely, he slept with his boots on.

Going back to the broken door, I'm stunned by a bright light in my face.

"Hands up! Don't move!" The voice comes over some kind of speaker,

91

and I raise my left hand to match my right, which was already trying to shield the light from my eyes.

"Turn around, face the wall."

I comply, the spotlight from what I assume to be a police vehicle following me as I take three steps to get out of the doorway and face the wall.

I hear footsteps coming up behind me. "Put your hands on the wall."

I mostly follow that order, trying not to put any pressure on my injured right hand.

"Spread your legs."

That one I have problems with. My knee doesn't want to hold my weight at that angle when I try to spread my legs, and I hobble a bit trying to get it there.

The officer helps by kicking my foot out wide, and I go down, my face smashing into the corrugated siding of the warehouse. I gasp with the pain.

"Keep your hands where I can see them!" His voice is no longer calm, and though he is behind me, and I can't see him, I have no doubt his gun is drawn and pointed at me. "Get up!"

"I'm trying," say, calmly as I can. "I hurt my knee. And my hand." I gently wave the swollen, purple right hand.

"Is that your blood?" His voice is not calm at all anymore. I realize I am still in the clothes from last night and my other sleeve is covered with dried blood.

"Yes, sir. I got injured at the parade last night."

"Yeah, I remember him," another voice says.

I hadn't realized there were two officers.

"The injuries are legit. I saw him getting checked out at the med tent last night. Can you get up?"

"I think so," I say. I put my good hand to the ground to take the weight off my bad knee.

"Go slow," the first voice warns.

"Yes, sir." I push my way back up into a standing position, and put my hands back up in the air, but don't turn around.

"You got ID on you?" The second officer again.

"Back pocket." I slowly reach with my jacked-up hand and fumble with my useless fingers, trying to get my wallet. I give up and try to reach it with my left hand but have no better success.

"Put your hands back up. I'll get it."

I nod, feeling like a complete failure. I can feel him reach into my pocket and it irritates the bruise I have back there, making me wonder if falling on my wallet caused the bruise in the first place.

"Jeff McKenzie."

It's not a question, but I treat it like one anyway. "Yes, sir."

"You know who this is, Tanner?" the second officer asks. I assume he's asking the first.

"Not a clue."

"Jeff McKenzie made that float with the bridge on it. The one with all the kids dressed up like little angels."

"Oh yeah?"

"Yup. It's his ex-wife's son what went missing last night."

"You don't say."

"Yup. Terrible thing, that. Gotta be rough on the whole family. I think we can trust him to put his arms down, don't you?"

"Sure. Why not? Go ahead and put them down, Mr. McKenzie."

I drop my arms, but I keep facing the wall. I've seen too many things on TV and the way things are going, I am expecting the worst despite the fact the one of the officers seems to know me. Or maybe that's what makes it worse. I can't think of any police officers I know, let alone why they would know me.

"You can turn around, Mr. McKenzie," the second officer says.

I slowly turn to face into the spotlight still shining on me from the car.

"Here you go," the first officer says, holding out my wallet. I take it with my good hand and shove it into my front pocket.

"Oh, now I recognize you," the first officer says and steps forward to get a better look at me.

Squinting into the light, I still can hardly make his face out.

"You were one of the parents who found Toddy McCurdy."

"No shit?" the second officer says.

"Who?" I ask.

93

"The dead guy in the park," the first answers. "You really get around, don't you, Mr. McKenzie?"

"Uh… I guess so?" I have no idea what he means, but I don't like how this is going, and I'm glad they haven't pulled out any nightsticks. There still feels like more tension in the air than just my fear, but I guess that probably comes from them finding me coming out of a broken door of a business just as the sun is starting to lighten the sky.

"Lemme check in with dispatch," the second officer says, "then I am pretty sure you are free to go, Mr. McKenzie."

Headlights sweep over us, and a truck pulls into the parking lot. The body posture of both officers change as the truck nears.

"That's gotta be Bill Petterson," I say. "He owns this place. I called him just before you guys got here, to let him know someone busted open the door to his warehouse."

"Oh, they did, did they?" The second officer shines his flashlight on the broken door jamb and then back to my face. "We might need you to hang out just a little bit longer than I thought, Mr. McKenzie."

Chapter 22

DRIVING MY TRUCK HOME FROM Dr. Stephen's office doesn't feel real. My eyes are everywhere except on the road, constantly searching the faces of each person I see, each place where a person could be, for Fleming. After I drive Main Street twice, I realize I'm not really headed home.

Which is fine. I wouldn't know what to do with myself anyway. Exhausted as I am, I know I can't sleep. It's been over twelve hours since Fleming vanished, and part of me keeps screaming we are running out of time, keeps bringing up the horrible idea that if we don't find him in twenty-four or forty-eight hours, we won't ever find him. I don't know if that's true, but I can't get it out of my head.

Even if I could, it wouldn't do me any good to go home. It hurts too much to even sit in the truck, let alone lie down, or even breathe, really. Two of my ribs are cracked, but nothing worse, and nothing to be done about them, according to Dr. Stephen, other than be careful so they heal properly. Six to eight weeks, he warned. Which is what he said about my hand as well.

Now splinted in a half-cast, half-elastic bandage concoction, I can't seem to do anything with it but scratch at my nose. Not that I could use it before it got splinted. Having a police officer fish around in my back pocket for my wallet for me hadn't exactly been fun.

My fears of the officers had been unwarranted. Once they had talked with Bill Petterson, they became much friendlier. After a quick look around in the warehouse, and Bill confirming he didn't think anything had been taken, they took my statement for their report and shooed me off to go see the doctor.

I take a deep breath, testing my ribs, again, and feel the sharp pain, again. I don't know why I keep doing this to myself. It's like self-flagellation for losing Fleming, I guess.

Dana hasn't answered my text or calls this morning, but Coney finally texted back while I was in Dr. Stephen's office and let me know that they hadn't heard anything, from anyone.

My phone rings and hope for good news surges through me like an electrical shock. Ignoring the tightness of the bandage on my palm, from where Dr. Stephen dug out the gravel, I tap the button to answer on my steering wheel with my mostly good hand. "Hello?"

"Jeff? It's Paige. I was wondering if you've heard anything about Fleming. Trent hasn't returned any of my calls." She sounds so distraught, so on the verge of hysterics, that it surprises me she's calling, and I wonder if she's still at the hospital or if they released her—possibly too soon.

"No. I haven't," I tell her. "They aren't answering my calls either. I'm guessing it's because they are busy with the police. But Coney texted me a while ago and said they hadn't heard anything yet."

There is silence from Paige's end of the phone.

"I'm sure..." I don't know what to say. I remember the photo on her phone, and Fleming calling her 'Auntie Paige,' and I realize she's more family to Fleming than I am. I try to be more sympathetic. "Paige, I'm sure they'll tell us if they hear anything."

I hear her take a ragged breath.

"Are you doing okay?" I ask hesitantly, not wanting to make a big deal out of knowing she'd been sedated and transported last night.

"Where are you? I need to see you." Her voice suddenly sounds calmer, more controlled, unnaturally business like, I think, because her business voice is usually overly upbeat and friendly.

"Uh... I just left Dr. Stephen's office, at the hospital." I wonder again if that is where she is.

I start to ask if she's still there, if I should turn around and come back for her, but before I can decide if that's something I really want to do, she asks,

"Do you know where my car is?"

"It's at Petterson's garage." I don't mention I have no idea how it got there after she was sedated. I suppose it doesn't really matter.

"If you hear anything, Jeff, you *will* let me know, right?"

"Of course I will."

"All right. Goodbye."

"Uh, goodbye," I say to an already dead line. Paige's abrupt shift from sounding so upset to sounding so cold leaves me feeling even more unsettled than I already was, and I wonder if she's got issues, the kind I never dreamed of, hiding behind her buoyant persona. It brings to mind how many times I felt like her smile didn't reach her eyes

I drive another couple of blocks and then pull the truck into the parking lot where I'd seen the man with the robe run away last night, not sure if this had been my destination all along or not.

Everything looks too normal. I'd been expecting crime scene tape all over the dumpster or something, but there's no indication that there had been police all over this area last night. No signs that a heartbroken family had stood here and lost their souls to an uncaring night.

I get out of my truck and squint up into the bright, late morning sun. My knee, still sore, is doing better after some ibuprofen, but I step gingerly on it anyway. The truck door almost shuts, but then opens up again after the weak push with my lame hand. I use my good hand to make sure it latches, then I lock it. Probably because I feel this area is crime-ridden and unsafe.

A quick glance around tells me there are no security cameras here. At least no obvious ones. I'm not surprised. Other than the terrible events of the last couple of days, Decanter is an almost crime-free town. A near perfect slice of Americana if there ever was one.

I follow the path I had seen the scraggly man in the Longhorns cap run. Scanning the ground with my eyes, as the officer had done with his flashlight, I wonder what kind of trail a person could leave here that could be followed.

Tracks, if it weren't paved. Scent, if I had a bloodhound's nose, maybe.

A plastic soda bottle glints sunlight at me from under a dry bush. Bicycle tires have left black smears of rubber on the sidewalk. People have left all kinds of evidence of their passing, but there's nothing I can really follow or even attribute to a specific person, let alone something from the bow-legged man in the Longhorns stocking cap.

I try to imagine that guy running through here last night, just after he got too far away for me to see. Then the officer, an hour later, coming through with a flashlight. What can I see now that the officer couldn't have seen in the dark? What would the man running away have seen?

Ahead, on the left, is a church, and for the first time I realize I am on Church Street, so named because of all the Churches. First United Methodist of Decanter, both the old one and the new one, are here, as well as the Decanter Church of Christ, the First Baptist, and a couple of others I don't really know.

I can see floodlights at each corner of the First Decanter building from here. Had those been on last night? I don't know. I hadn't come far enough out into the street look down this way last night. But if they were, and I was the one running away, I would have stayed on the dark side of the street, out of the light, where the person chasing me would have a harder time seeing me.

I start up the street, keeping to the right, paying attention to the houses and buildings as I walk by. Most of them are only one lot off from being on main street, and are older, brick style houses. But there are no signs of anything other than what I would expect to normally see. Some trash here and there, but not much. Not much of anything really.

Where did he go? Why was he *here?*

My thoughts are starting to feel like one of those cold case shows where an old guy is talking and says, *you have to get into their minds and understand what they are thinking.*

The thought of Fleming being a cold case makes me ill. I take a deep breath, unintentionally hurting my ribs this time. Clenching my fists doesn't work well for my damaged hands either, so I let my breath out slow and look off to the horizon, trying to calm myself.

As I look to the treeline in the distance, I suddenly realize where the man was going.

Chapter 23

I TURN OFF THE TRUCK ignition and step out into the small dirt parking lot. The weather is warmer than it should be for late December, and there are a double handful of cars parked here. People are out enjoying Decanter Lake and the hiking trails around it.

Walking around the fence, which is nothing more than a handful of thick wooden posts with a rope reaching across them, intended to keep motorized vehicles out, I follow the trailhead toward the lake, but my eyes are on the dry thickets around the path. I'm looking for smaller paths, the ones most people don't take. The ones made by homeless people and drifters who set up camps out here in the preserve.

I don't know much about the homeless population around Decanter, other than they've been in the news because it's growing and, from time to time, for some terrible thing they did, or that someone did to them. But I know in my gut that this is where that guy had been heading.

Church Street dead-ends into this trailhead, and it is likely, in my uninformed opinion, the most popular place to set up a home base, because of the quick access to free meals from the churches and then to the businesses right next to them on Main Street. In my experience, homeless and transient people don't usually have much use for a print shop, so they tend to pass me by without a glance. And in the past, I hadn't glanced back either. But some of the other shop owners occasionally had problems, either trying to keep their bathrooms for customers only, or chasing off panhandlers who were too aggressive.

At first, I don't spot anything other than what are likely rabbit trails through the leafless bushes, but as the main walking path splits, with one fork heading for the water and the other off to follow the curvature of the lake, I spot a third trail, a worn place off to the side. The dried weeds are nearly rubbed down to dirt from foot traffic here, and, at the very far edge of where I can see into the brush, there is a place where the mud and dirt trail, and especially a tree root, has been worn smooth and shiny.

The dormant, skeletal fingers of the bushes pull at my sleeves and scratch at my face as I push through, like they are starving and cold, begging me to stop and help them. Moving through them, crunching the dead leaves underfoot, brings to mind the body of the dead boy in the park. Toddy McCurdy, the police had said his name was.

He'd looked like a Toddy.

Something else one of the police officers had said was still eating at me. *You really get around, don't you, Mr. McKenzie?* I had no idea what he'd meant by that at the time, but the more I think about it, the more sense it makes. He'd seen me next to the body of Toddy McCurdy and then, just two days later, in the First Aid Tent at the parade, and the next morning, at a break-in at a warehouse.

I completely agree that is probably too many times for an officer to run into a fella in such a short while. So why can't I shake the thought there was something more about his comment?

I reach the polished root in the path to find it is at the top lip of a gully, almost eight feet deep. At the bottom of the ditch, hidden from sight until I got close, is a small collection of tents, in various states of disrepair, huddled around a small, cold firepit. Piles of ash, dumped off to the side, indicate it has been cleaned out many times.

For a long moment, I stand there looking. It appears there are five tents, maybe seven, depending upon what someone could consider a tent. I can't tell if anyone is down there inside of any of them or not. With my knee, ribs, and this hand, I'm not sure I'm up for climbing down there to see.

But I am sure I can't live with walking away without checking for Fleming.

After a couple of minutes of seeing nothing move, and hearing nothing from the tents, I decide I have to go down. I have to know before I can move on.

Leaning down, I try to get a good grip on the smooth root with my good hand, which, being my left hand, is not normally my good hand, not to mention the bandage on my palm makes it even harder to grip with, and I work my feet over the edge. Wishing I'd worn boots, I try to dig the toes of my tennis shoes into the dirt bank, but like the path just above, it has been worn smooth and hard by repeated use. I end up lowering myself nearly entirely by the strength of my left arm. Which is even weaker than usual for an off arm, because of my broken ribs. Which means I get less than half-way down the bank before I fall.

I land on my feet, but even the short drop jars my knee, and I stumble two steps sideways to catch my balance. When I do, I look up to find I can see right into one of the tents, and someone is looking back at me.

Chapter 24

HER EYES NEVER LEAVING MINE, the woman in the tent pulls a long knife up from her lap and holds it so that I can see it clearly. I'm sure Rambo would find it acceptable. She slowly rotates her wrist just enough to flash the metal of the blade at me, to make sure I can see how big it is. I also notice the wicked looking sawblade teeth on the back edge of the blade.

"I'm not here to hurt you," I say, holding up my hands. "I'm just looking for someone."

Her face hardens. That seems like it was the wrong thing for me to say.

"A boy. A little boy. He's only five. Have you seen him?"

The woman could have held down a job as a statue.

"I'm going to take that as a no," I tell her. "Please, if you do see him…" I get lost trying to figure out what to say. "Do you know the print shop, on Main Street? Print-a-Rama? That's my place." I grimace. I hate saying the name. I hate the name altogether, but, although it would cost less than two hundred to do the paperwork to change the name, getting the approval of the City Council would be a pain, and then the cost of a new sign, and getting that approved, would be thousands.

"If you see him," I tell her, "please come tell me. His name is Fleming. He vanished at the parade last night. Right off the fucking float…" My voice cracks, and I have to wipe tears out of my eyes as they blur the image of the woman pointing a knife at me.

I take a breath, but not too deep, and compose myself.

"I'm sorry to have disturbed you." I take a step back and lower my hands.

Looking around, I'm not liking the idea that I might have to climb back up that bank. Not just because I'm not sure I even can, but I am already imagining that knife plunging into my back when I'm not looking, those saw teeth jaggedly grating across my spine, like she was trying to saw me in half.

"Is there another way out of here?" I ask without looking at her. I don't want her to think I am trying to confront her. Then I feel weird for not looking at her, so I turn to her. She has lowered the knife, and her eyes are not quite as hard as they had been. "I don't think I can climb that," I say, and lamely wave my splinted hand at it.

Not saying anything, she picks the blade back up and points it in the opposite direction I'd come from.

I pick out what looks like another trail through the brambles, barely more than all the other rabbit trails.

"Thank you," I tell her. "And please, really, if you see or hear anything…"

She doesn't move, so I vacate her camp quickly as I can, pushing through the meager path encased by naked winter foliage. The bushes disappear on one side and the path opens up at the base of an old, dead tree, surrounded by a dormant tangle of pepper vine. The remaining bushes steer me toward the tree trunk, and the woody vines catch at my feet, forcing me to high step to get through them. I'm sure I sound like an elephant crashing through, and I'm not sneaking up on anyone.

At this point, I'm not sure I care. I'd never really thought there was a danger of getting lost out here before. There's a road that goes all the way around the lake, which means if you pick a direction, you have to eventually find either water or asphalt. But looking around… I really am in the middle of nowhere, with nothing to be seen anywhere except thicket.

I'm breathing hard now. A side effect of letting myself get so far out of shape, I tell myself, just like Coney said. Definitely not just because I'm getting old.

My knee says otherwise. I remember how it hurt when I was a teenager. It was a different kind of hurt. Then it was more of an immediate, localized pain, somehow with a promise it would eventually get better. Now, though the pain is still localized, it doesn't feel like it is my knee. It feels like it is *me.* And it doesn't really feel like it'll get better, it feels like it just is. Get used to it.

I'm lost in self-pitying thoughts when I come out into the open, and I find myself in some kind of inlet.

Even in the dead of winter, the still, clear water, surrounded by dense trees and hidden from the rest of the lake—heck the rest of the world—is inviting. So much so, that as I stand there admiring the small forest enclosure, I think about soaking my knee, which I can feel is hot and tightening up again.

Something white catches my eye, and I realize I am looking at a pile of clothes on the ground. The longer I look at it, the more it looks like the thing on bottom is Fleming's robe.

Chapter 25

I MOVE CLOSER TO EXAMINE the pile of clothing and, at the same time as I see the Longhorn stocking cap on top of the pile, I hear a furious splashing behind me.

The scraggly man, buck naked and soaking wet, is charging up out of the water at me. "Mother fucker!" he yells. He can't hardly be more than five foot tall, shorter than I remember, but I remember those eyes. And that weird run.

His bowed legs swing out wide as he runs up the lake bank, and his thin frame makes him look like some sort of stick-man. The snarl on his face matches the way I feel at seeing him.

I envision myself punching this bastard in the face when he reaches me, dropping him to the ground like a pile of broken matchsticks. But as I try to make a fist, the splint on my right hand, and the pain of the broken bones, stops me. He's two steps away now, coming at full speed. Unbalanced and unready, I switch to clenching my left hand and throw the punch.

He easily ducks my clumsy swing and puts his shoulder into my gut, into my broken ribs. The force of his attack lifts me off my feet and carries me backward, and the sudden rush of pain, and loss of air, instantly takes all of the fight out of me. I find myself helplessly draped over his shoulder like a wet blanket.

"Mother fucker!" he screams as he and I go flying into the dry bush above the clothes pile. He yells it at me again and again. As much as I want to scream it back at him, pick him up over my head and throw him back into the lake, I can't.

Trapped between him and the bush, pinned in from all sides by stabbing, broken branches trying for my eyes, it is all I can do to breathe. He backs up and charges me again, cursing the same words, over and over, like they are the only ones he knows. I try to dodge to the side, but I'm tangled in the branches, and I can't get far enough out of the way. He clips my side, my bad ribs, again, as I finally break out of the bramble trap.

With an uncontrolled spin, I fall forward and hit the ground hard, pain flashing white in my vision, unable to breathe.

Then he kicks me.

And he kicks me again. Twice to my gut, and then a third blow to my chest sends me rolling down the bank and into the icy water. My muscles, my whole body, constricts from the sudden cold. I continue to roll over one more time and end up face down in the lake.

My oxygen-starved lungs, still fighting for air since the first time he hit my ribs, struggle against me now, trying to trick me into breathing the icy water. I can't seem to right myself. I can't get my feet under me; I can't get my head up out of the water.

I know it can't be very deep here, but somehow it keeps pulling me down, and I can't tell which way is up. My wet clothes are too heavy, my traitorous body is too weak, and I can't manage a single coordinated swim stroke to save my life.

I feel faint, thoughts slipping from my head. I panic. It can't end like this. I have to get out. I have to find Fleming. I have to tell someone I found the guy who took Fleming!

My foot kicks something solid, and the contact brings my mind back into focus, gives me something to concentrate on. Desperately, I search with my foot, where I thought something was, and then it happens again. My foot lands on the semi-solid bottom, sinking into the lake muck, and suddenly I know which way is up again. My body responds quickly, putting my other foot down, and I push, throwing myself up above the surface and into the precious air.

Now that I am oriented, I put my feet down again and stand up, still gasping for air. I find myself barely chest-deep in the lake. Wiping the streaming water from my eyes, I see the bastard, still yelling the same two words over and over again while he pulls on his clothes.

He sees me looking at him and stoops to pick up a rock. His aim is good, and I have to dive aside. He barely misses my face.

I right myself again and start clawing my way up the muddy bank, slipping and getting heavier with every inch of me that comes out of the water. My shoe comes off, stuck in the muck below. The bastard looks like he is going to grab another rock, and I don't know if I will be able to dodge it again, but then he scoops up the rest of the clothes instead.

"Where's Fleming?" I try to yell, crawling up the bank, but the words are hoarse and broken. "Where's the boy?"

He looks at me, eyebrows together, as though he's confused, but he keeps spouting the same curses.

"What did you do to him?"

Out of the water now, I force myself to my feet, raising up to my full height, and I snarl like I'm some kind of an animal. It takes everything I've got, but rage prepares me to charge him, as he had me.

This time he does throw another rock, and his aim is better, hitting me in the arm before I can turn to avoid it. When I turn back, he's already running, moving his scrawny body through the tight path as fast as any rabbit, and there's no way in hell I can catch him. Even if I wasn't completely beaten.

But I don't need to.

I drop to my knees as I watch him go. I can clearly see the white robe clutched in his hand as he runs away. It's not Fleming's choir robe. It's a goddamned full-body chef's jacket, stolen from a goddamned kitchen supply company dumpster.

Chapter 26

THE COLD WIND SENDS MY soaked body into uncontrollable shivers and wakes me up. I have no idea how long I've been passed out on the ground. The clouds have moved in, and the temperature has dropped.

My ruined phone is still clutched in my hand. I vaguely remember trying to call for help after I collapsed. Mostly I remember thinking about Toddy McCurdy and how I was going to die out here, and be just like him, when I realized the lake had killed my phone.

And then I woke up.

I could have been dead.

Shaking, I push myself up into a sitting position. The wind swirls around my body making the side I hadn't realized was kind of warm against ground suddenly colder, and I find myself shivering so hard I can hardly control my movements as I try to put my phone back in my pocket. I don't know why I feel like I need to keep it, and I feel stupid for it, but I keep struggling until I manage to get the phone into the pocket on the fourth or fifth attempt.

The sound of the growing wind rustling through the dry weeds is haunting, lonely, and this isolated place, which I'd thought was so beautiful earlier, feels like a graveyard waiting to happen. Trying to happen.

I'm in trouble, and I know it, but I'm not dead. I thought I was. Maybe I should have been, but I'm not. That scrawny bastard whupped me but good. I want to tell myself it's because I was already injured, but the fact the injuries had contributed to my failings isn't the whole truth. The real truth is that guy, despite being homeless and whatever else he was, was in a hell of a lot better shape than I am and probably would have put up a better fight than I could have even if I'd been uninjured.

A gust of cold wind directly to my face takes my breath away. Shivers nearly overwhelm me, sending me into an uncontrollable fit of tremors. I have to get out of here, back to someplace warm, or I *will* be dead. I imagine my face is already pale as Toddy McCurdy's was. My lips feel blue. My fingers are numb.

My bad knee won't bend, and it's all I can do to stand up, pushing off the ground with my good hand, the dirt pressing into the small wounds exposed by the missing bandage. My front is covered in mud from lying in the dirt while wet. I can't feel my foot that is missing a shoe. I wriggle my toes, trying to get some feeling in them. They move slowly, like a kid pretending to be on the moon, but I still can't feel them, and it doesn't help. Looking around, I find my shoe, stuck in the mud, half-submerged, right at the edge of the water.

I don't want it. I don't feel like I have the strength to walk to it, let alone to bend down and pick it up, or even put it on. But I have to walk out of here, and doing that on a numb, frozen foot sounds like a really bad idea.

It takes me two tries to pick up the shoe, and I'm afraid I'll fall into the water again, but I get it, and then I move far enough away to make sure I won't fall in the lake when I put the shoe on. I plop down hard on my ass, probably bruising it even more but I can't feel it, and then I stare dumbly at the shoe in my hand.

I don't know how the hell I'm going to get it on a foot on the end of a leg that won't bend, using a hand that won't close, when I can't feel either of them.

The wind rips hot tears of fear, anger, and frustration from my eyes.

Telling myself I have two choices, do it and get out of here, or don't do it and see what happens.

But I know what will happen, and I'm not ready to be found looking just like Toddy McCurdy. Nor am I wanting to walk my foot down to a bloody stump because I can't feel it.

I begin struggling with the wet shoe. I get my toes in but can't get the rest. The back of the shoe folds in under my heel, and I can't reach it well enough to pull it out. I decide that will have to do, and I force myself up to my feet again.

I search the area for any sign of another path, one that doesn't lead back to a steep bank under a shiny root I have to climb up. And to where I might possibly have to face the guy who'd left me here to die. And maybe his girlfriend with the knife.

That's not fair, I tell myself. He thought I was coming after him, which, I was. And when he left, he probably thought I wasn't hurt that badly. Which, if I hadn't already been injured, I shouldn't have been.

Thinking a little more clearly about the encounter, now that the cold has cooled my temper, I can put myself in his shoes, and suddenly I become the weirdo, the stranger, the person attacking. He couldn't have known why I was there or what I wanted. Only that I was going to steal his clothes, in the wintertime, when he was wet and butt-naked, and that I was being aggressive about it.

Being out here, freezing wet in this cold, makes me think I would likely have fought just as hard to keep someone from taking my clothing.

I finally make out another, even less used path, heading away from the lake instead of alongside it. I don't really have a choice, so I take it.

Pushing through more leafless bushes that claw at my face and try to steal my loose shoe, I keep going until I see a larger, well-worn trail. Hoping I'm not making a mistake, I take it, assuming that because it goes in the general direction I'd started from, it will take me back.

I go into a kind of fugue state while I walk, forcing my feet to move. I'm grateful for the clear path. I couldn't have navigated any more brambles or roots. Although the pain is a beacon for me to follow in my haze, a way to keep me conscious, my knee hates me as much as I hate it, and we'd probably part ways, if we could.

I don't know how long I walk, but I'm exhausted and limping hard by the time I reach my truck. Despite taking less than an hour to find the guy in the Longhorn cap, it has taken me more time than I can guess to find my way back to my truck, and, though the exertion has helped, I am still freezing my ass off.

Chapter 27

MY CELL PHONE IS RUINED beyond repair. No amount of rice is bringing it back, I am sure. I can see water moving back and forth under the screen when I tilt it. I toss it onto the truck seat and watch it slide all the way across and fall down between the seat and the door. I stare dumbly at where I had intended for it to land until more shivering forces me to climb in after it.

Nothing like a refreshing December swim in the lake.

I hate myself for thinking I'd wanted to soak my knee in it. Be careful what you wish for, I guess.

I start the truck and turn the heater up to high. Though my shirt has dried out a bit walking in the cold wind, my pants and shoes are still soaked. Every speck of dirt along the way stuck to my already mucky tennis shoes, making them look like fuzzy night slippers made out of mud and straw, and every step back to the truck had been a miserable exercise in trying not to slip or trip and fall. The only good thing I can say is that my hands are so cold, I can't feel the broken one hurting anymore.

Which is in a soaking wet splint that's probably not doing me any good now. Not only do the bones likely need reset again now, the splint is never going to fully dry, and then it'll start rotting my skin and stinking. And it already stinks from lake muck. I definitely have to go get it replaced, and I've only had the damned thing on for three hours. If that.

I wonder if my insurance will authorize it a second time, or if I'm going to end up paying more than the deductible.

A sense of calm comes over me as I sit in the truck and realize I'm going to be all right.

I've heard people think about the stupidest things when their lives were in danger, and here I am worried about smelly splints and health insurance. I seem to be full of stupid thoughts lately.

With a deep sigh, I lean my head back against the seat.

It feels unbelievably good to be out of the wind, and I'm tempted to close my eyes and go to sleep. But the voice in my head, counting hours since Fleming disappeared, won't let me. Sitting in the truck seat presses the wet clothing against my skin, and I suddenly realize how much mud I've tracked into the truck. My entire front side is muddy, and my legs, from the knees down, are mud.

I start stripping off my clothes, wishing I'd done it before I got in. It's a struggle to get the wet shirt off over the splint, but I notice most of the bloodstain from last night is finally gone. Not that it matters. The shirt is ruined. The pants, with my knee not bending and a steering wheel in the way, are even worse to get off. By the time I am in my underwear, the heater is blowing warm air, and I want to curl up close to the warm air vents. I almost feel like I'm going to be okay.

Except I've accomplished nothing. That scrawny bastard had nothing to do with Fleming, and this entire trip, and telling the cops last night, had all been a waste of time.

Staring down at my belly, I try to see where the ink stain ends and the bruises begin, but it's a lost cause.

Since I can't call anyone to tell them what happened, I decide to head for Trent and Dana's, to let them know I was barking up the wrong tree. They can call Detective Littlejohn and let him know, maybe free up some resources that can be used to look somewhere else.

If the police are even looking at all.

I never heard from anyone other than Paige before I drowned my phone. At the very least I think Coney would have texted me, even if no one else thought to. Which probably means that she hadn't heard anything, which means nobody has.

While I can understand not calling me, to me, not keeping the parents in the loop sounds a lot like the police admitting nothing is being done.

I fight off the weight of my eyelids pressing down, my body badly wanting to sleep. I can't help but think that however helpless I'd felt laying out there, however terrible that whole damned experience was, it had all been my own doing. Whatever Fleming is going through, whatever he's feeling, likely none of it is his fault, and it's probably worse.

Chapter 28

I WAKE WITH A START. The truck is still running, and I'd fallen asleep slumped against the steering wheel. The dashboard clock says it's after two. The horrid voice in my head tells me I've wasted two more hours of the few I have to save Fleming's life.

I rub my eyes and shift the truck into gear, trying to think of the best way to get to Trent and Dana's house from here. My bare foot, pressing on the brake pedal, still burns like it's on fire from being nearly frozen. My whole body shivers again, though a small one this time, and realize I'm not wearing any clothes, and I don't have any to put on.

I need to go home first.

Heading out of the little dirt parking lot, I glance at it one last time in the review mirror and try not to think about how that scrawny little asshole kicked my ass. If he'd tried any harder, I'd still be laying there.

With a phone that couldn't call for help.

I speed all the way home, not caring if I get pulled over, knowing that if I do, I can tell the police to let Detective Littlejohn know the guy from the dumpster didn't have anything to do with Fleming.

When I get home, Coney's car is in front of my house. I push the button on the garage door opener attached to my visor and pull into the driveway, waiting for the overhead door to finish raising. Pulling in, I intentionally park the truck smack dab in the middle of the garage, and then carefully slide out of the seat with my bad leg sticking out like a ruined corkscrew blade on a Swiss Army knife. I hobble around to the passenger side and grab all of my muddy clothes out of the footwell and then head into the house, leaving behind the ruined cell phone, lost somewhere in the land of old french fries and hair ties.

Knowing Coney is here, I forgo my usual routine of brooding as I enter the house, trusting the overhead garage door to close on its own without supervision. I can hear the television in the living room, squawking out high-pitched voices of some anime show, and I hope I can get past her and into the shower before she realizes I'm home.

I make it less than two steps before she appears. She's got bags under her eyes and looks like a hundred-year-old teenager. Her heavy eyes give me an exhausted once over.

"And you give me crap about what *I* wear out of the house." Her voice is tired, and the humor is strained.

"I didn't wear this out," I correct her. "I just came back this way."

"Walk of shame?"

I grimace. Despite what had happened not being what she means, that is a more accurate description than I find comfortable.

"Have you heard anything?" I ask. But I already know the answer. She wouldn't look as bad as she does if there had been any good news. And she wouldn't have been able to joke if there'd been bad.

Coney just shakes her head.

"Are you okay?" she asks. "You are a walking bruise, and your knee looks like an overripe cantaloupe."

I give her a circular nod of my head that doesn't mean yes or no. "I need a shower."

"Yeah, you do." She scrunches her nose. "You smell like you were playing in a sewer. What happened?"

"I fell into Decanter Lake."

"And I'm Billie Eilish."

"Hi, Billie. That's your new name, you know," I say, limping past her, "because that's really what happened."

"Seriously? How in the hell did you end up in the lake?"

"Language!" I shut the door on her as I make it to the bathroom. "I'll explain when I get out."

I drop the filthy clothes in the corner and catch sight of myself in the mirror in my filthy underwear. I look terrible. I didn't even know I had a black eye. It matches the ink stains and bruises across my hand, ribs, belly, hip, thigh, and…other places. And Coney's right about my knee. Leaning in closer to the mirror, I gingerly poke at the purple bag under my eye with my finger on my good hand. It's sore, but not bad. I'm sure it'll be worse later. Just like the knee.

That guy must have kicked me in the face, and, with all the other pain, I didn't even realize it. Or maybe it was when—

I suddenly remember I need to tell someone that it wasn't that guy who took Fleming.

"Coney!" I call, cracking open the door.

She's still standing right there, trembling. Tears are in her eyes.

"Hey, baby," I say. "Are you okay?"

She shakes her head, and the tears start falling. "You look terrible! What happened?" she demands.

I'm not even sure where to begin, so I do what fathers always do; I start with reassurances. I open my arms and pull her to me. "Hey. I'm okay, just a little banged up, okay. But I need to you call your mom and let her know that the dumpster guy wasn't involved, so she can tell Detective Littlejohn, okay?"

I can feel her hot tears on my shoulder as she nods. "Did he do this to you?"

"Some of it, yeah. But most of this is from last night."

She pulls away from me with a strange look on her face. "Last night?"

"Yeah."

"What happened last night?" Her question, like the look on her face is strange, not right.

It's my turn to give her a strange look. "Honey, are you okay?"

She slowly shakes her head and asks me again. "What happened last night?"

"You were there. You know what happened."

"I want you to tell me."

I look into her eyes. Beyond the tears welling up, beyond the pain, there is something else there. Confusion, maybe? Has she somehow blocked memories from last night? Is Fleming's disappearance somehow affecting her like some kind of PTSD? Is that why she is here? Did she come here to be in familiar place, a place with nothing to remind her of him, of what happened, so she can…forget about it all?

"You remember Fleming disappeared last night, right?" I ask.

Her face scrunches up, and she looks like her dam of emotions is going to break. "*Of course* I fucking remember Fleming's gone! I mean what the fuck happened *to you* last night!"

"Oh, baby." I try to pull her closer, but she moves back, pulling out of my arms. "I thought you already knew because you saw me at the First Aid tent. I'm sorry." I guess I hadn't actually talked with her last night, other than briefly coordinating as we all looked for Fleming.

"Do you remember Luca, your friend from elementary school? He was on stilts, and he wasn't very good. He took a fall, and I tried to catch him." I held up my bad hand. "I mostly caught him, but I got a little banged up in the process." I pointed to the bruise on my ribs and my swollen knee. "We landed on the sidewalk curb." I grimace at the memory.

"You didn't have that last night." She points to my eye.

"Yeah. That's new. I went to go find the dumpster guy—"

"And he did that?"

"Yeah."

"And that's how you ended up in the lake?"

"Yeah."

She wipes the tears from her cheeks. "So, I bet he looks a lot worse, huh?"

I kind of laugh, kind of wince as my ribs hurt with the effort. "Depends on what you think of the guy in general. I never laid a hand on him."

Her eyebrows go up. "Then why did he punch you in the face?"

"Kicked," I correct her. "Because he thought I was going to lay a hand on him."

"Were you?"

"Yeah, I guess. Mostly I just wanted to find out about Fleming, but I probably came across a little aggressive."

"And you got your ass kicked." She nods knowingly, the disappointment evident on her face.

"Yeah."

"…And your face." She shakes her head. "Jesus, you stink. Go take your shower."

Feeling chastised by my daughter, I don't even bother to correct her language. She's right. And while I can wash the stink off, I don't know if I'll ever be able to wash the sting off. I slink back into the bathroom as she walks away from me.

"Call your mother!" I say, shutting the door.

Chapter 29

I GET DRESSED AND COME out of the bedroom feeling more like a torn one-dollar bill than a million bucks. Coney is still here, asleep on the couch, with the television still playing the anime show with squeaky voices. Her face, slack and free of judgmental expressions, makes her look like a little kid again. Sometimes, because she is so grown up, I forget how young she really is.

And as much as I want to sit down and just be here with her, I can't. I wouldn't be able to live with myself. I have to do something. I can't just pretend Fleming's not missing. I can't just sit around and do nothing, watching the clock tick down until it's too late.

Which is what Trent and Dana are doing, if they are doing what Detective Littlejohn told them to do—and that has to be terrible for them, even worse than it would be for me. My heart hurts for Dana. And for Trent.

And my little Coney. How terrible it must be to lose her little brother.

I can only imagine how much worse they are all hurting than I am.

Seeing her phone next to her head, I consider using it to make sure she called them but reject the idea quickly. I don't invade my daughter's privacy. I'm sure Coney would have called them after I asked her to, and I really don't want to wake her just to find out. For the first time in years, I regret taking out the landline phone.

I decide to head over to their house, to see how Trent and Dana are doing while I try to figure out what I can do to actually help. Instead of getting my ass kicked for no reason.

With a limping step toward my keys on the kitchen table, I change my mind. I need to go get my knee looked at. It's much worse than before. Coney was right, it looks like a rotten cantaloupe. And I need this splint replaced. Add in the ace bandage I'd been thinking about putting around my ribs, and my new beaut of a shiner, and I'm halfway to being mistaken for a low-budget remake of the Six-Million Dollar Man.

The thought strikes me as funny. That price tag is so outdated, I might actually be uncomfortably close to that number when I get my final medical bill.

"Where are you going?" Coney asks, sitting up and looking at me just as I reach for the keys. She rubs her tired eyes, still looking like a little kid, and I wish she hadn't woken up. I wish she could have stayed in a wonderful dreamland and not had to face today, not wake up until after we found Fleming and everything was right in the world again.

"To get this replaced." I hold up the splint. "It's going to smell like lake muck for the rest of eternity, I'm sure."

"And to get your knee looked at, right?"

"Right." Mentioning it makes me realize how tight it feels inside the leg of my jeans, and I wonder if I should have put on shorts. Thinking of the chill I'd barely managed to disperse from my bones with an extra hot shower, I quickly reject the idea. I may never wear shorts again.

She looks at me with a strange expression. Thoughtful, but strange. "Where were you last night?" she asks. Her words are strange.

I frown, again wondering if she's repressing memories or something to cope with the stress, though that didn't seem to be the case. "Honey, you already know. I told you. I helped look for Fleming, and then saw the dumpster guy—"

"No. I mean overnight. You didn't come home last night."

Again, her words don't feel right. Like they're not hers. They are stilted, accusing, like she'd been waiting a long time to ask me that. Like she is confronting me. Like her mother used to. Not to mention, how would she know if I came home or not? She'd been asleep in the back of the car.

"I slept on the couch at the print shop." Keys in my hand, I limp back over to her. If I learned one thing from all of the arguments with Dana, it is that when something is bothering someone enough to lead to a direct confrontation like this, it's time to stay calm, try to be understanding, and answer their questions. Or the shit hits the fan. And the last thing I need is to have any problems with my daughter.

"I decided it was too far of a walk to get back to my truck, at Petterson's warehouse," I tell her. "You know, with this knee. Admittedly it wasn't this bad last night, but it wasn't good either."

She nods but doesn't seem satisfied with the answer. Why was she asking? Had she needed me last night? Had she come looking for me, looking for help or consolation, and I wasn't here for her? Why hadn't she just called me?

"How did you know I wasn't home? Did you come here? Have you been here all night?" Another thought crosses my mind. "Is everything okay with your mom? She and Trent aren't fighting, are they? He didn't get abusive, did he? Is that what you were upset about the other day, when you came over here? Is he abusive?"

I finally stop asking questions long enough she has a chance to answer. Her eyes are wide, and she looks shocked. I realize I've gone into overprotective dad mode, and I take a small step back to give her space.

"No, Dad! Trent is *not* being abusive! How could you even think that?"

"I'm just stressed and upset, and I worry about you. I'm sorry. I—"

She holds up her hand to stop my rambling. "That's *not* why I was upset the other day. Trent is very nice. He would never hurt anyone."

"I'm sorry," I say lamely. I put the keys in my pocket. I'm not going anywhere while my daughter is this upset with me. I shift my weight to keep it off my bad knee while I wait for her to decide just how upset she is.

After a long moment of silence between us, I take a deep breath and compose myself. "Did you call them and tell them about the dumpster guy?"

"Yes. I told them. They already knew."

"They already knew? How? And why didn't they tell me?"

"Maybe because *somebody* hasn't been answering their phone."

"Yeah," I sigh. "It's dead. It went swimming in the lake, too."

We both go quiet again.

It occurs to me that Dana and Trent would have to have found out the dumpster guy wasn't involved sometime *after* I got to the lake, or they would have called and told me, and then I wouldn't have gotten my ass kicked. But…the guy was *at* the lake when I got there, that means the police would have to have known *before* I got there. Maybe…since they went looking for him last night?

"I…I was upset the other night because some of the kids at school were calling me names." Coney interrupts my thoughts.

She turns her head and looks away from me, not wanting to make eye contact. Obviously, she's still upset about it. "It's all stupid though," she says. "I mean," tears begin to roll down her cheeks, "it doesn't matter. It seemed like such a big deal, but now, it seems so unimportant compared to…"

She can't seem to finish the sentence, but I know she means Fleming's disappearing.

I hobble over and sit down next to her and try to tackle the problem I can take on, hoping it will take both of our minds off the one neither of us can handle.

"Why would kids call you names?"

She shrugs and still doesn't look at me.

"What kind of names, honey?" I put my hand on her knee and she jerks it away.

Her voice is barely a whisper. "Names like… slut. And whore."

It feels like there is a rock sinking down into my gut, and my heart suddenly hurts so badly for her. Being a teenager is hard, being the parent of one can be worse. "Why would they do that?"

"Because…because I dated a bunch of different guys." She keeps whispering, as though if she tells me quietly enough, I won't hear, but she still gets to tell me.

I don't know what meaning she intends behind the word 'dated,' and I don't ask. I don't know if this is the moment I've dreaded since it first occurred to me that she had become a young woman, but I'd determined a long time ago that her choices were hers, and hers alone, and I would be supportive.

As the words pour out of her, they come faster and faster. "I didn't want to end up like you and Mom. I didn't want to marry someone and then have a divorce. I know you guys got divorced because she never dated anyone else except you and she regretted it.

"I didn't want to make the same mistake. I wanted to date a lot of people. I wanted to make sure that when I thought I found the right person, I would really know that I had. I didn't want to have regrets." The wracking sob that stops the rush of words proves to me she does have regrets, and it makes me even more sure of what she'd meant by 'dated.'

"Oh, honey…" I swallow, trying to find the right words, words that won't make this worse after she took the chance and opened up to me. I hold my arm up, inviting her to lean in for a hug, and I'm relieved when she does.

Pulling her close, I kiss the top of her head. "That's not why we got a divorce."

Chapter 30

"YOUR MOTHER AND I," I hug Coney tight as I talk, "love each other very much, but sometimes..." I sigh. How do you explain the death of a marriage? How do you put it into words that make sense, when it never really made any sense to start with?

"It wouldn't be true if I said that your mother not dating other people wasn't a part of it. Because I don't know. Maybe it was. But for the record, she did date other people, I was just her first, and only, serious relationship." *Until Trent*, I think but don't say aloud.

"The thing is, nothing is ever really black and white easy to understand. The whole world is a gray area, especially when it comes to people. I can't tell you *exactly* why we divorced, but I can tell you this: people change.

"When we're young, the changes are quick, and obvious. Little kids grow fast. They change their personalities quickly. They pick up new interests and lose old ones in an afternoon. They make friends easy and move on easy. As we get older, that still happens, but it's slower. And we still change, but that's slower, too. Our personalities change, our interests change. And one day, sometimes, two people who love each other very much, discover that they don't have much in common anymore, maybe nothing in common anymore, and maybe they aren't really even friends anymore. Just...roommates who've known each other for a long time."

Coney doesn't say anything, and I don't know if what I am saying is helping, making things worse, or what. So, I keep talking.

"Your mother and I… We both changed. She became more and more focused on her career. Which is a good thing for her. Don't think I'm saying it's not. But it bothered her that I don't have any ambitions beyond a silly little print shop that doesn't make hardly any money.

"Eventually, other than you, we discovered that we didn't really have any common interests anymore. We didn't have any common goals. We didn't have…"

I kiss the top of Coney's head again and hold her tight. "I hope you don't ever think it had anything to do with you. Because it didn't. We both love you more than I could ever say or even than you would ever believe."

I listen to the shrill voices coming out of the tv for a moment and wish I'd turned the TV off when I thought Coney was asleep. I don't know what else to say.

And I'll be damned if I bring up the topic of Coney 'dating' again before she does.

"Do you still love Mom?"

"Of course, I do. Very much."

"But you're not friends anymore?"

"That's a little harder to answer. I mean. We are, but…it's hard, you know?"

"Do you think she still loves you?"

"I know she does. There's not a doubt in my mind about that."

Coney sighs deeply, and I remember how it felt, when she was a baby, and she'd fall asleep in my arms, and, just for a moment, everything in the world was perfect.

"Do you think you guys will ever get back together?"

"What?" The question surprises me.

"Don't you want to get back together with Mom?"

That question pushes past surprise and actually flummoxes me. Despite all of my daydreams about still having Dana around, or waking up thinking she's beside me, or leaving space for her to park in the garage, the actual idea of getting back together has never really crossed my mind. Not really. Not since Dana made it perfectly clear she was moving on. I had accepted her decision as permanent, whether or not I liked it, even before she met Trent.

Even if I still accidentally called her my wife instead of my ex-wife from time to time.

Would I really want to get back together? Even if Dana said she wanted to, would I want to?

All of the hard feelings would still be there. All of the things I did that drove her nuts, the things she did that pissed me off... The nasty things we had said to each other, that were true, but mean-spirited and nasty nonetheless. They would all still be there, still be barriers in our relationship, wouldn't they?

Some people got divorced and then remarried each other again. Or so I've heard. I've never met anyone who did.

Could that even work?

"Dad?"

"I uh... I don't think so," I finally answer her question.

"Really?" Coney sits up and looks at me. I'm expecting an accusing look, one that says, 'how could you *not* want to get back together with Mom?' but instead, she looks confused.

"Yeah. I mean I never really thought about it until just now, but, as much as I love your mother, as much as she will always be a part of me, of you, of our family, she's a different person now. Our relationship is different now. And I think she's happier because of it." I realize I really believe that as I say it.

"Are you happier?"

"No?"

"Then why wouldn't you want to be with her?"

"Because... Honey. Just like I love you so much I don't ever want you to grow up, but I have to let you. I have to let you live your life. I have to let you go do your own thing. I love your mother so much that I have to let her go. I have to let her live her life that makes her happy. Even if that is without me."

Tears well up in my eyes. I already knew all of this, somewhere deep down inside, some part of me did. But I just hadn't let myself think about it. Saying it out loud somehow makes it all real, makes it so I can't pretend and ignore it anymore. Somehow it changes something inside of me, and more than knowing it was all true, finally admitting it to my daughter means I can finally admit it to myself. And I know I can accept it.

Coney's tears are streaming down her cheeks again, matching mine, but she isn't sobbing anymore. Her face contorts into an expression of... anger? Disgust?

I lean back and look at her, confused. "Are you okay?" I don't understand why she's upset, not in this way.

She shakes her head and stands up, pulling something out of her ear. "No! No, I'm not okay!" She pulls something else out of her shirt and holds it up in front of her face. "And I'm not asking any more of your stupid questions!" she screams at it.

Before I can figure out what the things she's holding are, she throws them across the room at the wall and then nearly jumps on me, throwing her arms around me.

"They think *you* took Fleming, Daddy!"

Chapter 31

CONEY STORMS OUT OF THE house, heading for her car, the light snow swirling around her as though she's a force of nature it can't reach. I want to talk to her more, but she is too upset. All she could say was that they thought I'd done it, they thought I'd taken Fleming. She couldn't even tell me who 'they' were.

As she hits the sidewalk, she puts a hand up in the air and flips her middle finger at someone up the street.

I look, expecting to see an ominous black van or maybe an exterminator's truck with a fake bug on top. Instead, I spot an unassuming tan sedan, just at the top of the bend, with a dusting of snow on it. The wipers have cleared two wide arcs off the windshield, revealing one person, all alone, sitting behind the wheel.

It occurs to me that the car has been setting there for quite a while if it was cool enough for the snow to build up on the hood. I feel the chill start to seep back into my body, working its way toward my soul.

The car starts up just before Coney slams her door and starts hers. She drives off with a squeal of tires that makes me cringe, and the other car pulls up and takes her spot.

Through the window I can see the driver is nearly bald, with thin, wispy hair combed across the top of his head, but I feel like I can't see his face around the stereotypical mirrored sunglasses he wears even on a gloomy day like this. His car door opens, and a boot appears. I start to have suspicions, and then I see the Stetson in his hand, which he places snugly on his head before standing up. The western belt with the holstered gun at his hip cinches it all, and I know I'm looking at a Texas Ranger.

He's not a big man, but he walks up my sidewalk with a swagger of confidence bordering on arrogance. "Mr. McKenzie," he drawls, apparently leaning into character. He stops an arm's length away.

"Ranger," I answer.

"Welp... No point in acting like I'm not keeping an eye on you anymore, so how's about answering a few questions."

I look away from his face, down to the brown winter grass of my front lawn, where the snow is just starting to stick. I look away partly because I'm tired of looking at the reflection of my own beat-up face in his glasses, and partly because I really want to punch this man in the face.

Not that it had gone so well the last time I'd tried to punch someone, but part of me is willing to try again.

"You put a wire on my underage daughter to question me already," I say with a low growl that sounds intimidating enough it would have surprised me if I wasn't so pissed off.

"We had permission from the mother."

"*The* mother?" I snarl back, shaking my head in disbelief. "My opinion of you is dropping by the *fucking* second." Even as I spit the words, I know it's completely the wrong thing to say, but it comes on out of my face before I can stop it. The heat in my ears feels like they are going to burst into flames. My heart pounds like a bass drum in a marching band. I am so pissed off at this man right now, it's all I can do to concentrate on thinking straight and not doing something stupid.

The ranger apparently has the same concern. Though his haughty expression hasn't changed, his hand, in a relaxed but not at all subtle motion, moves up to rest on the butt of his gun.

"That's not where you want to take this," I warn him. "Won't look good on your record, killing an innocent man after spying on him with his teenage daughter when you were supposed to be finding her missing step-brother." The words roll out of my mouth crisp, and sharp, and confident, like they were someone else's, like some part of my brain, some part that thinks and

129

acts more clearly than I usually do, has taken over and put me on the back burner to watch and take notes on what happens.

Deep down inside, it scares the hell out of me. I'm not sure I really am in control of my body anymore. Not really sure of what I'm about to do or not do.

"You're the one drivin' this train, Mr. McKenzie. I'm just along for the ride." He doesn't move his hand.

Staring at the snowflakes catching on the brim of his hat, I force myself to take a deep breath and try to calm down. The sharp pain in my ribs helps pull me back toward reality, toward a rational understanding of the situation I am in, but more words roll out of my mouth anyway.

"What kind of questions can you possibly have that I haven't already answered in my statements or that you haven't gotten my daughter to ask me?" Mentioning Coney makes my chest tighten again and raises my blood pressure more. Forcing my mouth shut tight, I take deep breaths through my nose.

"I'll get straight to the point," the ranger says. "Where's the boy?"

I shake my head. "I don't know. You know I don't know. I've been fucking looking for him! Like you mother fuckers are *supposed* to be!" I scream the words and spit flies out of my mouth, and I realize I am almost out of control. Maybe I already am out of control.

"Jesus!" I smash my face into my hands and squeeze, trying to make the rage go away. Make the ranger to away, make the world goddamned world go away. All it does is hurt my hand and my bruised eye.

Which grounds and calms me a little. Which is, I am sure, a good thing in this situation.

When I think I can trust myself again, I drop my hands and look into the mirrored glasses concealing the ranger's eyes and emotions. "I'm sorry," I force myself to say. "This has all been very, *very*, upsetting. I'm going to go inside and sit down, because this," I point to my knee, "hurts a lot. You are welcome to come in with me. You are welcome to see if you can find your equipment Coney threw at the wall. You are welcome to search my house from top to bottom. I will answer any questions you have despite the fact I got my ass beat by a homeless dude because you didn't see fit to tell me you'd already talked to him because you thought I was the one who kidnapped my ex-wife's stepson." My heart starts pounding again as I speak, and that other part of my brain takes over my body again, and I look him in the mirrored glasses where his eyes should be. "But if you use my daughter again, so help me, God, I will track you down..."

I barely manage to keep my finger out of his face and regain control of myself before I say the rest of the words and likely commit a felony.

I clench my jaw and purse my lips, hard, so that nothing else stupid will come out, and then I go back into the house, not waiting to see if the ranger is going to follow me, arrest me, shoot me in the back, or what.

Chapter 32

I HOBBLE UP THE SIDEWALK to Dana and Trent's house with the crutch under my arm, on the same side as the knee in the brace. Dr. Stephen wasn't happy that I couldn't use it on the other side, because of the hand he'd just re-splinted, and he'd cautioned me to stay off my feet as much as possible, or it would get worse. In general, Dr. Stephen hadn't been very happy to see me again.

I'd been right about my knee. It was a torn meniscus. Cold comfort in being right, as I struggle to get up the two cement steps to the front door. Even ringing the doorbell is a challenge. Do I let go of the crutch and lean on it while I reach with my good hand, or do I reach across myself with my splinted hand and hope I don't have to try multiple times with fingers nearly devoid of any strength?

"Allow me, Mr. McKenzie."

I startle at the drawling voice and wobble on my crutch as Texas Ranger Cole Murry steps past me to ring the doorbell.

Standing on the same level, I find myself looking down upon the brim of his hat, though I've never considered myself taller than average.

I take a step back, not wanting to be so close to the man. I don't necessarily want to kill him anymore, if that was really even what I'd wanted when I was so pissed off, but I don't exactly like the man either. And I don't expect that to change any time soon.

Or ever.

Coney answers the door, and for a moment, I think she's going to slam it in Ranger Murry's face. Then she sees me and steps back to let us in.

Ranger Murry doffs his hat as he enters, not bothering to look at Coney or back to me to see if I'm following or having problems.

I don't expect he cares too much for me either.

Our conversation, or rather his interrogation of me at my house had gone fine, for what it was. He asked the same stupid questions and didn't like that he got the same damned answers. In return, he'd answered none of my questions for him.

He'd done a cursory look through my house, but I was pretty sure he spent most of the time watching me more than actually looking around, as though he were some kind of mentalist who thought I would have body language that would show him where I didn't want him to look.

"What did the doctor say?" Coney asks me, pulling my attention away from the ranger. Her face is contrite. She's still upset. I want to hold her close and tell her I'm not upset with her, that she was just doing what had to be done, that trying to help find her brother was the right thing to do, but the way she stands tells me she isn't ready to be forgiven.

I suspect she's still too pissed off at Ranger Murry to think straight, too. And I completely understand that.

"I'll live," I tell her.

She rolls her eyes at me.

It works, and I tell her the facts. "I've got appointments after the holidays to see specialists about both the hand and the knee, to see if I should have surgery or not, but I probably won't need it."

Trent comes into the living room with a hurried step. He looks like he hasn't slept in years. The skin on his face seems loose, and his eyes are sunken. Dana is not far behind him, and she enters the room looking no better. They both glance at me with quick, nervous looks, and then they only have eyes for the ranger standing in their living room, holding his hat in some semblance of politeness but still looking like a cock daring you to approach his henhouse.

I suddenly realize they must've bought in on the idea that I was the one who took Fleming, otherwise Dana never would have agreed to let Coney get wired up, and it kills a little part of my soul that they could have thought that about me.

"Any news?" they both ask over each other as Detective Littlejohn follows them into the room, holding a cup of coffee, despite the fact that it's near dinner time.

"I'm afraid not," Murray says. "Our best lead dried up."

I get the feeling he is specifically not looking at me as he says that. Dana looks at me out of the corner of her eye again, but only for half a second, and suddenly I feel like everyone in the room is specifically *not* looking at me.

"They still think you did it, Dad," Coney says.

The looks on their faces, especially the irritation on Murry's, tells me she's right. Littlejohn coolly takes a sip of his coffee, watching me over the top of the mug.

I curse under my breath. "Why?" I ask, looking from Trent to Dana. They both drop their gazes. Murry meets mine with a cold stare. No one says anything.

"Coney?" I look to my daughter. "What did they say that made you think I could have done this?"

"I'll thank you to not impede our investigation any further, young lady," Murry drawls before Coney answers. "—For the sake of your brother."

His faux politeness, mixed with talking down to her and then mentioning Fleming in a way that couldn't possibly feel more tacked-on, more fake, goes too far and pushes Coney's button again, and she explodes. "For the sake of my brother, you should be out looking for him instead of..." At a loss for words, she waves her hand angrily in a circle, and I get the feeling she wanted to point at Littlejohn and his coffee, but actually feels like he was more worthwhile than Murry. *"Fuck this!"*

For the second time today, I watch her storm out of a house because of Ranger Murry, and, if it's even possible, I like him less each time.

"Coney!" Dana, close on Coney's heels, hurries past me, following her. "Coney! Where are you going?"

"To look for my brother! Because no one else is!"

I hear her car door slam again, and I look at Murry and shake my head, wishing the way he made me feel could be made tangible and I could force-feed it down his throat. "Well, that sounded familiar, didn't it?"

Out of the corner of my eye, I see Littlejohn's eyebrows go up in surprise at my tone.

Murry's steely eyes narrow. Barely. "Do you make a habit of seeking out and assaulting homeless people, Mr. McKenzie?"

"What? Of course not!"

"Tell me about McCurdy."

"Who?"

"Don't play coy with me, Mr. McKenzie. I know the officers who spoke with you at the warehouse this morning told you his name. Now, I want you to tell me what you know about him."

"I don't know anything about him. I never saw him before...before I saw him dead at the park."

"That's not what other witnesses say. They say you saw him Thursday night."

"I looked for him, for *someone*, Thursday night, but I never saw anyone." Murry's blindsiding me with that question seems to have worked. It shut up the voice in my head that seems to know what to say, that wants to tell him off, and I'm left struggling to defend myself. "Ask Oliver Parkin," I tell him. "He was with me."

"There's always a convenient witness, huh, Mr. McKenzie? Someone else who was with you who knows you didn't do it." Murry, confident in his position, hasn't rested his hand on the grip of his weapon again, but Detective Littlejohn switches his coffee mug to his left hand.

"Well, while we're on the subject of witnesses," Murry continues, "I should inform you that the *other* homeless man you assaulted this morning has decided to press charges."

My jaw drops. "Mother fucker."

"That is exactly what he said."

"I never laid a hand on that guy. Look at me!" I point to my eye. "He did this! And he nearly drowned me, and then he fucking left me for dead!" My anger is rising. I'm losing my shit with Murry again. Probably proving his point that I was an unstable person who *would* kidnap my ex-wife's kid.

Murry, his stance still unchanged, somehow manages to look like he is prepared to take me down if he has to. In fact, without changing his expression, he somehow even looks like he wants to. Littlejohn, on the other hand, is wearing a deep scowl, his dark eyes taking in everything happening and seemingly not liking it.

Trent looks back and forth between Murry and me, obviously confused and obviously not wanting to be anywhere near this.

"I want to press charges back!" I snap at Murry. "That guy assaulted *me!*"

"Do you have any witnesses that can corroborate your account of the incident?" Murry's voice carries a smug satisfaction that says he knows I don't.

"Does he?" I say snidely.

Dana comes back into the house behind me, distracting me just enough I realize I've lost it again and really need to calm myself.

"He does," Murray answers.

"Bullshit," I say, lowering my voice. "We were alone in the woods."

"If you were alone, then there is no one else to say that is where you were this morning, is there?"

My jaw drops again. Murry is playing me. I don't think the guy in the woods is pressing charges at all. I don't think anyone has talked to him since I saw him, and I think Murry knows the guy will deny ever seeing me.

Murry is baiting me, trying to talk me into a corner, trying to make it so it looks like I am lying.

So that I look like I'm guilty.

"There was someone else," I say, carefully keeping myself under control. I can't let myself fall into this asshole's trap.

"You just said there wasn't, Mr. McKenzie." Murry's eyes seem to twinkle.

"She wasn't at the fight, not exactly. But I talked to her before. She pointed out the path I took. She'll tell you I was there."

"I doubt it," Murry says. His lips are barely pursed, and I think he is disgusted that he didn't catch me in a lie after all. "She doesn't talk."

"So, you know who she is?"

"I do."

I don't know what to say. I find myself waving my hand around, palm up, waiting for some kind of explanation. This man is near impossible to deal with, and I hate him so much. "So, we can go ask her."

Murry doesn't say anything. Littlejohn is watching him more than me now, and I can almost see the wheels turning in Murry's head, trying to find some other way to trick me into saying something conflicting enough that he can say he's caught me lying about it.

In what seems an uncharacteristic move, Murry suddenly responds to something I said. "I can send back the officers who went looking for your 'dumpster guy' last night—the same ones who found out he most certainly was *not* the one who took the child. They know who your *witness* is."

Petty as Murry's dig at me is, both Trent and Dana wince. Littlejohn's face is too controlled, he's trying too hard not to show anything, which makes me think he's not exactly a fan of Murry's either. I don't know if they are reacting to Murry's admission that he already knew about the dumpster guy, that I got attacked for no reason at all, thinking the police weren't doing anything to follow up, or if it is that Murry's choice of words is something they dislike as much as I do.

Either way, my thoughts catch up with all of the accusations he's been throwing at me, and I realize not only is he accusing me of murdering Toddy McCurdy, but, thinking I was a murderer, he *still* risked my daughter's life by sending her in to talk to me.

Fighting to keep control of myself, the words come boiling out of me again. "You mean Fleming," I say, trembling with anger, afraid this man is going to push me over the edge, maybe has pushed me over. "His name is Fleming. Not *the child*. And she is Dana. Not *the mother.*" Shaking, I let the angry words keep flying out of my mouth, heedless of consequence. "And you are a goddamned *asshole!*"

I pivot on my crutch, too angry to keep speaking, resentful of the injuries that stop me from just tackling Murry and beating the living shit out of him. "He thinks I killed someone," I say to Trent, Dana, and Littlejohn, my voice quavering. "And *y'all let him* send Coney..."

I can't finish the sentence. I nearly break their screen door as I stumble out, tripping over my crutch, tears of rage flowing down my face.

Chapter 33

MY NEW PHONE RATTLES IN the truck's cupholder as I start the engine up to drive home. Not only did the latest model—which was conveniently the only one in stock during holiday shopping—cost me an arm and a leg, almost literally, the damned thing doesn't want to connect to my truck. In fact, the guy at the store was unable to restore any of my contacts, apps, or anything to the new phone, and I am feeling pretty bent out of shape about the whole thing.

He promised me that when I got home to my own Wi-Fi, if I had my account and password, I would be able to get it all back myself, but the way things have been going lately, I have a zero-confidence level in that, and I'm sure he was shoveling me off to whichever customer service rep is there when I come back. I'm sure both he and I hope it's not him.

The snow is coming down heavier now, something we don't normally see in Decanter. Big flakes fly at the windshield like moths coming to the porchlight at night, creating a hypnotic effect in the dusky evening that I know I need to be wary of in my exhausted state.

The new phone's preset ringtone suddenly blasts out of my truck speakers, scaring the hell out of me.

I reach across the steering wheel and push the answer button with my left hand because I can't apply enough pressure with my right hand to do it. No response. It doesn't answer the phone, and the ringtone continues blaring louder than I have ever had the volume turned up in my truck. After three tries, I give up trying to use the truck to answer the phone and I awkwardly lift the phone out of the cupholder with my splinted hand, which can't hold the phone and swipe to answer at the same time, so I miss the call.

With all of my contacts missing, the only thing the caller ID shows is the phone number, and I don't recognize it.

At the next stop sign I pull over and park the truck so I can use both hands to call back. I have no idea if I'm calling a spammer back or if it's someone I know, but if the call is about Fleming, I need to know.

"Jeff?" the voice on the other end of the call asks. I immediately recognize Paige's voice, and I can tell she's still stressed out. "Where have you been? I've been trying to reach you all day! Have you heard anything?"

"No, I haven't heard anything. Sorry. My phone died, and I had to go buy a new one. Have you heard anything?"

"No. Lock, I'm at your shop. I want you to print up posters for Fleming. How soon can you be here?"

Her directness would normally have sent up red flag warnings, and I am still concerned that she had to be sedated last night and about how strange she was on the phone this morning, but I'm grateful *someone* finally seems to be doing something, and that they have something for me to do, too.

"I'm only a couple of blocks away," I tell her. "I'll be right there."

"Hurry." She hangs up, so I put the phone back into the cup holder and pull the truck back out onto the road.

It only takes a couple of minutes to get to Main Street. The Christmas lights are starting to come on as night sets in, and some places are lit up while others are still dark. The print shop comes into sight, and I spot Paige while I'm still an intersection away. She's standing in front of the three-foot tall, blue and white plywood mountains of the Island of Lost Toys diorama set up in front of the print shop. The falling snow is melting where it hits, and she looks cold, wet, and miserable.

I pull my truck in next to her car, filling the second of the three angled parking places reserved for my shop. Normally I would have parked in back and saved the space for customers, but between my knee and her anxiety, and the fact the shop isn't open and there are no customers, this seems a better choice.

Not to mention I have no desire to deal with any customers right now. God forbid if Margret Atwater were to show up, demanding last minute special hymnal flyers so everyone could pray for Fleming instead of actually going out to look for him, I don't know what I would do.

"Oh, thank God you're here," Paige says before I can even get out of the truck. "I brought my laptop." She pulls it out of her bag, talking a hundred miles an hour. "I still can't connect to the damned internet at home. I wanted to send emails out to everyone, but I can't, so I made this flyer for Fleming, and I need to you print up as many of them as you can as fast as you can." She holds the laptop for me to see the screen, but the glare from the last vestiges of light in the gray sky washes it out. I can't see anything on the screen at all.

She fidgets impatiently, glaring at me, as I pull out my crutch and shut the truck door, and I'm sure whatever meds they had sedated her with have completely worn off a long time ago.

"Well, let's see what we can do." I limp past her, still not taking the laptop she is trying to put into my hands, and unlock the door. Holding it open, I let Paige in first. She bustles in, still glaring, obviously upset that I am not doing things fast enough. I follow, carefully wiping my wet shoes and the rubber tip of my crutch on the welcome mat, so as not to slip on the linoleum floor. When I'm pretty sure I won't be ending up on my bruised ass again, I finally take the computer from her and set it up on the customer service counter where I can look at it without balancing it in one hand while leaning on my crutch.

On the counter, I spot Detective Littlejohn's business card, where I'd left it last night. I scoop it up and shove it into my pocket. I might need it to turn myself in, after I strangle Murry, if I ever end up alone with him again.

Despite the grim satisfaction the thought brings, I push it away, knowing I would never do something like that, and focus on Paige's laptop.

I can see her homemade poster now. It has two side-by-side photos of Fleming, one from just the other day at the Reindeer Games and one from last night, in his white robe and white face paint. Bold print at the top declares a ten-thousand-dollar reward and gives the same phone number she just called me from.

"Can you get the file off my computer without the internet?"

"Don't worry. We can use a thumb drive if we can't get it connected to my Wi-Fi," I tell her. "This is your phone number, right?" I ask, pointing to the number on the poster.

"Yes." Her tone is sharp, irritated. Obviously, she just wants me to hurry up and print the posters.

"Shouldn't you have a police number or something here? Like a tip-line?" I ask.

"Those bastards didn't want to listen to a thing I had to say." She snaps the words sharply at me. "I don't trust them to answer the calls. They've got too many *better things* to do, I'm sure."

If I hadn't already met Texas Ranger Cole Murry, I might have thought Paige was just upset, or overreacting, but I have met him, and I strongly suspect if she's met him too, he's been just as crass with her as with everyone else.

"I can have five hundred printed up in fifteen minutes," I tell her.

The look on her face tells me that's still not fast enough.

Chapter 34

PAIGE GRABS THE SMALL STACK of posters out of the tray while the copier is still spitting them out. "I'll be back for the rest," she says to me, pulling her coat collar up and already walking for the front door.

I don't bother to answer. I'm pretty sure she's not interested in anything I have to say. She's done nothing but grunt and glare at me since I started trying to get the file for the poster off of her computer. The only time she stopped actively glaring at me was when, after I got her laptop to connect to my Wi-Fi, she realized she could finally send out the emails she'd originally wanted to.

That had taken her about two minutes, and then she'd gone right back to being impatient with me.

Instead of the bell indicating her going out the front door, I hear her rustling around near the entrance. I look up to see her holding a two-pack of clear packing tape she's taken from the sales rack near the door. "I need scissors," she says when she sees me looking at her.

"Top drawer, this side of the sales counter." I point to the drawer under the cash machine, trying not to feel…violated, I guess. Her just demanding the posters and taking the tape without asking bothers me more than it should. I would have offered or given them freely, but to have her demand and take… And with the attitude she's got. I feel like she's angry with me.

And then it hits me. And it all makes sense. Someone must have told her that the police think I'm the one who took Fleming, and she probably, at least to some extent, believes it is possible.

I watch her pull the scissors out of the drawer and determinedly head out the door with the posters. Snow swirls in from the night as she goes through, leaving me alone with my thoughts.

The color copier behind me keeps whirring and pushing out pages, the sound barely filling the print shop. With Paige gone, despite the thinly veiled hostility, I've lost my feeling of usefulness. The posters will all be printed up in another couple of minutes, and then what do I do? Grab some tape and another pair of scissors and follow Paige's example? Go put posters up everywhere? Will that really do any good?

For the thousandth time, my brain reminds me time is running out. It's been over twenty hours since Fleming vanished from the float, and no one knows anything, and I have no idea what to do about it.

I go over everything, trying to remember what was going on around me when Luca was falling. The only clear memories are during the time everything seemed like the world had gone into slow motion around me, when I was sure Luca would fall and hit his head, but those memories are like having tunnel vision. I can only remember exactly the things I was looking at: Luca, the sidewalk curb, the kids on the curb trying to get out of the way.

Me, rushing in like some kind of idiot, hand out to catch Luca's head and stop it from smashing into the curb.

No. Not some kind of idiot. I push that thought away. I did what I thought I had to do, what I *knew* I had to do, and I'm still positive Luca would have hit his head on that curb. And then, instead of a missing Fleming, I'd be upset over a dead, or brain-damaged Luca, whom I maybe could have saved, and I couldn't live with that.

And maybe Fleming would have disappeared anyway. Maybe, like everyone else, I would have been watching Luca fall and I still wouldn't have any idea what happened to Fleming.

The copy machine goes silent.

I stare at it for what feels like a long time, then I pick up the stack of posters and carry them to the counter, trying to decide what to do. I can't stand the idea of just staying here, waiting for Paige to come back, but I don't know what else to do. Going to Dana and Trent's, to try and be supportive, seems like it's not really an option. I have no idea where Coney went, but I suspect it isn't back to my house or anywhere else Dana or I could easily find her.

If I had my druthers, I'd be with her. I really feel the need to hold my baby close right now.

She probably really is looking for Fleming, like she said she would. But where? Aimlessly driving around, like I had been? Even now I don't have a better idea. Search the park? The mall?

The first one implies that I think he's dead and I'm looking for a body. I don't want to let myself think that. The other is stupid. Why—how—would a five-year-old get to the mall. Or anywhere? He couldn't take himself anywhere. He wouldn't have gone somewhere. Someone *has* to have taken him.

Where would they take him? Not someplace like a mall. Not anywhere public, likely. They wouldn't want to be seen. They'd hide. Which means they won't be someplace I can just go *look* for Fleming. They will be someplace I would have to know where Fleming was in order to find him.

Which, added together with a probably incorrect factoid that floats through my mind about most crimes being committed by family members, makes me realize that this is probably why the police seem to be watching me instead of doing something that looks, at least to me, like it is useful.

Despite the lack of options I've come up with for where to look, I can't bring myself to just stay here. The unyielding sick feeling in my gut pushes me to move, to do something, *anything*—even if it is more aimless driving.

Maybe I'll at least spot Coney driving around and make sure she's all right.

I turn off the copier, grab the finished posters, and put them in a small plastic tub with a lid. Then, hobbling my way to out the front door and into the Christmas decorations-lit night, I use a quick, crutch-supported lean forward to set the tub down and pick up the colorfully painted rock I sometimes use for a doorstop. I drop the rock on top of the tub to make sure the wind won't blow it anywhere and straighten myself back up. There's no way Paige won't find them here, right in front of the door, and five hundred copies should be enough to keep her busy putting them up for hours.

I lock the print shop door and go back to my truck, tossing the crutch in ahead of me before I climb in. I don't know where I'm going, but I have to go.

Before I can back out of the parking space, the speakers nearly burst with the preset ringtone again, damn near giving me a heart attack. I grab at the phone and answer it, thankfully, before it can ring again.

"Jeff? Are you okay?"

I recognize Summer's voice. "Yeah. I'm banged up a bit, but the doctor says I'll live."

"I'm glad to hear that. I was a little worried about you last night."

I decide not to mention that getting my ass kicked by a homeless guy this morning was a lot worse. "I'm doing okay," I tell her. "Thank you. I take it you didn't have any luck asking around last night?" I ask, meaning when she'd gone to the warehouse after the parade.

"Not really. No one seems to have seen anything. Say, are you busy?"

"No?" *If anything, I am kind of the opposite of busy right now. I've run out of ideas on where to look for Fleming, and I don't know of anything else I can do to help. I don't seem wanted at Trent and Dana's. And I don't know where Coney is. And the police think I did it. And, to top it all off, they think I killed the kid in the park, too.* Though all of the other thoughts tear through my mind like a tornado, and I want to scream them at the world, I keep them to myself.

"Can you meet me at the middle school library?" Summer asks.

"Yeah." The question surprises me. "Is everything okay?"

"Oh, yeah. Everything is fine. I just had some work stuff I had to get done here."

When she doesn't elaborate, I just say, "Okay." I don't really know how to respond to that. Summer's words remind me of how strangely Coney had talked to me when she was wired up for Ranger Murry. And how Paige has been treating me. And everyone else, too.

Maybe even Summer thinks I took Fleming? The thought makes my heart hurt more than I would have expected.

Before I can think of anything else to say, Summer says, "Okay. See you soon," and hangs up.

I put the phone back into the cup-holder and stare out my windshield, watching the snow slowly falling into the diorama. Is this some new kind of trap set up by Ranger Murry? Is Summer going to be wired up now, trying to catch me in some kind of lie so Murry will have an excuse to arrest me or something?

It doesn't matter. I've got nothing to hide and there's nothing else I can think of to do or that I have to offer that will be of any use or help in finding Fleming. I might as well go. Maybe I can finally convince them it wasn't me and they will stop wasting time.

I put the truck into reverse, feeling better in some ways that I have some sort of actual destination to head to, worse in that *everyone* seems to think I took Fleming, which isn't helping find him at all.

Before I start backing out, I have the first intelligent thought I can remember in a while: I turn off the goddamned Bluetooth on my new phone so it can't blow my speakers out anymore.

Chapter 35

SUMMER MEETS ME AT THE front entrance of Decanter Middle School and opens the door for me. I struggle getting through with my crutch, and she steps outside, holding the door for me while I come in.

In the entryway, I shake off the snow, which is coming down in big flakes and sticking to the ground. Looking back to Summer as she closes the heavy door, I can see my tracks in the snow, a trail of two footprints and one dragging crutch mark off to the side, leading off in to the dark, all the way back to my truck in the mostly empty parking lot.

Summer, as I should have expected, looks the perfect part of the school librarian. With black-rimmed glasses, which I'd never seen her wear before, and her hair up, also in a way I'd never seen before, she could be the poster child for supporting libraries. Her Christmas sweater is anything but an ugly one. It looks like it was handmade by someone in a traditional Nordic style and custom fitted for her. And it perfectly matches her probably faux, but perfectly fashionable, gray fox fur winter boots.

"I think you're supposed to use that on the other side," Summer says, pointing to my crutch. There's a hint of concern in her eyes but a bit more teasing in her voice, and it lightens my mood.

Maybe she doesn't think I had anything to do with Fleming's disappearance after all.

"Unless you can't." I smile and hold up my splinted right hand.

"I didn't realize you'd hurt your knee, too. And that's new." She points

147

to my eye, the concern on her face growing, turning into a frown. "Last night was a bit rougher on you than I thought."

"In all honesty, it isn't all from last night." Summer isn't the kind of person who deserves lies or half-truths, and I find myself explaining about the guy I saw at the dumpster and then confronting him this morning. All of it had happened since the last time I saw or talked to her.

She nods and listens as I tell her about it, and, somehow, I don't feel judged at all. Instead, she seems thoughtful. Even when I admit the guy was a scrawny little dude and that he kicked my ass but good.

I finish telling her about it as we walk through the empty halls. Still looking pensive, in a way I would guess only librarians can, she doesn't say anything, so I switch topics before she has a chance to make up her mind about whether or not I'm an asshole for what happened.

"I thought the school was closed for Christmas break."

"Some of the admin staff have to work through Wednesday," Summer says. "One more day."

"And you?"

"Well, a librarian's job is never done. There is always something that needs my attention. Nowadays, though there aren't so many books left to reshelve, there are still computers that need to be fixed and updated, and sometimes I just need time to do a thorough cleaning of all the little nooks and crannies that the janitors don't get to, but things like gummy worms, and lost earbuds—and grosser things—do."

We reach the library entrance at pretty much the center of the school, and she gallantly opens the door again and waits for me to enter ahead of her. When I'm in, she motions me to the back of the library where desks have been set up like a cube farm office, with computers in each cubicle.

"Are we going somewhere specific?" I ask.

"To the one on the far end. There's something I want to show you."

I make my way to the desk she pointed to and carefully sit down in the too-small plastic chair. Summer moves past me and takes a seat in the chair for the next space, looking as though it was perfectly natural to sit in a tiny chair.

"Jeff," her voice is low, and I think she's being quiet because it's the library, but then, as her eyes intensely catch and hold mine, her words change that. "The police think you have something to do with Fleming going missing."

I feel my face and my ears flush. I'd already assumed she'd been told that, that she maybe even believed it, as Paige seems to, but hearing her say it out loud cuts me to the quick. "Yeah, I know."

"You do?" Her eyes widen.

"Yeah. They put a wire on Coney and tried to get her to ask me questions." I feel hot tears start to burn my eyes, reliving it all in my mind. I start to choke on the words, but more come out anyway. "My little girl. They put a wire on my little girl." Before I know what's happening, the tears are falling, burning down my cheeks like the anger burning in my soul.

And then Summer's arms are around me, holding me tight, and I put my face into her shoulder and just try to breathe around the sobs that I can't stop from coming out.

When I catch my breath, I pull back away from her. "I'm sorry," I say, wiping away tears with the back of my wrist.

Summer magically produces a tissue that somehow doesn't even look rumpled up, and she offers it to me. I take it and self-consciously wipe my nose.

"There's nothing to be sorry about," Summer says, her gaze holding mine. I don't see any of the judgement I had expected. Which I shouldn't have, I guess, because, well…because she's Summer.

"This has all been just awful," she says, gently taking hold of my hand, "and that had to have been like the straw that broke the camel's back. There is just no reason for that. Is Coney all right? That has to have been terrible for her, too."

I shrug. "I'm not sure. She was pretty upset, and then the fu—" I can't bring myself to cuss like that in front of her and catch myself. "The guy that put her up to it, Ranger Murry, is a special kind of an ass, and Coney got pissed off and left. I haven't heard from her since."

"Have you tried calling her?" She cocks her head at me, leaning forward, coming closer, making sure I keep looking her in the eyes.

I feel myself flush again. "No. I was trying to give her space. I mean—"

"You need to call her." Summer reaches up and takes me by my chin, gently forcing me to look her in the eyes again. "That little girl needs her daddy, and she needs him right now. Call her."

I nod and she lets go so I can pull out my phone. I open up the lock screen before looking back up to Summer's intense scrutiny. "Um... You wouldn't happen to have Coney's number, would you?"

Chapter 36

"SHE'S ON HER WAY HERE," I say, putting away my cellphone.

Summer had been right. I had needed to call Coney. And not just for her. I felt a lot better knowing she was okay, and Coney *had* needed me.

Coney had picked up my call on the first ring, and she was crying. At a loss for where to go, because she felt like Ranger Murry had invaded all of her personal spaces, would find her again at either home, she'd parked her car near a place where we'd picked wild blackberries from time to time when she was younger. And then she'd just sat there, not knowing what to do, watching the snow slowly pile up around her.

"Thank you," I tell Summer. "That was the right thing to do."

"Of course it was. Little girls always need their daddies, whether they realize it or not. And when things get really bad, when they think they definitely *don't* need their daddies, that's usually when they need them the most." She puts her hand on my shoulder and gently squeezes reassuringly.

"So," I start, not really sure I want to broach the subject, but really wanting to know the answer, "how did you find out the police thought I had something to do with Fleming missing?"

"Well. It was a couple of things, and that's also why I asked you to come here. First, last night, when Paige lost her damned mind and about killed everyone by almost running her car into the crowd—"

I raise my eyebrows at Summer. I hadn't ever heard her curse before. I almost didn't think it was possible that she *could* curse.

"—she kept spouting off a bunch of junk about you trying to break up Dana and Trent's marriage."

Summer stops talking and looks me unflinchingly in the eye. "Which actually sounded plausible, you know, given the way you always look at them. Or, more specifically, the way you always look at Dana."

Unlike Summer, I do flinch. "Yeah. Oliver mentioned something about that to me just the other day."

"Yeah, I know. He told me. Oliver is not a secret keeper. He also mentioned it to the police when they questioned him about what Paige was saying. Paige may be wrong, but Oliver's not. You need to let it go. You need to let *Dana* go."

"I know." My tone is way more defensive than I intend, and I take a breath and drop my voice. "I just had a talk with Coney about that…"

I realize that whole talk happened while Ranger Dickhead was listening in and asking the questions through Coney. How much of Coney's concerns and worries were really hers, and how many of them had just been planted by Murry?

Goddamn I hate that man.

I can feel the heat returning to my face and my blood pressure rising. Summer doesn't seem to notice, or, more likely, she tactfully ignores it. Likely she thinks I am more embarrassed than angry. Which, normally, I would have been.

"Anyway," Summer continues, "the police, and everyone else within earshot, listened to what Paige was screaming, and then, of course, the police really had no choice but to consider you a suspect, right? They were pretty much forced into investigating you."

"Everyone within earshot?" I wince, wondering just how many people that would have been.

"And then," Summer gently ignores my interruption, easily handling me like one of her students, "this morning, the police themselves basically told me you were their primary focus, though not in so many words."

She turns to the computer in front of her and starts typing, logging herself in. "After I drove Paige's car and float back to the warehouse last night, I started asking around to see if anyone had seen or knew anything, but no one had. I mean, *no one* saw anything. Everyone on that side of the float was so distracted by you and…" she scrunches her eyes as she tries to remember, "…Luca, that even if they did see something, they don't remember it."

She pauses and points at the computer. "So, I came here, accessed the school district records, and got the email addresses of the parents for the entire Decanter Elementary School's student body, and I sent out a request for any and all photos and videos taken of the float and the parade around that time."

"Is that legal?"

"Asking for the videos? Sure."

"I mean—"

Summer waves me off. "I know what you mean, Jeff. And I don't know, and I don't care. It's a gray area, I'm sure. It is all school related, right? And Fleming is a student. And it happened during a school sanctioned event." She taps on the keyboard some more and opens up a file folder.

"Anyway, a lot of people have sent me a lot of stuff, and I've been going over it all night—"

"You've been here all night?" I ask.

"Like I could sleep? Did you sleep last night?"

I think of the couch at the print shop, and I'm not sure if that counts. She doesn't let me answer anyway.

"As I was saying, one of the videos I've seen captured pretty much the whole thing with you and Luca, which proves that you really couldn't have been responsible. And when I called the police this morning to try to share it, they sent a ranger out here to see me, but they basically blew me off."

"They didn't want information about what happened?"

"Oh, they said they did. And I gave them a link to all of the files, but really, they only wanted to ask questions about you." Her voice grows colder, and her lips purse tightly as she speaks. "They asked me about our relationship, how long we'd known each other, who all of your friends are, why you were in the park where the body was found, why you were at the parade, where you were when Fleming disappeared, if I had seen you since the parade, if I knew your favorite places to hang out…" She shakes her head, her lips tight in disapproval. "But they never once asked anything at all about Fleming, or anyone, or anything, else. And as far as I could tell, they ignored pretty much anything I had to say that wasn't about you."

"That feels terribly familiar. That wouldn't happen to have been Texas Ranger Cole Murry, would it?"

She glances from the computer screen to me. "Yeah, that was his name. Is he the one who…?"

I nod, feeling sick.

Summer sighs and shakes her head.

"Anyway. Like I said, I sent a link with him, so they could access all of the photos and videos everyone gave me…and they have *never* bothered to access it."

Raising her wrist, she looks at her smartwatch. "It's been almost twelve hours now, and they haven't opened a single video or photo file that might help them find Fleming, that might give them a clue or maybe even show them what actually happened to Fleming."

Summer stands up and paces along the bookshelf lining the back wall. "The whole situation disgusts me. I was there, and I know what you did, and why. And he ignored me. He ignored me when I told him I was there, and he ignored me when I told him I knew you didn't have anything to do with it. And he ignored me when I told him I could show him a video that basically proves you didn't have anything to do with it. And now he's ignored the ton of evidence I gave him, already gift-wrapped and just waiting to be sorted through!"

Her eyes are flaming with anger and determination now, and I realize the Summer Christmas I thought I knew is barely the surface of who this woman is.

"I want to find Fleming, too," she says. "And I feel like the police are chasing their own tails trying to prove themselves right about you for some stupid reason, rather than try to find out what really happened."

She stops pacing and looks at me. Her gaze is hard, but not cold. Her eyes flick back and forth, looking from each of my eyes to the other, searching for something in mine, trying to determine if she knows me well enough to know for sure I didn't take Fleming, that I had nothing to do with it.

"So, I finally decided to call you," she says. "Even though he told me

I should stay out of it and let him know if I heard anything from you." Her anger and frustration builds, and she gestures at me with a quick, agitated hand. "It doesn't look to me like you've been too hard to find. All I did was pick up the phone and call!"

"Yeah, well... It is a new phone. The old one went into the lake with me." I smile lamely.

Her face hardens at the wisecrack.

I finally recognize what I am seeing in her face, what she is looking for from me.

It's not exactly what she'd said about Coney, about a little girl needing her daddy, but it's close. It's along the same vein. It's a basic fundamental need we all have; Summer needs someone to help her be strong. Someone she *knows* she can rely on, no matter what.

And I'm good with that. I'm feeling pretty much the same need right now. And of all the people I know, I think I would probably trust her the most.

"Summer, I give you my word," I say, "I swear on everything that is holy, I had nothing to do with it."

She pushes her glasses up on her nose and shakes her head at me. "I know that, dummy."

Chapter 37

I WAIT IN THE BACK of the library, clicking through the photos of the parade that people sent to Summer, while she goes to meet Coney at the school entrance. Apparently when Summer asked for everything, she got everything. A ton of them are completely unusable, and I assume it is from people looking at things while snapping photos rather than looking at the screen of their camera to see what they are photographing, and even more are of other parts of the parade, which is good, I guess. I keep hoping for angles that will catch something in the background.

Videos are both easier and harder to decide if they caught anything worthwhile. I figured out that the kids were singing "Here Comes Santa Claus" before Fleming disappeared, "Frosty the Snowman" after, and "Jingle Bells" during the time he vanished, which made it easy to tell if a video was anywhere near the right time frame, but, because so many videos have moving elements to them, I feel I need to watch them two or three times to make sure I'm not missing anything important in the backgrounds.

I've also determined, thanks to timestamps on so many photos, that Fleming disappeared from the float sometime between 8:24 and 8:28. That helps me speed through other timestamped files that are nowhere near that time frame.

Nonetheless, I grow more frustrated as I go through the photos. Either it's the wrong side of the float, or Fleming is there, or he's not. There aren't any photos of *when* it happened. If it's a video of the right time, it's of the wrong side float again, or, infuriatingly, it's of me in a tangled pile of arms and too-long legs with Luca.

In nearly every one of those I can hear someone in the crowd yell out, "Jesus! Why'd you tackle that kid?" and it makes my blood boil every time.

I wish even just one would have caught who the guy was, so I could personally thank him for his consideration and observational skills. I would have settled for at least hearing Mark call him a fucking dumbass again, but that never seems to show up either.

I hear voices growing louder, coming from the hallway, and look up to see Coney and Summer walk into the library. When Coney sees me, her face scrunches up and the waterworks start.

"Are you okay, honey?" I ask, grabbing my crutch and using it to stand up.

"No," she blurts out, rushing forward and embracing me. "I'm so sorry, Daddy. I'm so sorry."

"Hey," I grunt in pain as she squeezes my ribs, but I don't complain. I wrap my splinted arm around her back and fight not to overbalance on the crutch. "It's okay. It's all right."

"No, it's not. I let him make me think you did it! I--I..." Her words, if there are any, are lost in sobs, smothered in my shirt as she holds me tight.

"You were just doing what you needed to do," I tell her. "If there was any chance at all that I was involved, you needed to know, baby. It's okay."

"But I knew you wouldn't ever! But he kept saying you did!"

"Shh." I wipe the tears off her face with the fingers of my splinted hand, which ends up being such a terrible job I pretty much poke her in the eye instead. She pulls back, kind of laughing, still kind of crying, and wipes her own tears.

"It's okay," I say again. "The important thing now is we need to find Fleming."

Coney nods and comes back in for another hug. I hold her tight and look up to see Summer watching us, a morose smile on her face. I mouth the words, "Thank you," to her and squeeze my daughter tight.

Summer nods and then comes over to look at the computer. I let Coney go and tell them what I've learned so far.

"That's pretty much all I had determined as well," Summer says. "I was hoping that by not biasing you with my thoughts that you would find something different."

"How many more files do you have to go through?" Coney asks, heading back to Summer's desk at the center of the library. She grabs a couple of tissues and blows her nose.

"I'm through maybe a fourth," I say.

"I've been through all of them," Summer says, "but I probably went through too quickly. I want to go through again, slower this time, and see if there's anything I missed. It would be great if you'd be willing to look too, Coney. Another set of eyes is always a good thing."

"Yeah," Coney says. "I want to do that."

Summer logs into the computer next to me and Coney comes back to sit by me, then Summer takes the cubicle on the other side of Coney, and in moments we are all silent, save for the occasionally tinny audio of videos.

Jesus! Why'd you tackle that kid? floats up from Coney's computer, and I cringe. Then, at long last, there it is:

Fucking dumbass.

Chapter 38

"FLEMING!" PAIGE'S VOICE IS SHRILL as she runs up the parade route, trying to catch up with the black and white bridge float. "Fleming!" She twists an ankle as her high heel goes into an imperfection in the asphalt, but it doesn't slow her down. Her cries for Fleming become shrieks the cheap computer speaker can hardly handle as she finally gets close enough to see that he's no longer on the float.

I see movement out of the corner of my eye and look up to see Coney looking over my shoulder, into my cubicle, to see the video I'm watching.

"She really lost her shit," Coney says.

I don't bother to correct her language. Besides, she's right.

The video shows Paige turning around and running back. To my surprise, she throws herself into Trent's arms, momentarily burying herself in him. I can't make out his words over the noise of the crowd around whoever is recording the video, but she doesn't seem to like what he says. She pushes off of him, and races past, away from the float. When she gets close enough to her car that it comes into frame, I can see it is parked askew and nearly up on the curb where spectators stand watching.

She tries to get in, but Trent catches her and pulls her back, ignoring the fists she pummels against his arms. After a moment a police officer comes in to help Trent, and then I hear my name shrieked from Paige's crazed mouth. Most of her words are lost, the sounds she's making are both incoherent and out of range of the recording.

"And that," Summer says, looking over Coney's shoulder, "is why the police think you did it."

Another officer shows up and takes Trent's place holding Paige back from trying to get back to her car. The video ends as Summer, wearing her Mrs. Claus outfit—with my blood on the white fur around the cuffs—is directed by one of the officers to move Paige's car.

"Her ranting was all about you being jealous of Trent and wanting to break up the marriage," Summer says. "I'm surprised you can't hear it on the video, because I'm sure everyone else there heard it."

"That's what that ranger told Mom and me, too," Coney adds. "And Trent had already heard it." She pauses before continuing. "It's been pretty obvious that you don't like Trent and that you still love Mom, so it wasn't hard to believe him."

Still staring at the last frame of the video, an image of Summer, mouth agape, eyes fearful, with my blood on her, standing in front of Paige's car, with Paige arm-locked by two police officers, and Trent—Trent's face looks like a man in hell having his guts ripped out—I realize, this is all on me.

While I had nothing to do with Fleming's disappearing, all of the people in that frozen frame are in that situation because of me. Because I couldn't let Dana go. Because I still called her my wife instead of my ex-wife. Because I stared at her across the room anytime I saw her. Because my actions, as small and petty as they may have been, or as I thought them to be, impacted all these people enough to make Paige think I would do something as drastic as kidnapping Fleming to break up Trent and Dana's marriage, to make her cause this scene—and they believed her.

"I'm sorry," I whisper. "This is my fault."

"What? No!" Coney leans in from her chair and throws her arms around my neck. "This is bullshit. This is people jumping to stupid conclusions, just like when I told you they called me names for dating people. *They* made stupid assumptions, and that's not *my* fault. This is not *your* fault."

I don't remember saying anything nearly that intelligent, but Coney is right, and if she wants to credit me for that life lesson, I'll take it. Not to mention I get to, at least partially, revise what I think she means when she uses the word 'dated.'

"And the police are stupid for wasting time on you when they should be trying to figure out what really happened," Coney says.

I kiss her on the forehead. "They're not stupid. Just misdirected. Like you were, honey."

Funny how you can see and say things more clearly when you're trying to explain things to your kid. I think the police are being stupid as hell, but somehow, some part of me knows they're not, that they're doing the best they can, they're doing right thing, but that knowledge, that admission, only really comes to the surface when I try to make sure Coney can see the truth.

"Paige yelling stupid stuff still shouldn't have been enough to make them stop looking at *anything* else," she says, obviously as disgusted about it all as I had been.

No longer thinking of just myself, but thinking more objectively so that I can pass that kind of thinking on to my daughter, things begin to fall into place, and I begin to understand why Ranger Murry focused in on me like he did.

"You know," I tell her, "It may not necessarily have been what Paige said that made me a *good* suspect, but rather it was probably one of the things that maybe made me look like the best lead. I mean, not only are there the accusations made by Paige, which I have to admit are not completely unfounded, there is the fact that I was one of the first people on the scene of that murder at the park—a murder of someone that had been at the warehouse, when I was there, just two nights earlier."

Summer looks up from her cubicle, and I look back and forth between her and Coney while I continue to reason. "On top of that, I *was* on the scene of Fleming's disappearance. And I did send the police running off on a wild goose chase looking for a homeless guy who had nothing to do with anything. And then, this morning I was at the warehouse when the police discovered it had been broken into. It's all circumstantial stuff. Most of which has nothing to do with Fleming, but…" I shrug. "I have to admit, that's a lot of times for me to suddenly come up on their radar. As much as I hate the fu— uh, Ranger Murry, I have to admit I can see why he thinks I'm involved somehow."

"The warehouse was broken into?" Summer asks.

"Yeah. But as far as I can tell, nothing was taken."

"So that's another reason for them to suspect you," Summer says. "Tampering with the crime scene."

When Coney frowns at her, Summer says, "The float."

"The float is the crime scene," I say, repeating Summer's words back to her while a thought tries to germinate in my brain.

"Yeah," she answers. "That's where Fleming disappeared from, right? So, it's the crime scene."

Staring at the image from the video still frozen on screen in front of me, Paige held by the police, Trent next to her, Summer standing in front of Paige's car…something finally clicks into place for me. "The float is the crime scene."

Chapter 39

"THE FLOAT IS THE CRIME scene."

"You said that." Coney frowns at me.

"Summer, you said you drove Paige's car back to the warehouse?" I ask.

"Well, I finished the parade route with it first. I couldn't really turn it around in the middle of the parade. But yes."

"Here," I point to the video on my computer screen. "I can't see the float. And the video starts after Paige got out of the car. You said she drove crazy, and I can see by where the car is stopped, she did something crazy."

"She got out while it was still running," Summer says. "Trent had to jump in and stop it before it hit people."

"So, she didn't drive crazy-crazy. Like not wild enough to have damaged her little house?"

"No... I didn't see it all, but I think she just slammed on the brake and then jumped out without putting it in park."

"So, you didn't notice any damage to her float?"

"No. Should I have?"

"Maybe not," I say. "It was pretty minor. Still..." I look from Coney to Summer. "Can you guys see if there are any pictures or videos of Paige's little house float *after* Summer started driving?"

"What are you thinking?" Coney asks.

"I'm thinking that if we can see that there is no damage to the For Sale sign at the parade, then it had to have happened afterward. Which would

163

have been at the warehouse. And that could mean Paige's float—not *our* float—was the target of whoever broke into Petterson's warehouse."

"Paige's float?" Summer says. "You think Paige had something to do with it?"

"No," I say, already flipping through more photos. "I don't. I don't know what her deal with Fleming is, but I don't think that was an act. I think she really freaked out when she found out he was missing."

"Her deal is she thinks of Fleming as her own kid," Coney says. Her tone is cold and disapproving.

I raise an eyebrow at her.

"You probably weren't ever in the right place to see, but she is as obvious with her feelings for Fleming and Trent as you are with your feelings for Mom."

Summer, looking at me from behind Coney, nods in agreement with the last part of Coney's statement. I keep my mouth shut tight.

"Paige took care of Fleming after Nancy died," Coney says. "Nancy was Paige's best friend and, from what I can tell, she all but took over taking care of Fleming when Trent went into mourning. Paige didn't like it when Trent and Mom started dating, probably because she's got the hots for Trent, but she *really* didn't like it when they got married, because then Fleming was with *us* instead of *her* all the time."

"I know you didn't just pick all of that up from people's faces," I say. I remember the looks that I'd seen pass between Dana and Paige and realize that I could be wrong.

"Not all of it. A lot of it I got right off Paige's social media. I mean, it's not like she ever really tried to hide it. Before Mom and Trent got married, there were all kinds of posts about how much Paige *just knows* Trent and Fleming need her. I mean, it was really kind of sad. At first it looks like she's talking about helping after Nancy's death, but later you can tell she's kind of gone all Single White Female over it."

I furrow my eyebrows.

"Tries to take over Nancy's life, like the old movie," Summer says to me. "Are you sure about that, Coney?"

"Oh, yeah."

"Then maybe Paige did have something to do with it…" Summer doesn't sound sure.

Coney shakes her head. "No way. She would never do anything to hurt Fleming, and I've seen her try to put on a show for people—that video was not an act."

"I agree with Coney," I say. "Paige isn't that good at hiding her feelings. I don't think she could fake that meltdown. Plus, look how bad it made her look in front of all of her potential clients. Paige is nothing if not putting up a good front for them."

"That's sad, but true," Summer says. "So where does her float fit in?"

"I don't know," I say. "Maybe it doesn't. Maybe it wasn't her float. Maybe it was her car. But the damage to the float was the only thing I saw out of place at the warehouse."

"I didn't see anything weird about the car," Summer says, "but maybe."

"Something else sad but true," Coney says, "is that I'm pretty sure no one took any pictures of Paige's real estate advertisement, even if it was a cute little house decorated up for Christmas. I say we keep an eye out for that but stay focused on figuring out what happened to Fleming."

"Smart," Summer says.

"Just like her mother," I add.

They both give me sideways glances.

Chapter 40

CONEY'S PHONE RINGS WITH THE ominous sound of the opening notes of Beethoven's 5th Symphony breaking the silence in the library. So far none of us have found anything useful. Coney picks up her phone and turns it over, putting it face down on the desk.

"Isn't that your mother's ringtone?" I ask.

Coney looks at me but doesn't say anything.

"What if it's about Fleming?"

"Then she'll text," Coney says. "I really don't want to talk to her right now." Or ever, the look on her face says.

"I understand that, honey, but she's your mother. She's gotta be worried about where you are after you stormed out of the house, and she really doesn't need that on top of being worried sick over Fleming."

"When she texts, I'll text her back." Coney doesn't look at me, but Summer does, and I'm pretty sure I see approval in her eyes, though I'm not sure if she's approving of my parenting or Coney's decision. Maybe both, though I'm not sure how much of the fallout between Coney and Dana this morning she's privy to.

I let my gaze linger on Summer as she turns back to her computer. Her approval carried more weight for me than I would have expected, and I'm really glad she doesn't think I did this.

I wish to God I knew who did though.

As I click on photos and dismiss them, I think the only advantage I have over what the police know is that I know *I* didn't take Fleming. Which is why I'm sitting here looking for evidence in these photos and the police are... doing God knows what.

I can feel the pressure of time weighing heavy on me. How many of the first forty-eight hours have gone by since Fleming vanished? *Stupid!* I chide myself. *Not real numbers.* But the odds that Fleming is all right are getting worse by the second, and that I know to be real.

So, if I were the police, and I knew for a fact that *I* didn't do this, then who is the next best suspect?

My mind goes blank on the question. I remember the idea that crimes are most often committed by family members. Obviously, it wouldn't be Dana or Trent. Or Coney, who only crosses my mind at all because I am listing family members. Trent's parents live on the east coast, and Dana's, who do live only an hour away, wouldn't possibly do something like this.

And that leaves me. Which is another reason why the police think I did it.

So really, the whole idea that it was likely a family member who took Fleming would mostly point to me, but, in the end, as I didn't do it, it is misleading. And if that theory is wrong, it has to be someone else, someone not family.

Which makes anything a possibility, from a targeted to a random thing. If it was random, it could be anyone, anywhere, for any reason, so I back-burner that thought. It's not helpful.

If Fleming was targeted, then figuring out a *why* would give clues to the *who*, right?

My mind goes blank again.

"You guys willing to try to talk things through while we do this?" I ask aloud.

"Of course," Summer says.

"About what?" Coney asks at the same time.

"I'm just thinking out loud here," I say. "Trying to work things through, so I'm hoping you'll spitball with me."

"Uck," Coney says.

I ignore her and continue. "If you take the idea that most crimes are committed by family, that means Fleming was likely taken by either me, Dana, Trent, Coney," Coney side-eyes me at the mention of her name, "Trent's parents, or Dana's parents. Right?"

"Or Paige," Summer says. Coney side-eyes her this time. "You said she thinks of herself as family, right?" she tells Coney. "I'm pretty sure that counts when it comes to crimes of passion."

"*If* that's what this is," I say.

"Conceded," Summer says. "But we're spit balling here."

"Could you guys please stop saying that? Uck!"

"So, let's take them one at a time. Skipping me because that is a waste of time."

"Is it?" Summer asks.

Coney and I, mouths gaping, both look to her.

"Well, you were going to list Coney in this thought experiment, right? So why not list yourself? Why would you take Fleming? If that was something you were inclined to do."

"Um…" I answer intelligently.

"To break up Mom and Trent's marriage," Coney helpfully adds. "At least, that's what Paige said."

"Right," I say. "And if I did that, where would I take Fleming? Where could I hide him until I got what I wanted?'

Coney leans back, swallowing hard, and she pales.

I put a hand on her shoulder. "Hey. It's okay, I'm just spi— Uh, doing a thought exercise."

"But what if whoever did this isn't hiding Fleming until they get what they want? What if they hide him forever? Like…"

Like hiding his body, I know she thinks but doesn't say.

"Let's try not to jump around too much," Summer says. "Let's see if we can find any logical conclusions. Where would you hide him, Jeff?"

"I don't know."

"Think. Try. Be creative," Summer says.

"Well, the only places I own are my house and the print shop. Those would be too obvious. Everyone knows I own them. Someone would find him there."

"Has anyone looked there?" Summer asks.

"No. Yes. Kind of. Coney was at my house. Did you look around?" I ask.

Coney shakes her head. "I mean…I did, but not really. The ranger asked me if there was a cellar or something like that, but I know there isn't."

"He looked around after you left. Poked in the closets a little, but I didn't feel like he was really looking," I say.

"What about the print shop?" Summer prods.

"No. No one has been there except me and Paige."

"And did she look around?"

"No," I thought about it for a moment. "She poked around a little, but she was getting stuff to put up the posters she wanted me to print. The only other thing she did was send out emails after we finally got her laptop working."

"Her laptop?" Coney asks.

"Yeah. Why?"

"Because Ranger Rick wanted to know if you would think it was suspicious if I had my laptop set up in the house. He wanted to use the camera for video, to see what you were doing."

"Paige's laptop is still sitting on the counter at the print shop," I tell them.

"I would say they looked around your print shop then," Summer says.

Chapter 41

"YOU SHOULD REALLY PROBABLY AT least look at that," Summer says after Coney's phone dings with a text for the fourth time.

We are all exhausted from looking a pictures and videos, and I feel like I've never slept in my life. I stretch and immediately regret it when my ribs scream in pain. Trying to hold myself together, I get up and collect the empty clamshells from the Mexican food Coney had delivered.

Coney, giving in to Summer's suggestion, even though she'd ignored me when I'd said it, picks up her phone and taps the screen.

Hobbling on the crutch, with the trash tucked under my splinted arm, I make my way to the trashcan, noticing the clock says 8:35. My heart sinks. Fleming has been missing for over twenty-four hours now and I feel like we just lost him all over again, like it's too late.

"Dad, you need to get out of here," Coney's voice is sharp in the empty library. "Mom says if I know where you are, I have to tell them right now, because the police want to arrest you." Her eyes are wild with fear.

My gut twists, but having Coney around has a calming, rationalizing effect on my thoughts. Having her around makes me feel I have to show her what's right and wrong, and then set an example by doing the right thing. "I can't run, honey. What good will that do? Make me look guilty? Make the police spend more time looking in the wrong place for Fleming?" *If it isn't already too late…*

I look to Summer, whose eyes are not wild like Coney's, but they are full of concern. "I know between the three of us we've pretty much been through all of the photos," I say, "but…"

Summer nods, and if reading my thoughts, finishes for me. "We should have called them a long time ago."

Coney frowns, looking back and forth between us.

"Call your mom, honey," I tell her. "Tell her and Trent about the pictures. Ask them to come help look. At the very least, it will give them something to do. At best, maybe they'll see something we haven't, and we'll find Fleming."

"Dad, you can't—"

"Can't what? There's nothing I *can* do, honey. We don't know anything. I don't know where to look." I hobble back over and kiss her on the forehead. "Tell your mom I was here, but I left five minutes ago to go to the police station, to see if there was any new information. That way maybe they can't accuse either of you of harboring a fugitive."

Summer looks surprised.

"I thought you said you met this Ranger Murry asshole," I tell her.

"Language," Coney says to me. She turns to Summer, "But that's true. Asshole."

"Hey!"

Coney gives me a sly smirk.

"If you need anything…" Summer says.

"Like bail money?" I laugh. "I won't call you to bail me out."

"But you can," she says.

I let my eyes linger on her tired face just a little too long. And she lets me.

I swallow and smile at my daughter. "Call your mother. Tell them to come help. I left five minutes ago to go to the police station."

"I got it!" she says. "I got it." She picks up her phone to call.

I look to Summer one last time.

Be careful, she mouths at me, her eyes full of concern now.

I smile and nod, and then shove my hand into my pocket to check for my keys. I find Detective Littlejohn's card there and pull it out and hand it to Summer. "If you do find anything, I think I'd call this guy instead of the dickhead."

I turn and head out of the library and into the empty hallway.

The glass doors at the end of the hall are black with the night, and the closer I get to them, the more I feel like I am going to open them up and fall out into nothingness. There is a surge of emotions tearing through me. Fear for Fleming, what he is going through, that we won't find him, that he's already lost to us forever. Fear for Coney, that there may be a permanent wedge between her and Dana, that the loss of her brother will scar her life forever. Fear of what's going to happen to me when I get to the police station. But there are other feelings there, too. I feel closer to Coney now than I have in months. And the look Summer gave me... There's a feeling there I haven't had in years.

But as big as all of those feelings are, or rather should be, they all seem small and far away, distant. Like they belong to someone else. Just like the pain in my knee with each step I take and the pain in my ribs with every breath. When compared to the feeling of nothingness out that black door ahead of me at the end of the hall, they are almost nothing.

I reach the door, feeling that if I open it, it's just going to swallow me up and I will be gone forever.

But I push myself through and out into the night, anyway. Because it's the right thing to do. It's the only thing I can do.

Chapter 42

THE TRUCK SLIDES A LITTLE as I come around the corner onto Main Street. The roads have been heavily travelled enough, and slick roads are rare enough, that it surprises me, almost breaking through the morass of detachment I feel. Almost.

While the unusual snow has built up, Christmas shoppers have come out in full force to enjoy the winter wonderland. Main Street is lit up again, and with all of the people and cars bustling around, the world finally looks alive again.

But I feel like I left a part of myself behind in the darkness at the school. The part of me that feels.

I'm numb. Mentally. Emotionally. Beyond cold and somewhere into being alive but not existing at the same time. It occurs to me this might be how an inmate on death row feels, and I realize what I'm experiencing is resignation.

Fleming is not going to be found, and I'm going to go to jail for it. Maybe even for the murder of some kid I'd never even seen before. I'm going to jail. Maybe for a day or a month now, and then, depending upon the judge and jury, maybe for the rest of my life. I've listened to enough news talk shows to know it doesn't matter that I didn't do it. What matters is the police think I did it.

Or at least Ranger Murry.

And I just don't care anymore. I would be okay with it if it would bring

Fleming back. If it would fix the rift between Coney and Dana. If it would bring that kid, Toddy McCurdy, back. If everything could just all right for everyone else again, I would be okay with it.

But it won't be okay, and to make it worse, mine is a hollow sacrifice, not even made of my own free will, but forced upon me by a ranger who doesn't seem interested in the truth.

The print shop catches my eye when it comes into view. Not just because I look for it out of habit, but because the lights are on, and, between the cut-out mountains of the Island of Misfit Toys, I can see Paige's laptop still sitting on the counter.

A mirthless chuckle escapes my lips. *Ranger Murry's* laptop, not Paige's, I correct myself. If that had really been Paige's laptop, she'd have had a shit fit trying to get it back. There's no way she could have ignored her clients for this long, whether she was upset about Fleming or not.

Some tiny bit of the little emotion I have left, a hateful dark bit, bubbles up to the surface and, on impulse, I pull into the only parking space left in front of the print shop, irritated that people have ignored the signs saying the spaces were for my customers only.

I like the irritation. It feels good. As I struggle to get out of the truck and into the slushy snow with my crutch, the frustration fuels me, and it feels like I could nurture the feeling, make it bloom into anger and feel something again. I unlock the print shop door, grinning at the thought of handing Ranger Murry's laptop back to him in person, and I manage to grow that anger up closer to actual hate, because I *hate* that fucker and what he did, making Coney wear a wire when he thought I was a murderer, calling Fleming *the child* and Dana *the mother*, and now, putting a spycam in my print shop.

I know it's all petty of me, that he is only doing his job, but I like feeling petty. I like thinking that, if I'm going to jail anyway, maybe I'll just break this fucking laptop across that fucker's face!

I lean on the crutch and grab the laptop off the counter with my good hand. The black screen flickers to life even as I slam it shut and shove it under my other arm.

But something I saw on that screen registers in my brain after the fact and stops me cold. A shape. A symbol in the corner of the screen. Something

174

at the bottom of a photograph. Something on someone's hand maybe.

My sudden surge of hate all but forgotten, I fumble with the laptop, trying to put it back up on the counter so I can see it again, so I can be sure my eyes hadn't tricked me. I have to see the image again. I have to know if Murry put what I thought I saw on that screen saver. Was he trying to torment me? Playing games with me because he thinks I'm a killer? Did he want me to find it, to rub it in my face, to tell me he knew I'd killed Toddy McCurdy? To see what I would do?

I lift the lid, and the screen glows back to life, but it's not what I'd seen. It's a lock screen, asking for a password. I curse under my breath then remember Paige's indifference to being secure with her laptop. Could this really be Paige's laptop and not Murry's?

I try to remember what I had seen on the laptop after she opened up the settings screen for me to connect to the internet. I hadn't seen anything. But she had logged in and sent emails to everyone, asking if anyone had information about Fleming.

Or she said she had.

If this was her laptop, would she really have let Murry use it as a spycam? The video of her in hysterics, in the middle of the street during the parade, comes to mind, I realize she probably would do most anything for Fleming.

I quickly tap out all ones on the password screen and hit enter. Her desktop opens up, but the image I saw isn't there. The image had been part of a screen saver.

It takes me a minute to go through the settings, but I find the screen saver and activate it. A photo pops up, of Paige and Fleming, and I recognize Fleming's Christmas Grogu t-shirt. The photo was taken just the other day during the Reindeer Games. I tap the arrow key and another photo replaces it. Fleming with the giant bag of foam presents on his back during the race. I tap the arrow key again and again, moving through more photos. Suddenly I've gone past the one I was looking for and have to hit the back arrow.

And there it is.

Paige with a young man. He has one arm around her neck, the other is extended out toward the camera, taking a selfie. The knuckles of his hand at her shoulder have stark black tattoos on them, and I recognize them.

Chapter 43

THE MAN WITH HIS ARM around Paige's shoulders has, if not the same, then very similar tattoos to the ones on Toddy McCurdy's knuckles, but this man most definitely is not Toddy McCurdy. His features are sharp and angular, and he looks nothing like a chubby little boy. He exudes confidence and has a flamboyant, reassuring smile.

The kind that makes me run when I see it on a car salesman.

My heart is pounding, and I am no longer a numb void speckled with only rage and hate. This is Paige's laptop, and Murry didn't leave this for me to see. I know this guy having the same tattoos can't be a coincidence. He *has to* know Toddy McCurdy.

Which means he might know what happened to the poor kid, or maybe even be the one who killed him. My gut twists in knots at that thought. But either way, at the very least, this could be something I can use to show the police that I am not the only one who should be questioned about Toddy McCurdy's murder.

Once I manage to stop staring at the twenty-something, chisel-jawed guy, I realize, based on what Paige is wearing, this photo was taken at the Reindeer Games as well. Which maybe moves me six inches further away from that life sentence I was resigned to just moments ago. But six inches may be all a drowning man needs to reach air—something I know from personal experience.

I awkwardly balance against my crutch so that I can hold my phone up with both hands, and I snap a picture of the laptop screen. I fumble to text the photo to Coney, to ask if she's ever seen him with Paige, if she has any idea who he is.

Then the thought of her getting into trouble for helping me halts my fingers.

I can't risk anything more happening to her. I have no doubt Ranger Murry would slap her with hindering, abetting, harboring, jaywalking or God knows what, in a heartbeat. If for no other reason than to try to use it as misguided leverage against me.

As much as I don't want to directly ask Paige who the guy is, that's what I need to do.

I stand there stupidly, phone in hand, for a long moment. I don't have any contacts in my new phone. I can't call Paige.

I feel like an idiot when I realize her phone number is on every single one of the thousands of things that I've printed up for her over the years, including the posters this afternoon.

It only takes me a moment to find her number on a test copy of her Christmas cards, and I dial her up. Her phone rings, but she doesn't answer.

Knowing Paige always answers her phone for her clients, I immediately dial again. When she still doesn't answer, I wonder if she's on the other line, so I dial again, hoping persistence will pay off and she'll answer because I keep calling.

It occurs to me that maybe someone is calling her with information about Fleming, after seeing one of her posters. Looking toward the front glass door, I can't tell if she picked up the rest of the posters or not. I hadn't noticed them when I came in the print shop. But then, I'd been too upset and too focused on the laptop to notice or care.

I wait another minute just in case she's getting important information about Fleming from someone, and then I try again. This time, my call goes straight to voicemail, and I remember that she thinks I had something to do with Fleming's disappearance. She's not going to answer my call.

I shove my phone back into my pocket. I'm not going to contact Coney, and I don't have any idea who else to call—and no phone numbers in my phone anyway. I was already planning on taking the laptop to the police station, having thought it was Ranger Murry's, maybe I should still do that.

But will they listen to me when I tell them about the photo? Pretty sure not. And if I just hand the laptop over, what are the odds they will notice the photo or attach any significance to it if they do?

None, I'm sure.

Maybe I could head back to the school real quick, drop the laptop off with Coney and Summer, let them look through it and see if the guy is in Paige's contacts or social media or something.

That idea falls apart as I remember I told Coney to call Dana and Trent and have them come help look at the photos, which means the police will likely follow them, or at least know they are going to the library, which puts me, if I go back there, in the same position as just taking the laptop to the police station: getting myself arrested and having the laptop ignored.

I close the screen saver, hoping I can find something useful on Paige's computer myself, but her desktop is a confusing morass of icons that mean nothing to me. After a moment of leaning hunched over, balanced on the crutch, I have to stand up straight and stretch my back. Which hurts my ribs.

I rub my tired eyes as best I can with one hand. Exhaustion is catching up with me, and I'm not functioning well. My whole body aches, and I can hardly stand here and look at the laptop, which doesn't do me any good, because I don't understand what I'm looking at.

Finally, a folder catches my eye. It's labeled 'Fleming.'

I open it to find a bunch of other folders named 'photos,' each with dates, but the folder at the top of the screen is 'contacts.' I click on it and find a spreadsheet. I open that and am amazed to find a list of thirty or so people. At the top, of course, is Trent. Dana's name isn't listed with his. I'm not surprised, based upon what Coney had said earlier. Under Trent's name are, I think, based on the state and last name, his parents. I finally do spot Dana's contact information. It's last on the list.

Her last name is entered as 'Homewrecker.'

I have to read it a few times to be sure I understand what it says. I feel sick to my stomach for so many reasons. Coney was absolutely right, and I wonder what kind of crap Dana has had to put up with the last few years. Does Trent even know?

And Summer's words come back to haunt me: *You said she thinks of herself as family, right? I'm pretty sure that counts when it comes to crimes of passion.*

Could Paige have had something to do with Fleming's disappearance? Could the whole hysterics thing at the parade actually have been a show? An act put on to deflect suspicion?

Flashing red and blue lights fill the print shop and my heart leaps into my throat. I look up to see an ambulance going by, and my knees go weak.

I have to get out of here. Unlike when I told Coney I should turn myself in, I suddenly think I may be the only one who really knows something, even if I'm not sure what it is yet. And I'm spotlighted here in the print shop with the lights on, at night. Not to mention everyone knows to look for me here.

Closing the laptop, I tuck it under my arm again and head out into the still falling snow. As I lock the door, I notice the posters I printed up are still in the plastic tub under the rock.

Chapter 44

THE HEADLIGHTS SWEEP THROUGH THE gently falling snow and then across my truck's hood, blinding me through the windshield. When they don't turn off, I find myself holding my breath, wondering if I've made a mistake.

Spotlighted, I feel like there are guns aimed at me, and someone with an itchy trigger finger might put a bullet in my head. When the bullet doesn't come, and the lights go dark, I take a deep breath of relief.

A dark form, a silhouette against the darker night, gets out of the car and stands, looking in my direction. I can barely make out the clouds of breath floating away into the night. They are quick, and I realize I'm not the only one wondering if he's made a mistake.

I open the door and slide out of the truck, pulling my crutch along after me, grateful I'd remembered to turn the cab light off when I'd parked. I don't like the feeling of being a target in the light. I'd arranged to meet at the blackberry patch Coney had taken refuge at because it was just far enough out of town and out of the way that the odds of running into anyone else this time of night were near nothing.

It's not nearly as nice of a place in the winter. The brambles, what I saw of them in the headlights when I pulled up, are an ugly mess of sticks and thorns, lacking the fairytale beauty the lightning bugs add in the summertime. And without crickets, it's dead silent out here except for the sound of my shoes squelching into the mud under the light snow.

"Thanks for coming," I say quietly, shutting the truck door with a gentle push so that it only clicks.

"Like I wouldn't take any chance in hell to find my boy?"

"I swear to God, Trent, I had nothing to do with it."

"If I really thought you did, I wouldn't be here, but that don't mean there ain't a doubt in my heart."

"I know. And I appreciate you putting it aside long enough to see this. Did you get ahold of Paige?"

"Goes straight to voicemail," Trent tells me. "Just like you said."

I nod, though he probably can't tell in the dark. I'd figured most anyone would think it was weird if Paige wasn't answering her phone, especially if they knew her well. Especially as desperate as she had seemed to hear news about Fleming.

"I've got her laptop, if you want to see it."

"I do," he says. Then his tone changes. "Using it to call me from the internet, so the police wouldn't know it was you, borders on criminal genius, don't you think?" I can't tell if Trent is being sarcastic or accusatory. Probably both.

"I was on my way to turn it, and myself, in to the police when I saw the photo. I'm still willing to turn myself in. I can go do that as soon as we're done here, if you want, but I couldn't take the chance that the police would ignore it. I needed to get it to someone who I knew would do something about it."

Trent starts walking to me. I think I see his silhouette nod in the dark.

"It's in the front seat," I tell him, pointing to the truck. "It was on all day, so I had to plug it in."

He stops walking when he gets close, and I realize he's waiting for me to give him some room. I hobble aside and then change direction, going wide around him to stand in front of my truck. If I were him, I wouldn't want to expose my back to me either.

I lean on the crutch, feeling it sink a little into the mud, and ignore the snowflakes hitting my face as Trent climbs into the truck. When he opens the laptop, his face glows blue, looking like the floating head of an angry specter. The light reflects eerily off his eyes as they flick back and forth looking at

181

the screen.

"I left the screensaver on so you could see the photo," I call to him, trying to be loud enough he can hear me, but still keep quiet in the night. "If it switched photos, just tap an arrow key."

He nods and the light flickers slightly a few times. After a moment, he lifts the laptop up and shows it to me through the windshield to verify we're talking about the same image.

"Yeah. That one," I say.

"That's her son. Tommy," he tells me. His voice is muffled though he left the truck door open. "You were gone by the time he came around and she re-introduced him. I hadn't seen him…" He shakes his head, thinking. "In four years? Didn't even recognize him."

"See those tats on his knuckles?" I ask, working my way back closer to him so I don't have to talk so loudly, and so that I can hear better. "They are pretty much the same ones I saw on the kid at the park."

"So, you think they know each other."

"Yeah."

"So how do you think that ties in with Fleming?"

I shake my head. "I don't know. I mean, it could all be coincidence, but there's something else I want you to see. Close the screensaver and open the folder with Fleming's name on it."

Trent gives me a funny look but starts working on the computer. I fill him in on the conversation Summer, Coney, and I had about family being the most likely suspects.

"That's what the police told us," Trent nods.

"Open the spreadsheet named 'contacts' that's under all of those folders full of photos," I direct him. "Now, go all the way to the bottom and look for Dana's name."

I can see it in his eyes when he spots what Paige had named her.

"When I saw that," I say, "I remembered how much Paige seemed to be a part of the family. Or at least, seemed to want to be…" I leave the words hanging there, hoping he will start putting things together himself. If it makes sense to him on its own, I'm sure he'll believe it more than if I just say it.

"So, you think Paige took Fleming."

By the look on his face, I can see he is wondering about it himself. "I don't know what to think. I know it could be anything or anyone. For all I know Fleming just ran away."

He looks up sharply at me, and I continue hurriedly. "But I don't believe that. And I know it could have been damn near anyone in the world, for any reason, that took him. But I can't let myself believe that."

I've moved close enough I am standing at the door now, and I drop my voice. I can see the hurt in his eyes, and it looks like the hurt I feel for Coney, for Dana, and for Fleming. "I know we haven't really gotten along. And I know that's my fault. You've been nothing but nice, and I've been…a shit. And I'm sorry. I really hope you can forgive me long enough for me to help find your son. Because I care, too. He's my daughter's brother. He's my ex-wife's son. That makes him my family, too.

"I have to work with what I can, with what I have, and so do you. And right now, all I have is you, and, whether you want it or not, you've got me, so I hope you'll take advantage of that and trust me."

Trent's eyes, tired and baggy, never leave mine, and I feel like he's at least willing to listen, and that's a start.

"I *know* I didn't have anything to do with this," I tell him, "and I am sure that you, Dana, and Coney didn't. I never would have even thought of Paige until…" I wave my splinted hand at the laptop. "And now, I can't stop thinking Paige might have done this."

Chapter 45

"DO YOU REALLY THINK IT'S possible Tommy is helping her?" Trent asks me for the fourth or fifth time. I'm cramped in his car, hardly able to bend my knee, and Paige's computer perched on my lap doesn't help any.

"I have no idea. It doesn't make any sense to me, really," I answer. "Obviously, if we assume Paige took Fleming, she couldn't have done it alone. How could she? She was driving her car at the parade when it happened. But, if he did, why would her son help her do it? I mean, it seems like an insane thing to do, right? So why do you help someone, even if it is your mother, do something insane? Wouldn't you try to stop them instead?"

"Maybe you or I would," Trent says with a growl hidden somewhere behind his words. "That doesn't mean other people would. Lots of people do stupid things in groups."

"Yeah, that's true." I look out the window at the houses, and the darkness reminds me of walking up and down Main Street this time last night, looking into the shadows, hoping to find Fleming, but praying I didn't find his body. How long ago had that been? *More than twenty-four hours*, the horrid voice inside my head reminds me.

Feeling sick to my stomach about that, the totally illegal plan Trent and I have to try to find Fleming doesn't make me feel any better, but at least it's something. Before loading into the car, Trent had called Dana to tell her everything he and I had talked about. I couldn't hear her side of the conversation, but she didn't seem happy about what we had planned either, or that we were going to do it without her.

She was at the library, still going through the images with Summer and Coney. When Trent sent the photo of Tommy and Paige and asked Dana to go through all of the pictures again, this time looking for any of Tommy, to see if he was even at the parade, I thought I could hear Coney groan in the background, but when Trent got off the phone, he told me she was asleep with her head on the keyboard.

When I asked about the police, still worried that Coney might get into trouble somehow, Trent told me the police had left the house back when Dana overheard Ranger Murry telling one of the officers to issue an arrest warrant for me, about the time she texted Coney about it, and they hadn't been around since.

They were probably all out looking for me. Which was why Trent and I had agreed that it would be better to not be in my truck.

"But still," I continue musing aloud, trying to wrap my head around our theory. "Four years since you've seen Tommy, you said? Did he come back to help her? Did Paige just spring it on him, and he thought, *that sounds like a great idea, Mom?* Or…" I run out of ideas. "I can't really wrap my head around it. But either way, I still can't believe that Toddy McCurdy's death is just completely coincidence, can you?"

Trent gives a heavy sigh and shakes his head but doesn't say anything.

Turn left at Marsh Lane, Trent's GSP says in an electronic voice. *The destination is on the right.*

"Look for 5892," I tell Trent. But looking for the house numbers isn't necessary. The For Sale sign in the front yard unmistakably marks the house.

Trent pulls the car up and parks on the curb. When he turns off the engine and the lights go out, the world is suddenly quiet, and everything feels surreal.

"Are we really going to do this?" he asks, but his voice is subdued, and I suspect he's talking to himself. I answer anyway.

"It's the only idea we've got."

"Dana is going to kill me."

"Not if we find Fleming, and then, even if she does, it'll be worth it."

He nods and opens his door. The cab light comes on and we both flinch. Trent looks at me. "It'll look more suspicious if someone sees us trying to turn that off now."

"You're right," I say and put the laptop in the seat between us. "Besides, I couldn't find the door handle anyway. You saved me from looking stupid."

He watches as I mess around forever trying to get out of the car with my bum knee and then turn around to reach back in and get the crutch from the back seat.

"Right," he says. "Stopped that from happening."

He catches up with me before I can limp my way up to the door. "I'll hold the light while you do the combination," I offer, holding out my good hand to take the mini-Maglite he's holding.

He hands me the light and turns his attention to the lockbox on the door. "What was the combination again?"

I look up to the house numbers above the dark porchlight and read them backwards to him.

He sees where I'm looking and shakes his head. "Doesn't seem very secure," he says.

"That's what I told Paige when she told me her password was all ones." I frown at the thought.

Trent opens the lockbox and takes out the house key. As he unlocks the house, I tell him, "Paige told me that, and I told her it wasn't secure… and then she said, *What have I got to hide?* That doesn't make any sense if she actually had something to hide, right? I mean, if she was planning to take Fleming, then she would have something to hide, and then she wouldn't have told me her password. Right?"

"You're over-thinking everything," Trent says, taking the flashlight back from me and going into the house. "Everything you are thinking about is a guess, so every guess on top of another guess becomes more and more shaky, until the whole house of cards falls. And then you're just starting all over, with the same guesses, which leads you to the same place."

He sweeps the flashlight through the empty living room and heads toward the kitchen. "You need to focus on what we know and rule out what we don't. Right now, we are ruling out that Fleming is in this house. It doesn't matter if Paige took him or not, if she planned it or not, we just need to make sure he's not here, and move on."

I follow him into the house wishing I could have that kind of mental discipline, but I don't. I'm susceptible to the random thoughts that float though my head. Like the one that if anyone is in this house, they'll probably shoot us dead, and it would be legal.

Chapter 46

THE DARK HOUSE IS CREEPY. Being in someone else's house, in the middle of the night, just feels wrong, even if it is empty and for sale. My phone rings, and I nearly fall over my crutch, catching myself against the hallway wall with my shoulder. Trent puts the flashlight on me, and, through the glare of the light, I can see the irritation on his face.

Grabbing for my phone, I answer it in the middle of the second ring, like an idiot, instead of declining the call. As soon as it's too late, it occurs to me it could be Ranger Murry or Detective Littlejohn calling to ask where I am, to tell me to turn myself in. And I don't want to tell either one of them I'm in one of Paige's client's houses, let alone that it's the fourth one Trent and I have gone into in an hour.

"Hello?" I try to sound like I'm just waking up, but I'm pretty sure I fail. They probably already know I'm not home anyway.

"Hey, Jeff, it's Summer. I finally found a photo of Paige's float that was taken while I was driving it."

"Yeah?"

Trent intently watches me, trying to hear what Summer is saying, so I hold the phone away from my ear a little to let the sound carry.

"The For Sale sign is *not* broken in the photo," Summer says. "I can't tell about the latch on the roof, though. It's too fuzzy when I zoom in."

"That could mean it got broken after it got to the warehouse. You said Petterson backed the float in for you, right?" I ask Summer.

188

"Yeah. There's no way I was backing that into his warehouse."

"I need to give him a call," I say. "I'm sure he'll know if that sign was broken when he parked the float. He's pretty damned meticulous."

Trent mouths something at me. I miss most of it in the darkness, but I'm sure I know what he said.

"Is there any news? Is everyone else doing okay?" I ask.

"No news. Coney is still zonked out. Dana is fine. She found a victim's advocate website that lets you search a tattoo database."

"I didn't know you could do that."

"Get with the times, Jeff. You can do anything on the internet. Dana's trying to find a match to Tommy's knuckle tattoos, to see if they mean anything. Maybe give us some kind of clue about that other guy, and if he had something to do with any of this. I'm still looking to see if I can find any pictures of Tommy at the parade, but I doubt if I'll be able to pick him out of the background crowds even if he's there."

"Thank you. I really appreciate you helping."

"Jeff..." she says.

"Yeah?"

"Dana told me what you guys are doing. Please be safe."

"I will." I hesitate to hang up, but Summer does it before I do.

Trent turns away and keeps heading for the back of the house, flashlight beam sweeping out in front of him. "You really need to ask her out and get it over with," he says.

"What?"

"It's obvious Summer likes you. Hell, she joined the PTO and the float team for an entirely different school to just try to get your attention."

"No. Of course, she didn't." I don't know why Trent is teasing me, but I hope it means he no longer has lingering doubts about me having anything to do with Fleming disappearing. Maybe he's trying to bond, create the friendship we could have had, should have had, if I wasn't such an idiot.

"The hell she *did*. Do you remember the first time you met her?" He reaches a bedroom and goes in, turning a quick circle. The empty room, devoid of furniture pending sale of the house, is easy to check.

"No, I don't. Wait—I do. It was at the school meeting, when she asked to join the float crew—" I stop, realizing that wasn't true. "No. I already knew her name by then." Where had we met?

"See? That's why she's interested. You, Jeff, have got to be the *only* single guy in three counties who *hasn't* hit on her. And," he squeezes back past me to get into the hallway and moves to check the last bedroom, "as she knows you're an eligible bachelor, that caught her attention."

I shake my head. "I have no idea what you're talking about."

"There's nothing here," he says, looking around the final room. "Let's get out of here."

He heads for the door and keeps talking. "You really have no idea what I'm talking about. And the thing is, that's what attracts her to you like a moth to the flame."

I follow him out and he locks the door and replaces the key in the lockbox. When he's done, he heads for the car and mumbles something I don't catch.

"What?" I ask, hurrying to keep up.

Trent stops and turns to meet me face to face. "I said, if you didn't waste so much time pining over losing Dana, you would know what I was talking about."

I feel my ears grow hot enough to light up the cold night. "Look, Trent..."

"I get it, Jeff. When I lost Nancy... It was the end of the world. I can't imagine what it would have been like if she were still here, but not with me. I wish to God she were, but, even so, if she were still walking around and doing things like marrying someone else. I would have... I don't know. Followed her around obsessively, I guess. So, I have to give you credit for not doing that." He slaps me on the shoulder and turns to head for the car.

I follow, not sure what to say. Not sure if there is anything to say. It's kind of all been said out loud now, and it seems Trent is willing to move past it. I have to, too.

I get in the car and help Trent find the next address to put into the GPS. There are only two houses left on Paige's sale listings that don't have sellers still actively living in them, and my hope that we'll find Fleming by doing this is waning.

As Trent fiddles with the GPS, I pull out my phone to call Bill Petterson and rediscover that I don't have anyone in my contacts yet.

"Do you have Bill Petterson's number?" I ask.

"No. Can you look it up?"

"Smart," I say, feeling stupid. I open up the web browser on my phone. A pop-up warning says I have to allow cellular data usage, so I go to settings and try to approve it, but it won't let me.

"I can't do it," I tell Trent. "My phone isn't set up right. The salesperson said I have to connect to Wi-Fi to finish setting it up. Can you look it up for me?"

Not having moved the car yet, he puts it back into park and looks the number up. I dial it as he reads it to me. When an answering machine picks up, I realize it's the warehouse number. I wait for the tone and then leave a message asking Petterson to call me back when he can.

Chapter 47

AFTER SOME DEBATE, TRENT AND I decide to go to Paige's house and see if the float is there before we check the last two houses on our list of vacant properties. The deciding factor was the realization that, because we are both idiots, we'd never even considered going to Paige's house to see if she was there when she didn't answer her phone.

"I blame it on the stress and exhaustion," I say as he drives us there.

Trent just grunts.

For all we know, Paige has succumbed to the same kind of exhaustion after dealing with her own stress, and then being held at the hospital last night, and then looking for Fleming all day today. Or maybe she's on sedatives again, which would explain her not answering the phone.

"If she's there, I'll just say I wanted to return her laptop," I say. "It'll seem perfectly natural at—" I look at the clock on the dashboard, "eleven fifty-two pm. On a Tuesday."

A heavy sigh comes from Trent's side of the car. My soul echoes the feeling. I wish I hadn't looked at the clock, hadn't thought about what time it is, about how long…

I force the bad thoughts away.

"I'm sorry. I'm an idiot," I tell Trent. "I got it stuck in my head that maybe Paige took Fleming, and then, because I'd already been thinking that whoever took him would be hiding him somewhere, it never even crossed my mind to just go to her house."

"You're not the only idiot here, Jeff. Let it go."

"But we're agreed about the float though, right? I'm not being totally stupid about that? Someone probably broke into the warehouse to get to the float?"

"I don't know anything anymore," Trent says. "I'm so damned tired I can't think straight. I'm half afraid I'm going to wreck the car."

The traffic had lightened up until, now nearly midnight, it was all but non-existent, and the snow had started covering the roads unimpeded before it finally lightened up. Trent's car was doing okay, but there were slick spots and icy patches.

"Jesus! How many fucking felonies did we commit tonight?" Trent finally says, slamming his palm against the steering wheel. "I can't help Fleming if I go to jail. Even if I don't go to jail, I'll probably be disbarred. Then I can't work. I can't take care of Dana." He tosses a frustrated hand gesture at me. "I can't take care of Coney...

"You know she's like a daughter to me, right Jeff? You know I'd do anything for her."

I see the desperation in his eyes and wonder if what I'd said when Coney was wearing a wire, when I had asked her if Trent was abusive, had gotten back to him.

"Trent, you have no idea how grateful I am to you that you take good care of ..." I catch myself before I call them *my girls*. "Look. I was jealous of you, all right? I mean, you have everything." The sentence seems to echo in the car. Because he'd *had* everything, but now he doesn't have his son.

I try to start over. "Trent, you're a damned good man. Dana is lucky to have you. I'm lucky to have you watching over people I love when I can't be there to do it myself." Suddenly tears hit my eyes, blurring the road ahead in the headlights, and my throat constricts. "I'm the one who failed you, when you trusted me with the ones you love. I'm the one who lost your son."

The car is silent but for my sniffles as I wipe away the tears.

"I'd be lying if I said that thought hadn't crossed my mind." Trent glances at me, but I can't meet his gaze. "But it's a bullshit thought, Jeff," he says. "It's just as bullshit as you thinking I took Dana away from you. We both have to let the bullshit thoughts go, or we won't get through this."

We drive the rest of the way to Paige's house without talking. When we get there, the lights are all off. I try to see into the backyard, through the wooden privacy fence, but I can't tell if the house float is parked back there again or not.

I wait for Trent to open his door before I open mine, but he just sits quietly for a moment, thinking.

"If we get through this…" he finally says.

"When." I correct him. "When we get through this."

Trent nods. *"When* we get through this, you and I need to sit down and figure some shit out. For the sake of the people we both love."

"Yeah. Look, I'm not saying I won't listen to what you have to say, because I will. I promise I will listen to every word. But I want you to know that I already know this is all on me. I'm the one who had the problems. You were…the better man. Better than I deserved."

I don't wait for him to answer. I open the door and start the process of getting my broken ass out of the car. I slip twice on the slushy curb but still manage to get out before he gets all the way around the car.

Trent heads up the sidewalk, and I follow, carefully testing for slippery ice with my crutch before each step. He rings the doorbell before I get there. When I catch up, he rings it a second time.

"How long do we wait?" I ask.

He shakes his head and shrugs, and we wait a minute longer. The snow has stopped, but the temperature is still dropping, and my nose and ears are cold. Trent pushes the button again, and, faintly, I can hear the chime working inside.

"I'm going to go see if the float is in the backyard," I say. I turn and carefully make my way off the porch and across the front yard, to the gate in the fence on the side of the house.

The light snow has filled in any tire tracks that might have been left earlier in the day but makes my passing through painfully obvious. I reach the wooden privacy fence and look over, my nose brushing a pile of snow on top of the slats. Against the lighter, snow-covered lawn, I can see the outline of the trailer and the little house float, back where it had been parked before.

Trent's footsteps crunch in the snow behind me. A small steam cloud puffs from his mouth as he looks over the fence with me. "Now what?"

"I think we should go look. See if we can figure out what was so important that someone needed to break into the warehouse to get to it."

I lift the latch and fight the dragging of the bottom of the gate with my bad hand.

"Let me," Trent says, stepping in and opening the gate far enough for us to get through.

His face is grim, and, as we head toward the float, I suspect he fears the same thing that I do. That the something someone had hidden inside that perfect little house was Fleming's body.

Chapter 48

THE ONLY SOUND IN THE silent night is our breathing and the snow and dead grass crunching underfoot. I point to the broken For Sale sign when I get close enough to make it out. Trent nods.

When we reach the float, I pull out my phone and turn on the flashlight. I use it to show him the splintered wood around the broken latch on the lid, where the screws had been torn out, ripped from the wood.

"That's what made me think someone broke into the warehouse for something inside the float," I say quietly, other thoughts that shouldn't be spoken aloud passing back and forth between us as readily as if they had been spoken.

Trent steps up onto the deck of the float. I'm resentful of my knee that prevents me from climbing up next to him, and simultaneously grateful that I can't see inside when Trent lifts the lid. He turns on his flashlight and points it into the float, waving it around, looking.

I strain to make out his face, to glean any clue of what he sees by his reaction.

Visualizing what the inside looked like when I was in there, I imagine the naked plywood and the half-dozen wires I'd replaced. I try not to imagine the tiny body of a five-year-old, baby-faced, looking like he is going to suck his thumb. I try not to imagine dark red and brown stains seeped into the wood.

When Trent's face holds steady, I am both relieved and disappointed.

Fleming is not there.

After a moment, Trent digs out his phone and holds it down, inside the box. The flash from the photo is like lightning filling the backyard, and it ruins my night vision, leaving green afterimages on my eyes.

Trent closes the lid and hops back down next to me. "What do you think of this?" he asks, holding his phone for me to see.

The interior looks just as I remember, but when Trent uses his fingers to zoom in, I see what he's taken a photo of. A white smear on the plywood.

"It looks like face paint," I say.

"I think Fleming was in there."

"That makes sense, I guess. That would explain how he vanished so quickly. He went into the float."

"Or someone put him in there."

I jump, and my sudden movement makes Trent jump.

"Sorry," I say, pulling my phone out of my pocket. "I put it on vibrate. I don't normally do that. It startled me."

Trent shakes his head and turns back to the float, I assume searching for any more white face paint on the outside.

My phone just shows a number, but I answer it anyway. If it's the police, I want to tell them what we found.

"Jeff? This is Petterson."

"Hey, Bill. Thanks for calling me back. Sorry it's so late. Hopefully my call didn't get you up again."

"Naw. It's been a long day. Spent the whole day trying to track down what I needed to get the door repaired right. Didn't want to do a half-assed repair, so it took me until about an hour ago to finally get it done. Got home before midnight, though, so that's a win."

"That's good," I say. "The break-in is actually what I was calling about. Did you ever find anything they took?"

"Nope. Not a thing."

"You parked Paige Walker's float in there last night, right?"

"Yeah. She picked it up with her car this morning. I almost wasn't sure I should let her drive, after last night—you heard about that, right?"

"Yeah, I did. Say, when you parked did you notice anything off about her car?"

"Can't say as I did."

"How about the float? Was the For Sale sign broken? Or that latch that holds the lid down?"

"Nope. I would have seen that. I walked all the way around it before I got in the car. Looked it all over. Just good practice to check everything yourself, even if you're only going to move it twenty feet. That little house looked just as pristine as when you put the paint away yesterday morning."

"Thanks, Bill. I knew you'd know."

"Why d'you ask?"

"When I was in there this morning, the only things I noticed out of place anywhere were the broken sign and latch on that float. That made me think it might have been the target of your break-in, which made me think that the float might have had some kind of evidence. Something that might tell us what happened to Fleming."

"Eee-yup," Petterson says.

"And I think I was right. I'm looking at the float right now, and there's something that looks like white face paint inside of it. I think Fleming was in there and someone broke in to get him."

"So," Petterson says slowly. "Here's something you might find interesting. My door wasn't busted in. It was busted *out*."

"Busted *out?*" I repeat for Trent, who has come back closer to me.

"Eee-yup. The door jamb, the deadbolt, the way they were broken, someone broke them from the inside out. Looked like they were kicked."

"Which means someone was breaking *out* of your warehouse," I say, "not in."

"Eee-yup. Got that automatic locking system, remember?"

"Only too well. Thanks, Bill. I appreciate it. Get some sleep."

I hang up and look to Trent. "Fleming couldn't break that door, there's no way," I say. "So, someone had to be inside of there with him. We need to call Murry or Littlejohn and let them know so they can come out here and check for fingerprints or DNA or whatever it is they do. If they can figure out who it was, then maybe they can find Fleming."

"I can tell you who it was," a man's voice says from behind me. Startled,

I whirl around on my crutch to face the man and then stumble sideways, nearly going over.

"And then you can tell me where to find him." As he grins, the man's messed up teeth shine in the night, matching the glint of light off the barrel of the gun he's pointing at us.

Chapter 49

WITH A WAVE OF HIS gun, the man motions for us to move back toward the house. "We're all gonna go in and have us a little sit-down kind of talk, a pow-wow," he says. "Get outta the cold and snow. Maybe have a nice warm cup of coffee. It's all going to be very civilized. As long as you two stay civilized."

I don't like the way the man's hand shakes as he points the gun at us.

"I'm just trying to find my son," Trent says. "Please, if you—"

"We'll talk inside." The man's tone, and the look in his eyes, backed up with the weapon, brooks no argument, and we head to the house in silence.

The sliding glass door is open, and I follow Trent in, fantasies of quickly spinning around and hitting the gunman over the head with my crutch floating through my head. They're dashed when my wet shoes slip on the kitchen floor and it's all I can do to stay on my feet.

"Take a seat at the table." The man points for us to sit on opposite sides of the table and then waits, scratching at his arm nervously until we're both sitting. He closes the back door and says, "You got here just in time. I just finished brewing my third pot. It's fresh."

Trent and I exchange looks. The man is not jittery because of coffee. And Trent's eyes show no signs he's got any better idea about what to do than I do.

Laying his gun on the counter, but keeping it close at hand, the man uses the dim glow of a phone screen to take down two mugs from the cupboard.

He sets them next to a third mug and pours steaming coffee into each of them.

"You boys are lucky you came here," he says, his voice sounding a bit strained, a bit rushed, "though you may not feel that way right at this moment." Picking the gun back up, he brings one mug over and places it in front of Trent before going back for one for me. "It seems you were following a predictable pattern tonight, and the police caught on to you." He winks at us and takes the third coffee mug in his own hand. "The police are waiting for you at the next house you were likely headed to. Didn't matter which of the two it was, they're at both."

Trent's eyes go wide. I'm sure mine did the same.

The man chuckles at our surprise and sits in the chair between us

"At least, I assume it was you boys," he waves his gun as he speaks, talking with it like he would with his hands, "going in and out of empty houses represented by a certain real estate agent whose house you have just now coincidentally turned up at."

He chuckles again, puts the coffee mug on the table, and holds up his phone. "Police scanner app." He taps the phone to a wireless earbud in his left ear and grins, showing us his horrible, possibly rotting teeth. "Never leave home without it."

He puts the phone away and takes a tentative sip of his coffee, looking back and forth between us before settling upon Trent.

"So," he says, scratching at his arm again, "you're looking for your boy."

"Do you know where he is?" The desperation is barely controlled in Trent's voice.

"No. But I know who he is." He picks up his mug, takes another sip of coffee, and, looking smug, watches Trent's reaction.

I furrow my eyebrows. "That's a strange thing to say, isn't it?"

"Who are you?" he asks me, the barrel of the gun following along with his gaze.

"A friend of the family."

"Out in the snow, in the middle of the night, on a crutch." His head bobbles quickly, in the tiniest of nods as he looks me over, taking in my splinted hand and my black eye. "Good friend," he says to Trent, but he sounds sarcastic about it, like maybe he's saying Trent should have picked someone who wasn't crippled.

One hand wrapped around the coffee mug, the other still holding the gun, he leans back, stretching wide, pushing his back against the chair, and groans. With his hand held out in front of him, so as to not spill the coffee, I spot the tattoos across his knuckles. I glance at Trent. He recognizes them too.

"I had a good friend once," the man says, finishing his stretch. Though he's looking at Trent, he moves his gun so that it is close to, but not quite, pointing at me. "He turned out to be an asshole. The kind of friend you wish you didn't have. And then," his gun points directly at me, "he killed my brother."

He slowly turns his attention back to me. "Are you that kind of friend?" His eyes have gone cold and hard.

I don't have an answer to give. I certainly have not been the good kind of friend, maybe even the kind Trent wished he didn't have, but I'm scared to death to admit that. I wish I had the confidence I'd had when I faced down Ranger Murry. I realize now that was just a false confidence, built out of my rage but based on the fact that, deep down inside, I knew a lawman wouldn't shoot me just for being an asshole.

I'm pretty sure this man will.

He seems to be waiting for an answer, and getting antsy about it, so I tell him the truth. "I'm the kind of friend that loses your son when I'm supposed to be watching him."

The man lets the barrel of his gun drift away from me a little. "So, my friend fucked up your life, too, huh?"

"Your friend took Fleming?" I ask.

The man bobbles his head again.

"Why?"

He looks from me to Trent, and then back to me. "Oh, you *really* don't want to know. If you were a good friend, you wouldn't want *him* to know." The wicked grin spreading across his face scares the shit out of me. My mind goes to all kinds of bad places, and I don't know what to think.

"Is he going to kill Fleming?" Trent blurts out.

"Ha! No," the man says. "My bad. I can totally see how you would have thought that. Sorry. No. Fleming is, I am sure, perfectly safe." He takes another drink of coffee and then puts the mug on the table.

"See what kind of friend you are?" he asks me, scratching his chin with the barrel of his gun. "You made your friend think all kinds of bad things that were wrong. Which means now I have to tell him about my friend, so he can understand—and that's going to be worse."

He looks to Trent again. "I'm sorry all we have is coffee. You're gonna need a drink for this one."

Chapter 50

"MY *FRIEND* IS THE *REAL* father of your son," the man tells Trent, using the gun barrel in a circular motion for emphasis.

Trent sits up straight in his chair, confusion and horror twisting across his face.

"Maybe I should start at the beginning," the man says thoughtfully, scratching at his arm again. "You up for a hell of a story?" Although he glances from Trent to me, he doesn't wait for an answer. He seems to be getting higher while he talks, and I wonder if he took a hit of something just before he found us.

"My brother and I were passing through here, oh…about six years ago. Just a quick flyby. Nothing big. And then we made a new friend. Tommy Walker. Not Johnny, not Black, not Red, but a worthless fucking Tommy.

"But we didn't know that at the time. What we knew was the kid knew how to party. And fuck could he party. His mom," the man waves the gun to encompass the house around us, "was a real estate agent, and there was always an empty house available for a party. And Tommy knew every drug dealer and bookie in town, and they all *loved* to party with him, because Tommy would get all the gamers together for an impromptu LAN party and we would all get high and play and bet against each other… We were like fucking rock stars, like that fucking song; we got our drugs and chicks for free."

He takes what looks to be the last drink of his coffee and puts the mug on the table. "*God-damn* those were good times." He leans back, tipping his chair up onto two legs, a reminiscing smile on his face. "But, like everything, I guess, all good things must come to an end. Tommy got a little wild one night, did some stupid shit. And me and my brother were too drunk, too high, too stupid to not be involved. Hell, like the idiots we were, we thought it was funny at the time.

"You see, Tommy had the hots for this older chick, a friend of his mom's. You might have known her." He looks to Trent and drops his chair back onto four legs with a sharp *thump*. "Her name was Nancy."

I see Trent tense up. It takes me a moment to realize the man is talking about Trent's deceased wife, Fleming's mother.

"She was a 'friend of the family,'" he says, looking to me with implied meaning, the wicked grin crawling back across his face. "And a fine lookin' piece of ass, if you don't mind me sayin'."

Trent's thin lips tell me he does mind. The man is enjoying telling his story now and doesn't seem to notice or care.

"But she hardly gave Tommy the time of day. Can't say as I blame her. I think she'd known him since he was nothing more than a diaper rash. Not to mention he was still a snot-nosed young punk. Wouldn't know what to do with a woman like that, anyway." The man picks up his mug and looks into it before putting it back.

"Turns out he didn't have to know what to do. A little date-rape drug in her drink one night at one of his mom's open house parties, and…" He chuckles. "Well, you get the idea."

Leaning forward, he looks closely at Trent, who's gone pale. "And just when you think that's bad, the story gets worse."

The man gets up and goes to the back door again. "Goddamn it's hot in here." He opens the door and then heads to the counter, where he uses the dim light from his phone to refill his coffee. He doesn't offer any to us, but then, neither of us have touched ours. With his back to us, I wonder if I could charge him before he could get his gun off the counter, but my knee…

The anxious look on Trent's face makes me think he might be considering the same. I grip my crutch, ready to do anything I can to help if he goes for it.

"Tommy had a little run-in with the law," the man continues, "for possession with intent to sell, and he did a little bit of time over it. About three years, to be exact. He got lucky. First offence. When he got out, me and Toddy, being the *good* friends that we were, we were there to meet him." He stands back by the open door with his refilled mug. "Did I mention my brother's name was Toddy? Anyway, two days and one helluva party after his release from jail, Tommy hears a rumor that a certain lady had a baby. A boy. Named Fleming. Who was just about exactly the right age…"

I can't bring myself to look at Trent. I can't imagine what he is going through right now. I wish I had the strength, the courage to hit this man over the head with my crutch, to tell him to shut the fuck up, but I hardly have the courage to whimper at him as he talks and waves his gun around. My hand hurts from gripping the crutch, and I play out how to swing it with my left hand, to help Trent if I have to, but all of my imaginations end like my left-handed swing at the homeless guy by the lake.

"So, Tommy goes looking for the love of his life, wanting to put things right, I guess. Didn't make no sense to me then, don't make none now. But he did. And when she didn't want nothin' to do with him, he lost his shit and punched her in the side of the head so hard she plumb just fell over dead."

Trent jumps like someone's stuck him with a knife.

"Oh, yeah," the man says to him, nodding deeply. "I told you you'd need a drink."

Twirling the gun barrel around in the air to indicate the house around us, he asks me, "Is Mom a drinker? If you know where her booze is, your friend could use a pull or three right now. I won't begrudge a man that."

I shake my head. It's all I can do to answer him, and that's only out of fear he'll shoot me if I don't. "I don't know. I don't remember ever seeing her drink."

"Well," he says to Trent with a shrug, "neither do I. Sorry. I tried. So, to wrap up the story, me and Toddy helped that fucking idiot load her into her car and run it off the road and out into the lake. You know, so's it don't look like a murder.

"'Cause that's what it was, I suppose. Didn't really think of it like that at the time. But if I'd realized how goddamned murderous that sonofabitch was—" He stops and takes a deep breath of the cool air coming in the back door. "But I'm getting ahead of myself. I've told the part that makes you need a drink, and now I need a little of the expression therapy for myself. The one thing I learned in prison that was actually helpful. Gotta let it out, right?"

Leaving the door open, he comes back and sits down.

"So, after we…" he looks at Trent and hesitates, some modicum of pity passing through his bloodshot eyes. "Afterwards, we got drunk and high. And then we ran out of stuff. On our way to find more, Tommy decides he needs the goddamned 'motherload,' he kept calling it, and just pulls right on into a winery, marches in, and demands they give him a whole fucking wine barrel."

The man snorts, a short half-laugh. "As if that would ever happen, right? Like it would even fit in the car. Like we could have even moved it.

"But Tommy, he's a hell of a guy when things are going his way, but when they're not… He fucking shot them both. Took the cash out of the cash drawer, all one-hundred and seven dollars of it, and grabbed two cases of wine." The man takes a deep breath. "And then, suddenly, we were all three of us on the run. Him a murderer three times over, and us accessories

"We didn't go to jail for any of that, though." He shakes his head. "I don't know how, but they never pegged us for it. Instead, we went to jail for possession with intent, all three of us, after Tommy got pulled over doing a hundred and thirty-eight across the panhandle. Me and Toddy were passed out. Didn't even know we'd been pulled over until we woke up in jail.

"Tommy told them the drugs were all ours, that we were the dealers, he was just the driver, working in exchange for getting to use. You know, because he didn't need a second offence for distribution, right? That's a life sentence. So, we all got three years this time."

He drains the rest of his mug and slams it down on the table. "But that's what friends are for, right?" He looks at me. "We get each other out of trouble, and then we get each other into trouble." His voice tenses as he talks. "And then, when we decide to do something really fucking stupid, like kidnap a kid, and our friend finally draws a line in the sand and says *No! This is too stupid!* and tries to talk us out of it, tries to stop us… What do we do then?"

He raises the gun again and points it at me and screams, "Then we fucking kill them!"

Chapter 51

"SO," THE MAN SAYS, LOOKING at Trent. The man is barely in control of himself and breathing hard. "I hope you understand how we've both got skin in this game." He points the gun back and forth between himself and Trent. "You help me, I'll help you, and we'll both get justice."

"What do you want?" Trent asks.

"Well, I know you don't know where Tommy is, or you'd be there already, but you figured the same thing I did. He's probably using one of his mother's houses somewhere. But I already checked the three that were listed on the internet. Somehow, if the police scanner was right, you had a list that included more houses. Where'd you get it?"

"It's on her computer," I say, still not wanting the man's attention, but needing to do something to stop all of the focus from being on Trent. In all honesty, I'm not sure if I'm trying to help Trent or just make myself useful enough to keep alive.

"Where is it?"

"In the car," Trent answers for me. I realize, had Paige been here, I would've blown the whole excuse of bringing it to her by forgetting it during my process of getting out of the car with my crutch.

"Well, let's go get it." The man waves his gun for us to get up.

I stand up and my shirt pocket starts glowing and vibrating. The man stops and points his gun at me. "Who's calling you after midnight?"

"Uh, it could be my friend, who's trying to help us find Fleming. Or, it could be the police, who think I killed your brother."

"Or it could be my wife," Trent says. "I didn't answer my phone a few minutes ago."

"Take it out, let's see."

I take it out and show him. The caller ID is just a number, but I recognize it as Summer's. "It's my friend," I say.

"Why isn't she in your contacts?"

"New phone. My old one died in the lake this morning." Those words suddenly sound terrible to me, and I wish I'd said something else.

"New phone, who dis?" The man laughs. "All right. I want you to answer it, on speaker, and be careful what you say." He makes sure I see the gun is pointed at me.

"Hello?" I ask, answering the phone.

"Jeff, I think Dana found something." Summer's tinny voice echoes in the kitchen. "There were three matches for Tommy's tattoo. One was the guy in the park, Toddy McCurdy, and the other was his brother, Matt. We've been trying to call Matt, hoping maybe he can help us, but so far there's no answer."

Matt McCurdy, keeping the gun on me, pulls out his own phone and looks at the screen. "What number are you calling?" he asks, startling both Trent and me.

Summer hesitates. I'm not sure if it's at the different voice or if she's looking for the number. After a moment she says the number.

"Yeah, that's an old one," McCurdy says. "What were you wanting to ask me?"

"Uh…" Summer stalls.

"It's okay," I tell her. "Matt is here with us. He found us. He's looking for Tommy, too." I hope I didn't say too much, but McCurdy doesn't respond to it, so I think I'm all right.

"We, uh, we were going to ask if you thought Tommy had anything to do with Fleming's disappearance, and if you knew where we could find him."

"Yes. No," McCurdy says. "Anything else?"

Summer is quiet for a moment. "I wanted to let Jeff know that there is one video, of him and Luca, that looks like it shows someone opening the roof on the little house in the background. But it was taken from way up the street, and it's too far away to really see anything."

"Does that mean anything to you, *Jeff?*" McCurdy asks me.

"Yeah. It means that's how Fleming disappeared from the parade without a trace."

McCurdy nods. "Okay then, that explains why you were poking around back there. I'd wondered." He looks back to the phone. "Anything else?"

Summer doesn't say anything.

"He's asking you, Summer," I say.

"No. That's it. We've run out of ideas of things to look for."

"Okay," McCurdy says. "We'll talk to you later." He reaches down and ends the call himself.

"Sounds like you really do have good friends helping you," he tells Trent. "What a pleasant surprise."

He waves the gun again. "Let's go to the car. Both of you."

Chapter 52

"YOU'RE STARTING TO IRRITATE ME, gimpy," McCurdy says, shoving me in the back, pushing me toward the car.

It's all I can do to not fall over, but I manage to use the momentum to make it to the car quicker. Trent is already there, waiting, carefully not doing anything to upset the man with the gun.

"Where's the laptop?" McCurdy asks.

"Front seat," Trent and I both say.

The gun waves in my face. "Get it, *friend*."

I balance on my crutch and try to open the car door.

"Let me get it," Trent says.

"Get back!" McCurdy growls, stepping closer and pointing his gun at Trent. Trent steps back, hands half-raised.

I fumble until the door is open and then I reach in and get the laptop computer and pull it out. Hopping on my good leg, splashing gutter slush, I turn around and hold it out to McCurdy.

He takes it and looks back and forth between me and Trent before taking a step back. Cradling the laptop with the arm holding the gun, he opens the computer up with his other hand. The glow from the screen lights up his face, and he scowls at what I assume is the lock screen.

Stabbing at the keyboard with one shaky finger, he grunts and then chuckles to himself. "Still all ones. Fucking stupid."

I shift my weight, leaning back onto my crutch and McCurdy quickly looks over the top of the screen at me, squinting with a nasty look. He takes long enough to focus on me that I realize the screen is ruining his night vision, like it had mine earlier. A brief hope flashes through my mind that I can find a way to use that to get Trent and I away, or get the gun, or something, but right now, gimpy seems to fit me too well.

McCurdy drops his eyes down again and works the trackpad. The whole laptop shimmies under his unsteady hands. After a moment, he nods and grunts again. "Here it is…" he mumbles.

"What-what did you find?" Trent quietly asks.

"The *other* places," McCurdy says. A toothy grin spreads across his face and he looks at us with those wicked eyes again. "Her list of places that aren't on the market because they are getting fixed up or some shit. Plus, something new. It looks like she's started dabbling in BnB's."

McCurdy adjusts his grip on the laptop, the gun in his hand making it even hard for him to hold it. I risk a glance at Trent who is wearing a strange mix of fear and hope on his face.

Suddenly McCurdy looks up, his twitchy eyes scanning up and down the street. "We gotta go," he says, quickly closing the laptop and moving forward. "Get in the car."

Neither of us moves as he approaches. When he sees the look on our faces, he taps his earbud with the barrel of his gun. "Never leave home without it, remember? Now, let's go."

When we still don't move, McCurdy becomes jittery again. He raises his gun and erratically points it back and forth at us. "Who has the keys?"

"I do," Trent says, pulling them out of his pocket and holding them up.

"You have two choices, *friend,* but only one second to choose. Are you giving me the keys or coming with me?"

Trent hesitates. I feel the same way. The chance that this guy might help find Fleming is too much to risk losing, but the risk is our lives. Then again, he's obviously messed up on something, and God knows what will happen if he does find Tommy and Fleming is with him.

"I'll go," I suddenly say, the words coming out of my mouth before I lose the courage to say them. Holding the passenger door open wider, I look at McCurdy. "Do you want me to drive or navigate?"

"Ah, the good friend. Enemy of my enemy, and all that shit, right?" McCurdy says with a wild smile. He looks at my leg. "Can you even drive?"

I don't know if I can bend my leg enough to drive Trent's sedan, but before I can lie to McCurdy, Trent speaks up.

"I'll drive." He moves toward the driver's side door, his face like pale granite in the night. "Jeff can navigate. You," he points to McCurdy, "figure out what we need to do next."

"Fuck yeah." McCurdy nods enthusiastically and moves toward the car.

"Front or back?" I ask him.

"Shotgun. You ride bitch."

I look into the front seat. It's not even a bench seat. There's no way we can all fit up front. Before I can object, McCurdy is shoving me in.

I do my best not to yell out in pain as my knee is forced to bend and my ribs are tweaked and then jammed by his elbow as he pushes in behind me. With my knees against the radio knobs, pressing right into the sorest spot possible, it's all I can do to try to keep my breathing regulated. I don't want to upset McCurdy and have him decide that I'm too much of a problem to deal with.

"Let's go!" McCurdy anxiously taps the gun on the dashboard in front of him and looks around me to see what Trent is doing.

Trent gets in, starts the car and pulls away from the curb.

"That way." McCurdy reaches across me, putting the gun in my face to point. "Through the neighborhood. Go the back ways until we get away from here."

For a moment, I consider going for the gun, but, folded up like a lawn chair, I know I don't have a chance.

Chapter 53

THE SOUND OF THE GUN barrel tapping against McCurdy's gross teeth is unnerving. He's grown even more anxious, excited, twitchy, something—I don't know what—since we left Paige's house. My best guess is that whatever drugs he's using are still rushing through his system, and he's steadily been getting worse.

He is mumbling incessantly, hunched over the laptop, looking at things I can't see. It bothers me the way he keeps scratching his face and head with the gun. Trent has been driving slow circles in the back streets around a random neighborhood while McCurdy tries to make a Wi-Fi hotspot with his phone and connected the laptop so he can access Paige's online files, beyond the spreadsheets we had seen before.

"Ha!" McCurdy says, looking up to laugh triumphantly at the roof of the car before putting his face back to the laptop. The gun is in his lap now, between the computer and his belly, as he types with both hands.

And I can't keep my eyes off of it. Like a siren's song, it calls to me, yet I know if I reach for it, it will be my doom.

McCurdy mutters something else at the computer. I can't tell if he is talking to us or to himself. It doesn't seem to matter. He's not waiting for either of us to answer anything he says anymore.

"Oh, look at that…" he babbles. "That could be interesting… Oh, yeah." He looks up at me with mischievous eyes and that toothy smile, pleased about something. "Security systems. That will save a lot of time." He nods at me and then goes back to the screen.

I look at Trent and give a tiny shrug. Neither of us have spoken unless spoken to for fear of getting too much of McCurdy's attention. Trent, huge bags under his eyes, looks as bad as a corpse in the light from the dashboard, but he keeps driving slow and steady through the wet streets.

"Fuck!" McCurdy suddenly shouts, making me jump and Trent jerk the steering wheel.

McCurdy looks at us wild-eyed, the gun suddenly in his hand and waving around wildly again. "You idiots! You goddamned idiots!" Scrunching his eyes tightly shut, he hits himself in the temple with the gun a couple of times. "You let them get you on video!"

He opens his eyes and bares his teeth at us, shaking his head and looking around as though thinking causes him incredible pain. Then he's pointing the gun at Trent, holding it less than two inches away from my nose.

I tense, ready to try for the weapon, when McCurdy screams, "Pull over!"

Trent, looking scared as I feel, starts slowing and looking for a clear parking place to pull over into on the residential street.

"Now! Fuck! Just stop the fucking car!"

Trent hits the brakes, and we all jerk forward. The radio knobs dig into my knee like someone trying to take scoops out of me with a melon spoon. The pain is unbearable and, even as we are all still jerking forward with the stop, I involuntarily begin to curl into the fetal position. My forehead slams into McCurdy's gun. The blast, bright even through my closed eyelids, deafens me and sprays burning gunpowder across my face. My arms reflexively come up to protect myself, and I find them tangled with McCurdy's arm—and the gun.

I push, hard, trying to force his hand and the gun into the dashboard, away from where he can fire at Trent again. Someone is shouting, but my ears are ringing, and I can't hear well enough to know what they are saying. I hope to God it's not Trent screaming for help because he's been shot.

I can feel McCurdy trying to pull the gun back. I swing my splinted hand at his face and feel it connect with something. Then the car jerks hard again. We both smash forward into the dash and suddenly the gun is free. I feel it fall away from both my hand and his, bouncing off my knees and to the floor

215

under Trent's feet. I try to hit McCurdy with my splint again, but he's leaned too far into me, reaching for the gun again, so I head-butt, not knowing if I will hit anything or not.

My head hits something softer than I expected, but he's still pushing against me, so I do it again, and again, grunting with effort and ignoring the explosions of pain in my knee and ribs. On the fourth try, I hit something solid. Too solid. It's unyielding and pain flashes white behind my eyes and sets me falling backward into the seat.

"Stop!" It's Trent's voice. "Jesus Christ, stop or I'll shoot!"

The pressure lets up off of me, and I feel McCurdy pull back. My vision clears, and I see blood running down his chin. His jaw looks broken, and his eyes are full of fear.

Trent's car has run into one of the parked cars. He's holding the gun, awkwardly reaching around me to point it at McCurdy. I lean my face back farther, fearing more explosions and powder burns.

"Fuck! I thought we were friends!" McCurdy slurs, hand going to his jaw. "I didn't mean to shoot. He did it!" He points at me. "Fucking assholes." He opens the car door.

"Stop!" Trent yells again.

"I'm not going back to jail because of you idiots!" McCurdy slurs. "They got you on video!" He half-falls out the door and starts running away into the night, the laptop still in his hand.

The gun in Trent's hand trembles as he aims at the retreating figure's back, and I cringe, pulling my head as far back, away from the weapon as I can.

Chapter 54

WHEN I FEEL MOVEMENT NEXT to me instead of the concussive blast of another shot, I open my eyes and look at Trent.

He's lowered the gun. Still staring into the night where McCurdy vanished, tears well in his eyes and he takes a ragged breath. "He took the laptop." He manages to say.

I nod.

"That was our last hope of finding Fleming."

He's right. And I don't know what to say.

"I couldn't shoot him in the back."

"No. You couldn't."

"I don't think I could have shot him at all."

I don't know if I could have. But I didn't have to make the decision. I reach out and put my hand on Trent's shoulder, but I don't have any words to offer.

A porch light comes on from a nearby house. A silhouette of a man with a gun appears in the doorway. "What the hell is going on out there?" he yells.

Trent and I look at each other. The look in his eyes tells me he's still badly shaken.

"What do we do?" he asks

I shake my head.

"We should call Ranger Murry," he finally says.

"Yeah," I agree. The terror is wearing off, working its way down to merely scared as hell, and a weird, numbing exhaustion is setting in. I feel like I don't have the energy left to raise an arm, let alone think or argue if I disagreed. Which, after just having had a gun shot in front of my face, I don't.

Trent reaches for his phone on the dash, where we'd been using it for GPS, and pulls back a shattered mess of glass and plastic. "I guess I know where the bullet went," he says.

I try to laugh but can't, processing with relief the realization that Trent *hadn't* been shot when the gun went off.

"You call," Trent tells me.

"I don't have the number," I say. "And I—"

"—can't look it up," we say at the same time.

Trent meets my eyes and shakes his head. "You and that goddamned phone."

I do manage a laugh this time, but it hurts my ribs. The sharp pain reminds my body to hurt and everything else begins to scream in agony as well. I unfold myself into the passenger seat.

"Don't move!" the man on the porch yells. "I'm calling the police."

"Well, that'll work, I guess," Trent says.

"Tell them there's a dangerous man on foot in the neighborhood," I yell back at the man, holding my ribs as I do it. "Tell them he carjacked us!"

The man hesitates and then vanishes back inside his house. Trent and I sit in silence for a moment.

"I'll call Summer," I tell him. "I've got her number. I can ask her to call the police for us, give them our side of the story. Maybe have her call Littlejohn instead of Murry. I feel like he'll be more open to listening than Murry will." I dig out my phone.

"I don't want to wait here for the police," Trent says. "I don't want to be here if McCurdy comes back. Who knows where he went. Right into one of these people's houses to find another gun? Or a knife? He's high as hell and there's no telling what he'll do. I think it'll be safer for everyone if we don't stay here."

"I agree. Can you drive," I ask.

Trent looks to the front of his car, where it's hit the parked car, and then at the bullet hole in the dash, above the steering column. "We'll see."

He puts the car into park and tries starting it. It turns over, so he backs up away from the wreckage. Something sounds like tearing cardboard as the two cars separate with a slight bump.

"So far, so good," Trent says.

"Hey! Stop! Or I'll shoot!" the man from the house yells again. He waves his gun, but it doesn't scare me like when McCurdy had done it.

"Get back inside," I yell back to him. "He's dangerous! Tell the police he went that way!" I point in the general direction of the man's backyard, where McCurdy had gone, and the man vanishes again. This time with his front door slamming shut.

"Shut your door," Trent tells me.

I pull the car door shut, and Trent aims the front of the car down the street, rolling slowly at first, testing the steering and brakes, but then picking up speed at he goes. As we move out of the neighborhood, the night around us becomes surreal. Like we'd just left a set on a movie studio tour and none of it was real. Like we could just pretend nothing ever happened.

"You gonna call?" Trent asks.

I look down at the phone I'd forgotten was in my hand. "Yeah." I go to recent calls and redial Summer's number. "Where should I tell her to have the police to meet us?"

"I don't know. Home, I guess. That seems safest, I guess. So that it doesn't look like we're trying to run away or anything. Make sure you have her tell them why we just left the scene of an accident with gunshots."

Chapter 55

TRENT PULLS UP IN HIS driveway just as I get off the phone with Summer. I'd taken extra time to tell her everything that happened, and what we thought was on the laptop that might help the police find Fleming, in the hope that, if they just arrested Trent and I and hauled us away, someone would still know what was going on.

He presses the button on the garage door opener and, as the door raises, I realize he is going to pull in on the right-hand side, where Dana always used to park at hour house.

I push the thought away.

There's no room for that kind of thinking in my life anymore. Never again. Then I realize I'll have problems getting out of the car after he pulls in.

"Let me get out first," I tell him.

He nods tiredly and waits while I struggle to get out and then look for my crutch. It's not in the backseat. "It's in Paige's front yard," I say out loud, shaking my head.

It got left behind when McCurdy shoved me into the front seat.

"We've got one in a closet somewhere. I'll get it after I park."

I nod and close the car door, hopping out of the way and grabbing the edge of the garage for support. Trent turns the motor off without pulling into the garage and gets out. "I decided I didn't want them thinking I was trying to hide the damage or the accident," he says, waving for me to follow him into the house through the garage door.

Using whatever I can grab along the way, I hop and limp my way in after him.

Their door doesn't open up to the kitchen table with a cavernous house behind it. Instead, it opens to a small mudroom with a bench and coat hangers. Trent points to the bench and vanishes around the corner and into the house. I take another hop-step and sit down while I wait.

He's only gone a minute, coming back with a crutch he's already adjusting for me. "It's from my ankle surgery," he says.

"Thank you." I take it but don't stand up.

We look at each other for a moment. I'm sure I look worse than he does, and he looks bad.

"Thank you," he says. "Tonight didn't go well…"

I laugh and shake my head. It makes him give a half smile.

"…but I appreciate that you were there. Thank you for trying to help me find my son. It means a lot to me."

"I'm so sorry, Trent—"

He waves me off. "No more bullshit thinking, remember?"

"Yeah. You're right. No more bullshit thinking."

There's room on the bench, and he sits next to me. After a moment he puts his head in his hands. "Know any good lawyers?" he asks.

I laugh again. He and Dana aren't those kinds of lawyers, but it's funny anyway. "No. I suppose we should use the time before the police get here to look one up."

He sighs deeply and then looks at me. "You know, you really should connect to our internet and see if you can upgrade that damned phone of yours before you need it to call someone to bail us out."

"You don't think Dana will bail us out?" I ask, teasing. But it's a good idea, so I pull my phone out.

"After all the illegal shit we did? No. I wouldn't want her too. It might risk her being disbarred, too. But I think Summer would bail you out."

"Yeah. Ha! She did tell me she would."

"See? I told you. You need to ask her out."

"Maybe someday. You know, if I ever beat the murder rap."

"No way that sticks," Trent shakes his head. "But the half-dozen felony

B and E's... Sounds like maybe they've got you on video for that."

"I'll...plead...insanity..." My mind wanders away from what I was saying as I look at my phone. My heart starts to pound.

"You okay, Jeff? Not gonna pass out and leave me to explain everything to the police all by myself, are you?"

I shake my head and show Trent my phone. My hand is shaking.

"That one," he says, pointing to the list of available Wi-Fi connections.

I shake my head. "No. *That* one." I point to the one at the bottom of the list, with the weakest signal.

Trent squints at it. "Pan..op...ticon?" he reads.

"I know that one," I say, my voice quavering. "Panopticon. The All Seeing Eye."

Trent looks at me.

"It's the name Paige said her son gave to the new routers she needed to install security systems in her houses."

Chapter 56

"HE'S HERE?" TRENT SAYS BREATHLESSLY, looking up from my phone, hope in his eyes for the first time in what feels like a lifetime.

"I think he's been watching from close by," I say.

"He's been watching my family…"

"Maybe," I say. "I'd bet he was trying to figure out a good time and place to take Fleming. But you guys kept too close a watch. He couldn't find a way to take him."

"So, he tried at the Reindeer Games, where he knew little kids would be out of sight of their parents," Trent says, thinking out loud.

"But McCurdy's brother knew what he was doing and tried to stop him."

"And got killed for it."

"So, Tommy had to improvise, had to watch for a new chance, find some other way…"

"And when you caused a huge scene at the parade, he was right there, close by, ready to take advantage."

"I think," I say, my heart pounding now, "that he's still close by. I think, if he was desperate enough to take an out-in-the-open chance like grabbing Fleming off the float, than he probably didn't have a *good* plan. And if he didn't have a good plan, he would need to go into hiding until he figured things out."

"And if he already had a safe place here," Trent finishes my thought, "he probably would have come right back to it, until things calmed down and he could figure a way out of the mess."

I nod. "That feels right to me."

"So how do we figure out which house it is? There's got to be a way to track down a Wi-Fi signal. Some app to triangulate it or something."

I start to ask if Trent remembers anyone in the neighborhood moving or any houses being sold or rented in the last few months, but before I can get the words out, I remember watching a perfectly formed smoke ring float in the morning air, just a few houses away from here. And the car that made it had looked just like Paige's.

"I know where it is." I jump up and grab the crutch, hurrying to the door and back out into the garage.

"Where?" Trent demands, following me.

"Three houses down." I point to the car. "Grab McCurdy's gun."

Trent opens the car door and grabs the gun and still catches up with me easily. I can see by the look on his face his adrenaline is pumping as hard as mine, and I hope to God I'm right and Fleming is there as I crutch my way down the sidewalk.

And, if I am, I pray we're not too late. We're way past twenty-four hours. *But not yet forty-eight,* the voice in my head adds, optimistically for once, spurring me on.

Trent falters, slowing down. "We should wait," he hisses.

I stop and look at him.

"The police will be here any minute. We should let them handle this."

I look at him, and I see so many things on his face. So many fears, so much pain. But more than that, I don't see *Trent.* I don't see the Hallmark Movie Hero with the perfect life I was jealous of. I see Fleming's father. Dana's husband. Coney's stepdad. And I see someone I consider a friend. And his family needs him. *My* family needs him. More than they need me.

"Give me the gun." I hold out my hand.

"What? No."

"Yes. I want you to think about this really hard, and then, whether or not you like it, I want you to give me the gun. No bullshit thoughts. Agreed?" I hold his eyes until he gives in.

"I'll agree to no bullshit."

224

"Close enough. If Fleming is in there, and if the police roll up in here making a fuss to get us, that will alert whoever is with him, and then they'll have a chance to hide Fleming, or escape, or something worse. Like maybe," I hate myself for saying it, but I need to be sure Trent understands, "a murder-suicide. Because once we tell the police we think Fleming is in there, they're going to fuck around and waste more time getting a search warrant or calling backup or some shit."

I can see understanding set in Trent's eyes as they grow darker, more determined.

"Give me the gun," I tell him, "and I can go in there and you can tell them I am in there with a gun. Then, because they already suspect me, because they already think I'm a threat, they can come right on in to protect people from me, right?"

Trent shakes his head. "No. I'm going in."

"Trent. No bullshit. They already think I did this. They aren't going to listen to me if I stay out here and talk to them. I need *you* to talk to them."

He doesn't move.

"We're running out of time. They're going to be here any minute. Give me the gun."

Trent hesitates and then hands it to me. "Don't do anything stupid."

I look him in the eye. "If anything happens, you tell *our* family that I love them."

Chapter 57

ALTHOUGH I CAN SEE A dim light in one of the side windows toward the back of the house, the front of the house is quiet, and the porchlight is off, as I approach the door. The white-trimmed aluminum screen door nearly glows in the night, and I realize it's because morning is finally coming to this never-ending night.

If McCurdy was right, and there are security videos of Trent and I at the other houses, then this house surely has a security system as well. But I don't know what I'm looking for, and I don't see anything. Not seeing any kind of camera near the door, it would be easy to tell myself that Paige hasn't set one up here yet, but the Wi-Fi name tells me I can't take that chance.

I'm sure I have only minutes until the police show up, and seconds until Tommy, if he is even inside, is alerted to my presence by the security system. Which, as far as I can tell, only leaves me the option of being direct.

I use the crutch to move up the steps as quickly as I can, and then, just as I am about to ring the doorbell, I hear a whisper, from right behind me.

"There's a keylock. Right there, on the ground next to the flowerpot."

"Jesus," I hiss back at Trent. "You scared the shit out of me."

"Good. You're being stupid if someone can sneak up on you like that. Were you really just going to ring the doorbell? That's stupid, too, isn't it?"

I don't answer. I don't have an answer. He might be right.

"I thought we agreed you'd stay back and tell the police he was in here," I growl at him.

He bends down and gets the keylock. "I don't think he would leave this out here if he was using this house, do you?"

I sigh, my heart sinking. "No. I guess not. I wish we would have thought of that before we went into all of those other houses."

"I blame it on the stress and exhaustion," Trent says, giving me a sideways look.

I try to laugh, but it comes out more of a grunt.

Trent looks at up the house number and unlocks the little lock box. "As long as we're here," he says, "I want to look. I don't think I can live with myself if we didn't."

I nod, feeling pretty much the same way.

"Let me go first," he says, taking the key out. "You keep the gun. Clearly, I don't know when to use them."

"That's bullshit thinking," I tell him, holding the screen door open while he unlocks the main door. It creaks slightly as it opens up to a dark living room. He goes in, and I follow.

The smell is horrid.

"Is that cat piss?" Trent whispers. "No wonder it's not on the list. It's gonna take a hell of a cleaning crew to get rid of that."

I leave the front door open, allowing what little light there is to come in so we can see better, and hoping it lessens the smell.

The gun is heavy in my hand. We hadn't had one when looking through the other houses. It hadn't ever occurred to me that we might need a weapon if we'd found Fleming. Now, I feel like it's an unbearable burden around my neck. Like Trent, I'm afraid I have no idea when to use it, and I'm afraid I will use it too late. Or worse, too soon.

I'm tempted to toss it, just to get it out of my hand, but I need to get it to the police, and I can't just leave it in a random house. I try to shove it in a pocket, but it doesn't fit, and I'll be damned if I'm going to stick it down the front of my pants.

A small nightlight in the kitchen shows there's a small table with chairs in there. Trent points to dirty dishes next to the sink. Someone is, or recently has been here.

Suddenly the house feels different to me, different than the other houses.

It feels terribly wrong to be in here knowing, or at least thinking, that other people were recently in here. Or maybe still are.

Before I can say anything to Trent, I spot a flashing red light on the wall. The house has an alarm, and we've tripped it. Before I can point it out to Trent, bright lights come on, blinding me, and a high-pitched keening wail pierces through my head.

Something hard hits me across the back, and I go down, twisting around my crutch, the gun falling from my hand. It clatters to the floor, and I hear Trent shout something over the din of the alarm, but I can't tell what it is. Rolling over, all I can see are dark shapes moving quickly in front of the blinding security lights.

And then the gun goes off.

Chapter 58

THE ALARM GOES SILENT, LEAVING me feeling like I've gone deaf. The blinding flood lights turn off and the kitchen lights come one. Tommy is standing over me with a baseball bat, looking like he's ready to bash my head in. Trent, standing against the kitchen wall, at the wrong end of a gun barrel, has his hands up. There is a bullet hole in the yellow wallpaper behind him. Paige, who is holding the gun on Trent, slowly takes her hand down from the alarm system.

Before anyone can move, a crying voice comes from the hallway, followed by pattering feet. "*Auntie Paige!*"

"Go back to bed, honey," Paige calls. "It's all okay! I'll be right there to tuck you back in."

"What was—?" Fleming, tears and terror on his face, comes running out of the hallway in pajamas and bare feet, and freezes. "Daddy!" He sprints and launches himself up into Trent's arms from three feet away. Trent catches him and pulls him in for a bear hug.

"Are you all better now?" Fleming asks him.

"Much better now," Trent sobs, tears running down his own cheeks.

Paige's face twists and contorts, emotions tearing her apart, and she lowers the gun so she's not pointing it at Fleming.

"He can't stay, buddy," Tommy says lowering his arm holding the bat but not moving away from me. "Remember what we talked about?"

Fleming squeezes his arms tighter around Trent's neck. "But he's not

229

sick anymore!"

"But he's not your real dad," Tommy says. "I am. Remember?"

Fleming, face buried in Trent's shoulder, shakes his head furiously.

Paige looks back and forth from Fleming to Tommy. "Maybe he can come with us," she whispers, taking a step toward Trent. There is desperation in her voice.

"Are you stupid?" Tommy says. "Give me that," he points to the gun, "and take the kid back to the bedroom."

Paige hesitates. I can't help but wonder if Ranger Murry had called Fleming *the child* in front of her, too, and if she had hated it much as I had.

"Come on. You're the one who wanted to be part of your grandson's life. I told you what might happen. You can't change your mind now—unless you want to spend the rest of your life in prison."

The look in his eyes, more wild than McCurdy's ever were, makes me think he wouldn't let her have that choice, that he'd kill her himself so he didn't have to go back to prison.

With nervous steps, Paige comes closer bringing the gun to her son. Then she looks down at me, sprawled on the floor at her feet, and all but spits on me. "This is all your fault. If you'd worked harder to keep your marriage, none of this would have to happen this way." I think she's going to point the gun at me, but then she hands it to Tommy and moves to take Fleming from Trent's arms.

Neither Trent nor Fleming wants to let go, and Paige struggles to take the boy out of his father's arms.

"Let him go," Tommy says to Trent, baseball bat in one hand, gun in the other. "You really don't want him to be around for whatever comes next, do you?" He loosens his grip and lets the bat slide down through his hand, lightly bouncing the end of it off the side of my head.

It's not much more than a tap, but it hurts like hell and leaves me seeing stars.

Trent, tears running freely down his face, gives his little boy up to Paige. Fleming starts screaming, kicking at Paige, but she holds him tight.

"It didn't have to be like this." I can barely make out her words to Trent over Fleming's cries. "I could have been everything to you. Fleming could have been our son—our grandson," she corrects herself. "I took care of you after Nancy died, just as much as I took care of him." The hurt on her face matches the deep pain in her eyes. "I *loved* you. You and Nancy were my family." Tears start running down her cheeks, too. "I didn't deserve the way you treated me. I didn't deserve to be abandoned for that— that *homewrecker!*"

"Who's the real homewrecker, Paige?" I ask.

"Shut up!" Tommy kicks me.

"Or what? You'll beat me? Shoot me? You'll show Fleming exactly why you could never really be his father?" The voice, deep inside of me, cheers me on. I'm in control of myself this time, saying it on my own this time. No matter how stupid I know it might be.

Tommy's face turns red, and he kicks me again, fortunately missing my ribs.

"See Fleming? He's a bad man!" I yell.

"Shut up!" He kicks me in the ribs this time, leaving me gasping.

"Stop it!" Paige yells, trying to cover Fleming's eyes and ears at the same time.

"Did Tommy tell you the truth, Paige?" I manage to breathe out as she heads for the hallway. "That he raped and killed Nancy?"

I see her freeze and look at Tommy with shock on her face, then I see the baseball bat, and then my head explodes in pain.

And then I'm retching, curling and twisting on myself like a decapitated snake in the grass. I can't stop the spinning of the world and the heaving of my stomach, though nothing comes out, which makes it ever worse.

"Tommy!" I hear Paige shout.

"Get him out of here!" Tommy shouts back. "And reset the alarm! You! Pick him up!"

I see and hear feet moving around me, but I can't focus. More dry heaving. Strong arms go under me, lifting me, but I can't uncurl myself to help get me up, I can't stop trying to vomit something that's not in my stomach.

Trent grunts as he manages to slide me a couple of feet across the floor. The movement triggers more heaves from me, and I involuntarily contort, folding over in on myself.

"Jesus! Fuck!" Tommy yells. "Fucking leave him. Go, that way. Go!"

I hear them moving away from me. There's a click of a light switch somewhere and the world around me goes blessedly dark, somehow relieving some of the pressure in my head. The cool tile floor feels good on my face as I retch and gulp air like a fish out of water.

"…now! Everything! Pack it up!" I hear Tommy's voice from somewhere else in the house. "We are leaving now!"

Trent's voice floats out, but I can't tell what he says. It's followed by a thump and Tommy yelling again.

I lay on the cool floor and feel the rotation of the Earth trying to make me heave again, but I fight it. I suck in air and fight it.

After a while, I'm not spinning anymore, or at least not as much, though my head hurts terribly. I tell myself I have to get up. I don't know what's happened to Trent, but I have to get up and get Fleming. No matter what, I have to get Fleming.

Just as I am about ready to try to get up, I hear footsteps coming back.

"Yes, I'm totally serious," Tommy says. "We blow it up." He reaches me and I do my best to play dead. A quick kick to the gut forces air out of me, and I can't help it. Tommy grunts and heads back down the hallway.

I watch him go, wondering what he means about blowing something up, and then I notice the blinking red light on the security pad. Had it been blinking before? My mind isn't clear, but I don't think so. The red light hurts my eyes. My head throbs in time with the flash of light. I'm pretty sure I would have noticed before.

A dark shape appears in the kitchen, then moves to the pad. I hear a quiet beeping, and the lights stop blinking.

The shape moves toward me and bends down close. A hand reaches out and pats my shoulder with a chuckle. "Too bad for you, *friend*."

Chapter 59

I WATCH MCCURDY'S SHAPE SNEAK down the dark hallway, toward the voices, and I push myself up off of the floor. The world spins and my head hurts like I've drank an ocean of tequila, but I take hold of my crutch and keep going, putting my shoulder against the wall for support. The cool metal of the crutch feels good and solid in my hand, and it helps to ground me.

I take a couple of steps down the hall, following the direction I'd seen McCurdy go. I hear a thump and a crash come from the room at the end of the hallway, followed by angry shouting, devoid of words. Paige opens a side door and hurries out, worriedly looking toward the room at the end. I misstep and almost fall, scraping the crutch against the wall and she turns her head and sees me.

Hate flashes across her face again. "You're not taking my boys away from me!" She turns and runs into the other room—and screams.

I can't see her, but another thump comes from the room and wild shadows appear on the walls. Strange, jumping shadows that move out of time with the yelling voices and crashing sounds.

As I hurry closer, fighting the world spinning around me, it takes my addled brain a moment to figure out that what I'm seeing is caused by flickering light. By the time I reach the door Paige had come out of, I realize it's fire. Suddenly the stench, the rolling smoke coming out of the room, is terrible.

Someone shoots out of the side room and grabs my leg, tightly, and I almost go down. Catching myself on the wall, I look down to see Fleming, face buried in my thigh.

"Hey!" I grab his shoulder, trying not to fall over. "Hey, look at me, Fleming!"

Not relaxing his grip, he tilts his head back and looks up at me with his big brown, tear-filled eyes.

"I need you to run, okay? I need you to run home!"

He shakes his head and buries his face again. More crashing comes from the room and Paige falls to the ground, landing where I can see her just inside the door.

Blood is streaming from her lips. She sees Fleming and me, and she screams. "No!"

"You need to go get help," I tell Fleming. "Your dad needs help. Your *real* dad."

Paige scrambles to her feet and runs toward us.

I raise the crutch and slam her in the chest with it as she tackles me. Her momentum carries her forward and all three of us go down, bouncing off the walls of the hallway. Shrieking, Paige wildly claws at my face, and I twist to get away, but my arms are pinned under her and the crutch, and the weight of her body on my ribs steals my breath.

Fleming, crying, pulls himself out of the tangled mess of our bodies.

"Run, Fleming," I gasp. Paige's nails find my cheek and tear what feels like giant rents. "Run out the front door and go home! Get help!"

"No!" Paige yells again, trying to crawl over me, trying to reach Fleming before he can stand up.

I grab at her, trying to hold her back. My splinted hand can't catch anything, but my left hand gets hold of her hair, and I pull, jerking her head sideways as Fleming finally runs. She stabs at my eyes with her fingers, and I squeeze them shut, turning my head away and trying to pull her hair harder. Her knee lands a blow between my legs and suddenly I'm retching and gasping for air again. I try to hold on to the fistful of hair, but my grip weakens, and I can feel her pulling free.

Then her weight is off of me. I scramble to chase after her, but she's not past me. I turn and look back.

McCurdy is there, looking like a demon from hell with the flames flickering in the room behind him and lighting up the hallway in an orange glow. His wicked eyes and blocky teeth glow in the light as he lifts Paige up by the throat and laughs. He looks at me and grins. "See? This is what friends are for, right?"

Shots tear through his body, spraying me with warm blood.

McCurdy looks surprised and drops Paige. She scrambles backward into the first room as McCurdy awkwardly turns to look behind him. Two more shots send him stumbling back toward me. I crawl to get out of the way as he falls. He lands hard, shaking the floor beneath me, revealing Tommy, on his knees, in the flaming doorway.

Tommy shifts his aim and points the barrel of the gun at me.

Chapter 60

TOMMY WOBBLES ON HIS KNEES and his hand shakes as he points the gun at me. His shirt and pants, covered in blood, look like a sick, mirror image of the ones I'd spilled ink on. There's a knife sticking out of his belly.

I wish to God I could get up, that I could do *something*, but I can't. I can hardly move at all. And even if I could, I know I wouldn't run.

I don't know where Fleming is, but I know he isn't behind me anymore, and I pray he did what I told him. I pray he ran out the front door, that the police are there, three houses away, looking for Trent and me, and I pray they have Fleming, and that he is safe with them.

All I have left is a little bit of time, and I intend to use it to give Fleming all the time I can.

So, I stay where I am, half-propped up against the hallway wall, and I continue to meet Tommy's hateful gaze. Time slows when I can tell he's going to pull the trigger. His body changes, tenses as he braces himself for the recoil. His shaking hand stills, and the effort of squeezing the trigger spins the gun slightly on the axis of the barrel.

The muzzle flashes and I hear the bullet, like an echo in a wind tunnel, whistle past my ear.

I throw myself down as he fires again and the wall above me rains drywall dust into my face. It takes everything I have to roll over, roll away from where I'd been, but I do it.

The third shot hits me.

It's a red-hot spear into my thigh above my bad knee, and I scream. The pain sends adrenaline and anger surging through me, helping me focus past the sickening, roiling world I'd been in since Tommy hit me with the bat. I roll over again, trying to move out of the way before he can shoot again.

When it doesn't come, I risk a look at him. He's stupidly pointing the gun at me and trying to pull the trigger, but nothing is happening.

Riding the surge of rage, I grab the crutch and use it to pull myself up. My bad leg has gone completely numb except for a horrible burning sensation from my hip to my knee. Somehow, it makes it easy to use, and I start toward him, despite him still trying to shoot me with an empty gun. I can see by his glazed eyes, and the blood pooling under him, that he's not a threat anymore. The flames behind him have grown big enough I can feel the heat, and acrid, black smoke is pouring out, filling the hallway.

I know I should leave, but I don't know what happened to Trent, other than they brought him this way, and I can't leave him. I carefully step over McCurdy's body, trying to move quickly, but not so much as to fall and lose more time. "Trent!" I call out, the word turning into a wheeze half-way through, the pain in my ribs smothering it.

Screaming, Paige rushes out from the bedroom, stabbing at me with screwdriver. My left fist connects with her nose, dropping her to the ground like a pile of broken matchsticks. She curls into a ball, holding her face.

I look into the room behind her, but don't see anyone. "Trent!" My voice carries a little better this time, but the crackling of the fire behind me is louder, and smoke is starting to burn my lungs.

"Where is he?" I nudge Paige with my foot. When she doesn't respond, I lightly kick her in the knee. "Damn it, Paige, I know you can hear me! The house is on fire. We have to get out of here. Where's Trent?"

She rocks back and forth, and I hear her sob.

"Paige, I want you to tell me where Trent is, and then I want you to go make sure Fleming got out of the house. Do you hear me? I need to you make sure Fleming got out of the house."

She looks up at me, blood dripping through her fingers as she holds them over her nose.

"Go make sure Fleming is safe."

Nodding, she stands up, wobbling on her feet.

"Where's Trent?" I ask again, nearly choking on the smoke.

She points into the room with the fire and falls into the doorway, barely keeping on her feet.

"Go," I tell her. "Go make sure Fleming is safe."

As she stumbles down the hallway, I turn back to the room, and Tommy. Still on his knees, barely upright, he's looking at me, but the hand with the gun is limp at his side. He tries to say something, but I ignore him and try to step around him into the room.

He catches at my crutch, but there's no strength behind it. I'm more bothered by the squishy wetness I feel in my shoe. I glance down to see my leg covered in the blood coming from my thigh and resolve not to look at it again. I pull the crutch out of his weak grip and move into the room.

A huge master bedroom, it is bigger than I thought it would be. But instead of a bed, I find myself looking at knocked-over benches, broken bottles and spilled glassware, some of which are dripping liquids that are on fire. A layer of smoke that pushes down from the ceiling to my chest. Five-gallon buckets and plastic chemical bottles line the walls of the room.

Resolving not to look at those again either, I bend down to get my face out of the smoke, scanning the room but I don't see Trent anywhere. Over the roar of the flames, I hear a muffled thump and spot what has to the be the bathroom door next to the burning bench. I hurry to it, holding my splinted arm up to shield my face from the heat of the flames.

When I open the door, smoke pours in with me, but I find Trent.

Chapter 61

"JESUS." THE CURSE SLIPS OUT as I realize what I'm seeing. Trent is face down in the toilet, with his hands tied together behind it and the lid tied shut on his head. I can hear him gasping for air as he struggles to keep his face out of the water.

"I'm here," I tell him, untying the rope holding his head down and flipping open the lid. "I got you."

Still unable to lift his head out because his arms are pulled so tight, he turns his head sideways, gasping for air, and burbles something at me. Dropping the crutch, and ignoring the way my bloody leg slides out from underneath me, I fall to the floor and reach behind the toilet to untie his wrists. "Don't worry. I got you." I fumble at the nylon cord, but I can't seem to figure the knot out.

Trent tries to talk more, and I make out Fleming's name.

"I told him to run out of the house. I told him to run home," I say, my face pressed against the porcelain.

Something in the room behind us explodes and the flames *whoosh* and roar louder.

Trent thrashes and yells something, jerking his hands around, and I can't find the knot again.

"Hold still!"

"Mmm-Flmmg!"

"I know! He's safe!" I lie, hoping that it's not a lie. Fumbling blindly, smoke burning my eyes and making my nose run, I can't untie his hands. "Fuck! I can't get it!

Trent thrashes again, and one clear word comes up. "Go!"

Another whoosh of flames from the other room tells me something else has caught fire, and I can feel greater heat on my back. If we don't get out of her now, we're not getting out.

"Go!" Trent screams, bobbing his head up and down for each word. "Our...family...needs...you!"

I try for the knot again, but Trent bucks and turns, moving to push me away and keep the knot out of reach. "Go!"

"Fuck!" I gasp. "I can't leave you!"

"Go!" He kicks a leg out wildly, trying to make me leave.

I don't know what to say.

"Go!"

I push myself out from behind the toilet, and pull myself up on my crutch, nearly blind by the smoke and flames.

"Go!" I hear him yell again.

I yell in frustration, hating myself for leaving, but knowing he's right. Our family needs at least one of us, and if I stay longer, we'll both die in here. I hurry to get out of the burning room, nearly tripping over Tommy, who has somehow moved himself to where he is leaning on the doorframe. He rolls his eyes to look up at me with a pale, slack face.

And I spot the knife still in his belly.

Reaching down, I pull it out. He shudders and his eyes roll up into his head, then come back to stare at me accusingly.

The smoke sets me coughing, shooting pain through my ribs. Already off balance, bent over, I fall to the ground, gasping for air. Under the layer of smoke, I finally get another good breath of air and start an awkward crawl back to Trent. With only one good hand and one good knee, both on the same side, I end up crawling on my elbows, dragging my bad leg behind me.

When I get back to the bathroom Trent isn't moving. I shove at his legs, trying to push him back around so I can get to his hands. His body jerks and I hear a gasp come up from under the toilet lid. He kicks at me again. "Go!"

"No! Give me your hands, goddamn it! I've got a knife!"

Trent twists around and I can finally reach the cord again. It takes me precious seconds to get the blade between his hands and start sawing. When I see blood, I feel bad, but I keep going. Suddenly I'm through the cord and his hands come apart.

Trent pulls his face out of the toilet, gasping for air, and gets a lungful of smoke instead.

"Stay down here." I grab him and pull him low. The smoke layer is down to not much more than ankle-height now.

"I told you to go!" he says, spitting water.

"We can talk bullshit thoughts later," I answer. "Hurry up and go. You're faster than me!"

Trent starts crawling out, and I follow on elbows, pushing with the toes of my good leg, working my way through the hell of Tommy Walker's flaming master bedroom meth lab.

I catch up with Trent at the doorway, where Tommy has slumped across the threshold. Tommy's chest is barely rising and falling, and Trent pulls at him, trying to drag him out of the inferno with us. I want to tell Trent to leave him, that he's not worth it, but Trent is a better man than me, and I can't bring him down like that.

So, I push at Tommy's feet, and together we slide him a couple of inches. After a couple more tries, we get our movements coordinated, and we manage to get Tommy to slide farther each time.

Until we reach McCurdy.

Trent grunts and tugs, crawling through McCurdy's blood and trying to get Tommy over the body. I crawl up next to them and grab Tommy's jeans. With a coordinated effort, we pull him over. Tommy's head hits the floor, and he opens his eyes, looking around. He spots Trent and gives a weak laugh.

He reaches up and grabs Trent's arm. With a smile he says, "I fucked your wife. She had my kid…"

Rage fills Trent's face and he roars at Tommy, using the anger to pull harder, dragging Tommy another foot, but Tommy's face is already slack, his open eyes unmoving.

"Go!" I choke on the smoke. "He's not worth it" And this time I know I'm right. And it doesn't matter. "Go!"

Coughing, we make it to the living room before boots appear around us and strong arms grab me and pick me up. Suddenly I find myself outside, sucking in fresh air in the light of dawn, firemen on either side of me, holding me up. The good air makes me cough harder, hurting my ribs. My bad leg feels like it's made of ice.

"Where's Fleming?" I hear Trent demanding.

"Is there anyone else in there?" one of the firefighters asks me, her words muffled though her mask.

"Two… dead…" I manage to get out around coughs. As she turns to go in, I call out, "Wait! It's a meth lab! It's going to explode!"

The firefighter hesitates.

Texas Ranger Cole Murry appears next to me, handcuffs already out and ready. His face hard as stone as he reaches for me. "Don't worry, son. Meth labs don't usually ex—"

The blast knocks us all to the ground.

Epilogue

OLIVER LOOKS DOWN AT ME, a plastic Christmas tree with blinking lights in his hand. The price tag from the hospital gift shop is still on it. "You look like hell. I can't believe all the injuries you got, and you just kept going."

"When you get to be my age," I tell him, "you'll see. Pain is just an everyday part of life. You ignore it and move on. It wasn't any different than any other day."

"Yeah, right." He sets the little tree on the table next to the hospital bed. "How long they keeping you for?"

"I don't know. My understanding is it's mostly an observational thing because of the concussion."

"That come with the goose-egg on the side of your head?" he points to my temple where Tommy had first lightly tapped me with the bat.

"Believe it or not, no. That," I reach up and touch the tender lump, "was about the mildest thing that happened to me over the last couple of days."

"Compared to getting shot, I believe it. Is it true Paige and her son were going to make it look like Trent killed you and then died when the meth lab exploded?'

"That's what I heard," I tell him. "I missed that part of the conversation." I point to the lump on my head again.

"Dad!" Coney rushes into the room and Oliver barely gets out of the way as she all but throws herself on me. The squeeze hurts, but it's worth

243

it. Fleming, coming in the door right behind her, imitates her and yells "Dad!" He runs to the other side of the bed and climbs up to hug me from the other side.

I put my arms around them and pull them both tight.

"I'm so glad you're okay," Coney says. "When Mom said you got shot—" She's already crying into my chest so hard she can't finish.

After a moment, wiping tears away, Coney whispers, "It's okay if he calls you Dad, right?"

"Me and Coney decided to have the same moms and dads!" Fleming whispers too. His eyes are alive with excitement.

"Oh, yeah," I tell them, giving them both a squeeze. "You can have the same moms and dads. And you can both call me Dad."

I breathe deep and hold onto the moment, squeezing my eyes shut as hot tears come for me, too. When I open them, Dana is at the foot of the bed. For the first time in as long as I can remember, she's smiling at me.

"How's Trent?" I ask her.

"Fine," Trent says, following Dana into the room. "A little smoke inhalation. A little beat up. Exhausted. But I'm fine. Thanks to you."

"Hey now," I say. "No bull—uh, no B.S. thoughts. We got through this together."

He nods. "Yes, we did. And we're going to keep doing it."

"Hey, uh, lemme get out of y'all's hair," Oliver says. He points to me. "I just wanted to make sure you were doing okay."

"I appreciate it," I say. "We'll have a beer soon, and I'll talk your ear off. You're buying."

"Sounds good." He waves and starts to head out but runs into Summer at the doorway.

"Oh! Excuse me, Oliver," she says politely, with a perfect smile, both gracious and apologetic.

He takes a step backward to let her in, and then she sees me. Her eyes widen behind her librarian glasses, and the smile fades. She nods to Oliver and moves past him to come into the room

"Look at you, Jeff!" she says. "I told you to be careful!"

"I was."

"You got *shot!*" She looks at me indignantly and comes around the bed. Her face softens and she reaches over Fleming to lightly touch the bump on my head. "Does it hurt?"

"Only when I breathe."

Fleming giggles, and I give him a squeeze.

Summer smiles at me with tight lips and shakes her head, somehow making me feel she approves and disapproves at the same time.

I look to Oliver, still at the door, and he smiles at me and gives me a salacious wink and a nod.

Turning back to Summer, I ask, "What are you doing tonight?"

Summer furrows her perfect eyebrows at me. "Why?"

"Would you like to have dinner with me?"

"Why, Mr. McKenzie, how very forward of you." She raises her eyebrows, purses her lips and shakes her head, but her eyes twinkle magically. "I don't know. I'm just not much for hospital food."

Coney chuckles and Fleming lets out a fake guffaw that shows he doesn't really know why he's laughing.

I nod and squeeze my kids tight. "Well, then what are you doing for Christmas Dinner?"

"Well..." she leans down and whispers where only Fleming, Coney, and I can hear. "I usually spend it with Father Christmas, but I might be persuaded to make an exception this year."

CASTLE BRIDGE MEDIA RECOMMENDS...

If you liked *Lost Angel*, you might also enjoy reading the following titles from Castle Bridge Media available on Amazon or by order at your favorite book store:

Austinites
By In Churl Yo

Bloodsucker City
By Jim Towns

THE CASTLE OF HORROR
ANTHOLOGY SERIES
Volume 1
Volume 2: *Holiday Horrors*
Volume 3: *Scary Summer Stories*
Volume 4: *Women Running From Houses*
Volume 5: *Thinly Veiled: The 70s*
Volume 6: *Femme Fatales**
Volume 7: *Love Gone Wrong*
Volume 8: *Thinly Veiled: The 80s*
Volume 9: *Young Adult*
Edited By Jason Henderson
and In Churl Yo
*Edited By P.J. Hoover

Castle of Horror Podcast
Book of Great Horror:
Our Favorites, Top Tens
and Bizarre Pleasures
Edited By Jason Henderson

Dream State
By Martin Ott

FuturePast Sci-Fi Anthology
Edited by In Churl Yo

GLAZIER'S GAP
Ghosts of the Forbidden
By Leanna Renee Hieber

Isonation
By In Churl Yo

MID-LIFE CRISIS THRILLERS
18 Miles From Town
By Jason Henderson
Lost Angel
By Sam Knight

THE PATH
The Blue-Spangled Blue
By David Bowles
The Deepest Green
By David Bowles

SURF MYSTIC
Night of the Book Man
By Peyton Douglas
Dark of the Curl
By Peyton Douglas

Nightwalkers: Gothic Horror Movies
By Bruce Lanier Wright

Yesterday's Tomorrows:
The Golden Age of
Science Fiction Movies
By Bruce Lanier Wright

Please remember to leave us your reviews on Amazon and Goodreads!

THANK YOU FOR SUPPORTING INDEPENDENT PUBLISHERS AND AUTHORS!
castlebridgemedia.com